D0434456

JENNIFER VANDEVER is a graduate of Columbia University's film program and the co-writer of the film *Just One Time*. *The Brontë Project* is her first novel. She currently lives in Los Angeles, California. Visit her website at www.jennifervandever.com.

the brontë project

project

A NOVEL OF PASSION, DESIRE,
AND GOOD PR

jennifer vandever

**POCKET
BOOKS**

LONDON • SYDNEY • NEW YORK • TORONTO

First published in Great Britain by Simon & Schuster UK Ltd, 2005
This edition first published by Pocket Books, 2006
An imprint of Simon & Schuster UK Ltd
A CBS COMPANY

Extracts from *The Brontës: A Life in Letters*, translated and edited by Juliet Barker,
are reproduced by kind permission of Penguin Books Ltd.

3 5 7 9 10 8 6 4

Simon & Schuster UK Ltd
Africa House
64-78 Kingsway
London WC2B 6AH

www.simonsays.co.uk

Simon & Schuster Australia
Sydney

A CIP catalogue record for this book is
available from the British Library

ISBN 1416511474
EAN 9781416511472

Printed and bound in Great Britain by
Cox & Wyman Ltd, Reading, Berks

for my parents, ruth and william vandever

acknowledgments

My gratitude goes to the many friends who became the first audience for this book and whose questions, ideas, and encouragement truly helped form it. I must also thank the early readers at Curtis Brown, Ltd., for their support, especially my agent, Kirsten Manges, whose dedication to finding this project a home never wavered and who always remained a source of smart and insightful advice. Thanks to the many good people of Crown Publishing and Shaye Areheart Books for their inspiring energy and enthusiasm, particularly my editor, Sally Kim, for shepherding *The Brontë Project* with such skill, wisdom, and good humor.

For spiritual, emotional, and Web support, I am indebted to Matt Sweeney, Christina Lazaridi, Alan Levy, and Jeff and Gay Landreth. Thanks to Andrés Soto for his patience, kindness, and knowledge of butterflies. Thanks to my parents for always encouraging me to follow my own passion and for supporting me in every way. More gratitude than I can express goes to Lisa Vandever and Scot Zeller for their unflagging willingness to read yet another draft; I consider myself remarkably blessed to have found two such thoughtful and generous first readers.

I owe a great debt of gratitude to those scholars and biographers whose efforts served as a basis for my research on the Brontës. Specifically, the biographies *Brontës: Charlotte Brontë and Her Family* by Rebecca Fraser and *The Brontës* by Juliet Barker served as a vital source of information. Ms. Barker's *The Brontës: A Life in Letters* was also a touchstone for much of my investigation of Charlotte Brontë's correspondence. I must also, obviously, thank Charlotte Brontë, whose life, fiction, and letters proved more compellingly modern and alive than I could have ever imagined at the beginning of this journey.

part one

The romantic stands, on the other hand, for the things that, with all the facilities in the world, all the wealth and all the courage and all the wit and all the adventure, we never *can* directly know; the things that can reach us only through the beautiful circuit and subterfuge of our thought and our desire.

Henry James, *The Art of the Novel*

Arthur says such letters as mine never ought to be kept—they are dangerous as lucifer matches—so be sure to follow a recommendation he has just given 'fire them' or 'there will be no more' such is his resolve. I can't help laughing—this seems to me so funny.

Charlotte Brontë, to Ellen Nussey, 1854

letters

It is painful to be dependent on the small stimulus letters give.

Charlotte Brontë, to Ellen Nussey, 1850

Fate affords some lovers only one opportunity to meet. Others it allows endless opportunities, so that their coupling seems more like the work of fate's fair-haired cousin, serendipity. Whatever the circumstances, any number of preconditions must gather around this fortuitous event. In the case of Sara and Paul it was the combination of a graduate seminar on the modern British novel, a boring holiday party, Anglophilia in general, and Paul's vague resemblance to a young Laurence Olivier in particular. They had so capitalized on their good fortune that six years after the fact they stood side by side, surveying the crowd, both eyeing the door and drinking a cheap merlot from plastic cups.

jennifer vandever

Even in the most generous accounting, fate has a lot to answer for. Romeo and Juliet met on a Sunday and were dead by Thursday. This was a fact Sara had picked up at an academic seminar, "Shakespeare's Love and Time: Counting Our Days"—something like that—wedged between lectures on Ophelia's eating disorders and Macbeth's compulsive gambling. Someone had actually taken it upon himself to count the days in that play, a ludicrous venture Sara had thought at the time. But it was an instructive fact, one that stayed with her. This was the true lesson of Romeo and Juliet: The course of destiny was hard and swift. That stranger you met on Sunday could be the corpse of your true love draped artfully over your own cadaver on Thursday. You just never knew.

Sara remembered this fact as she watched Paul chatting joylessly with the Vice Dean, the cheap merlot coating the back of her throat like syrup. The wine was actually very expensive, she thought. Not that the wine was any good, but it's a particular brand of wine that a particular brand of people will stand around in bright rooms drinking out of plastic cups, people who must believe this activity will bring them some advantage. In terms of lost time, dignity, and energy, the wine actually came at a very steep price. Sara had time to think of this as she set down her cup and approached the cheese platter, realizing the same theory applied to cheese.

"The wine's actually pretty expensive, if you think about it," Sara whispered to Paul. They were in need of the quiet intimacy of a shared joke.

"Sorry, what?" Paul asked, distracted.

4

"The wine. It's expensive. If you factor in the lost time and . . . dignity . . ." Sara said, faltering. It was less amusing out loud and Paul gave her the indulgent smile of a joke unrealized.

"Then let's go," Paul said.

"Not yet."

It happened every year in late August, the old faculty welcoming the new. It seemed a strange custom to celebrate newness by offering up the same old: bad wine, bad cheese, new teachers, welcome. Paul was ready to leave and find a proper drink elsewhere. He'd learned there wasn't much advantage to be found here while Sara still hadn't, and it was creating a rift. Paul didn't need these events like Sara did. He'd already published—at twenty-seven, no less—and wrote about sexy topics like language and power that attracted grants and the attention of Vice Deans.

Sara was not so lucky in her research, which concerned letters and, more specifically, lost letters. She was looking for Brontë letters. Charlotte Brontë in particular was a famously avid correspondent and her husband a scrupulous destroyer of her letters, such was his Victorian horror of private revelation. The bulk of her research consisted of dead-end correspondences with cranky old ladies in Belgium and England who may or may not have lost Brontë letters languishing in their attics. They had gotten to be an occupational hazard, these lonely widows who would tease out Sara's interest in their forgotten archives. They would tell her of their cat's indigestion, their lost pension checks, visits to the doctor, cataloging in minute detail their various physical complaints. They would describe the boorishness of neighbors, the ingratitude of children, the sad, failing light on their kitchen's windowsill before getting down to Sara's real purpose in writing them. Invariably the investigations ended in disappointment.

Sara would probably never find an authentic letter, and she had to admit during quieter moments that perhaps this search was simply an attempt to delay the inevitable: writing her thesis. There was a long list of missing Brontë letters and writings, but by now most people assumed they'd been destroyed, and who really cared? Not Sara's thesis adviser.

"D'you think there might've been some sexual abuse in there?" her adviser once asked hopefully.

"Good God, no," Sara replied.

"Oh, well, can't hurt to look, can it?" the adviser suggested merrily.

With most English Ph.D. candidates scrambling for the last crumbs of employment, Sara knew she was poorly situated. For the time being, the department would plug her into Lit. 101 courses, sopping up the excess of unlettered freshmen. Her research grant, which provided the bulk of her living expenses, was due for renewal soon and she was becoming keenly aware that unless she did something vaguely fashionable, something vaguely sexy as Paul had, her days were numbered.

"Let's go," Paul whispered again.

"We can't."

"Why not?"

"We're celebrating newness," Sara reminded.

"Oh, right," Paul sighed.

Something always compelled her to believe that five more minutes would rectify a brief academic career distinguished mostly by its silence. Even this pathetic celebration of newness gave her hope. She knew Paul was mostly there for her benefit this year and he was eager to leave at the first opportunity. Then there was a collective rustling in the room. Sara looked up to see that Claire Vigee, the bestselling Princess Diana scholar and the faculty's most dazzling new addition, had arrived.

"Excuse me, everyone," Claire began.

The crowd turned to face Claire, who was dressed like a cross between Rita Hayworth and a seventeenth-century courtesan and was flanked by two very buff black men dressed entirely in leather. This was new.

"These are Derek and Lester, my bodyguards," Claire announced in a lilting accent that sounded to Sara like an indefinable mix of French, British, and pretentious. "There have been some death threats. Anyway, they're passing out directions to the launch party tonight for my new book, which you probably all know about. I'm afraid I have to be off, but I just want you all to know how much I look forward to teaching here this year and learning from all of you and all that. Thanks."

Something about the way Claire had thanked them provoked the crowd to give her a round of applause, as though they had just given her an award. The book party was being sponsored by the journal Claire edited, *Labia*, and Sara overheard Ed Grimes, the drunken medievalist, snicker triumphantly about never turning down an invitation from "labia" as bodyguard Derek thrust an invitation into her hands. General merriment erupted as the crowd that had lowered its sights to Free BadWine learned that it was now being treated to an Open Bar. Sara was about to toss her invitation away when she caught Paul's eye and realized that, of course, they were going.

Sara already knew Claire and knew she hated her. She had mistakenly sat on a panel Claire conducted a couple of years ago. Mistakenly, because Sara had written an article about the Brontës an editor had unfortunately titled "Sister Power," and for a full year after that, Sara had been invited to speak at symposia of all kind to discuss her role at the forefront of the gender wars. Sara had no desire to be at the forefront of any war, much less one so indeterminate, but she had accepted Claire's invitation before realizing she'd been mistakenly dubbed a campus firebrand. Modern readings of the classics were generally pretty indulgent affairs, Sara thought. She realized her attitude was unfashionable, but what could she do? She sat on Claire's panel (to decline after accepting would have aroused speculation) in stony silence. After an hour of tepid debate among the other panelists about quilting and women murderers, Claire turned to Sara and asked if she was giving a demonstration of "Victorian feminine silence." Sara mumbled something incoherent about corsets and wished she were dead. Or Claire were dead.

Luckily, a woman on the panel, Toi from Syracuse, who'd been spoiling for a fight ever since Claire dismissed her life's work as "that whole Otherness thing," redirected the debate toward her sphere of inquiry: "It's always about some white lady gettin' laid—that's all those books are. Why doesn't she step aside and let some of her Latina and African-American sisters get some of the action?" The audience cheered. Sara thought perhaps she should point out that in the "gettin' laid" category the Brontës were notable failures with the exception of Charlotte, who possibly got some action during her six-month marriage before dropping dead at thirty-eight. But then perhaps she'd misunderstood Toi's point.

But that was two years ago. Sara was sure Claire wouldn't remember her.

"The silent Victorian! I wondered what darkened corner you'd receded into!" And in fact Sara did look around for a darkened corner, but she could feel Paul tugging her toward Claire.

"I'm so glad people from the department are coming. Did you see my bodyguards? They're very sexy but not very attentive." Claire gestured toward Lester and Derek, who were drunkenly flirting with each other in the far corner.

"I'm telling everyone to get bodyguards these days. Even if you don't need them, which I do, they make one feel, how can I say, so valuable?"

Sara tried to exchange a look of disbelief with Paul, who was staring at Claire, disturbingly entranced.

"I'm Paul."

Claire inexplicably flicked the edge of her bustier with her thumb before taking Paul's hand.

"Of course you are, I know. You do Orwell and she does Brontë. It must be reassuring to have professional interests that are so conventionally gendered. Some mornings I wake up and say, Claire, just one day without sexual ambiguity, please, because living with ambiguity is actually very difficult, it requires a very complex mind like mine, which I know scares people, but then most of my friends are very famous and they don't mind. Excuse me."

Claire waved at someone across the room and ran to embrace her. Or him.

"What a freak," Sara muttered under her breath.

"Oh, I don't know," Paul said, gesturing to the bartender for a drink. Sara took a deep, stabilizing breath. Claire was like the anti-Sara: Where Sara was slim-hipped, small-breasted, and quiet, Claire was shapely and loud. Where Sara had straight dark hair, Claire had a shock of coppery red curls. Sara favored the practical and the classic in clothing and colors that, as her mother liked to point out, occurred naturally in bruises—blacks, grays, and blues— while Claire went for the blatantly trendy and expensive. On Claire even black looked red.

She was everything Sara was not, so Paul's passing interest in her bothered Sara. But she and Paul matched, she reassured herself. Hadn't they simultaneously thrown out the bulk of thrift-store clothing that comprised their early-twentysomething wardrobes and jointly acquired tailored, professional clothes, with only the random thrift-store purchase to maintain their prior claim to hipness? Paul would look ridiculous standing next to Claire, doubt-less part of her appeal, Sara figured. His closet now bulged with nice suits and sweaters, but an accusation of conven-tionality could still cut him to the core.

"She called us conventionally gendered," Sara re-minded him.

"She called me searingly nihilistic," said Meredith, who joined them. Meredith taught poetry.

"Well, you are," Paul replied.

Meredith was developing a reputation for her ability to recover painful childhood memories and relate them in verse that was invariably described by reviewers as stark, scathing, or searing. Less charitable members of the fac-ulty enjoyed the game of speculating as to what new tragedy Meredith would recall for a sequel.

"Screw you, Paul," Meredith said, waving off one of the toga-clad waitresses.

"Is this a theme party?" Paul asked.

"You're being served a fig tart by a Roman slave—what do you think?"

"You're in a good mood, Meredith," Paul said. Mere-dith smiled and indicated to the bartender another round, whispering, "This turns into a cash bar in twenty minutes—we better hurry up and get ripped." A woman in a sleek black suit grabbed Meredith's shoulder.

"There you are. There's a promising young filmmaker you might want to meet over there next to the column."

"Doric or Ionic?" Paul asked the young woman. She stared at him, uncomprehending, then ran a hand down the front of her suit.

"Donna Karan."

"This is Maura, Claire's publicist's assistant," Meredith intoned with mock interest. "Paul's also an author." This information produced a calming effect on Maura.

"Where have you published?" she asked.

"Mostly in Hungary and the back of men's magazines."

Maura frowned slightly.

"Right now I'm editing *The Complete Idiot's Guide to Writing a Complete Idiot's Guide*," Paul added.

Maura brightened. "I love those books! I learned all about mutual funds. You'll have to let me know when it comes out. What about you?" Maura wheeled around to Sara.

"I'm working on my thesis," Sara said, carefully avoiding anything that might provoke interest.

"On?"

"The Brontë sisters."

Maura thought, cross-referencing with speed-dial celerity. "You know, I love all that old Motown stuff." She noticed a young man in baggy trousers and tiny eyeglasses. "That's the one," she told Meredith.

"Who?"

"The promising filmmaker. He also won an award!"

"Terrific. I'll have to go have a chat once I'm good and drunk."

"Great. Ciao!" Maura said before buttonholing another award winner.

"What was that all about?" Sara asked.

"Oh, the publicist's upset, last-minute changeover and all," Meredith explained. "Seems Claire's trying to shore up the old sure-I'm-a-bestseller-but-I'm-actually-quite-brilliant image, but instead of inviting award-winning novelists and spiritual leaders, the publicist mistakenly invited all the old transvestites-and-models crowd."

"So what award did you win?" Paul asked.

"The Anne Sexton Incestuous Poetry Award. Maura's beside herself with confusion."

"Congratulations," Sara said dryly.

"It's another beautiful night in New York," Meredith said, raising her glass. "The booze is free and everyone's a promising young filmmaker."

to the heart

. . . no young lady should fall in love till the offer has been made, accepted—the marriage ceremony performed and the first half year of wedded life has passed away—a woman may then begin to love but with great precaution—very coolly—very moderately—very rationally—If she ever loves so much that a harsh word or a cold look from her husband cuts her to the heart— she is a fool . . .

Charlotte Brontë, to Ellen Nussey, 1840

Sara reminded herself of Brontë's advice as she watched Paul and Claire chatting. But, she also recalled, Brontë had written her most coolly pragmatic advice on love long before she'd experienced it herself and certainly didn't follow it once she had.

Sara had fallen in love with Paul when she was very young. It was difficult, too. Hearts had to be broken for their love to be satisfied. They had been together for six years—most of that living together—and now were going to be married during the winter break, all of which ignored superstition and certain Brontë admonitions regarding (1) living together, (2) long engagements, (3) winter marriages, and (4) falling in love before the wedding, certainly before a half year of marriage.

Even so, Paul was never a fan of the Brontës, his tastes generally leaning toward the modern and the masculine. This was ironic because he was one of the prime beneficiaries of the Brontës. Sara fell almost instantly in love with him upon realizing that her study partner, in a certain light, with his head cocked at a particular angle, was almost the exact image of the young Laurence Olivier in *Wuthering Heights*. When she was nine, Sara saw the movie on TV and was shattered. She immediately read the book and was devastated.

Her parents, both therapists, tried to snap her out of it. "Now, how could Cathy and Heathcliff resolve this problem by communicating their feelings before it leads to a fatality? What about the ending disturbs you? How could you change that? Could Heathcliff have worn a warmer coat? How about Cathy paying more attention to her health?" They didn't get it. Sara didn't want them to be cured, she wanted to wallow in the awful morbidity of it all—she'd never felt so alive. Her parents could keep their self-actualization and power communication; Sara was obsessed with dying on a heath, cold and alone, her only comfort being the sound of her lover's name. Her parents were deeply disturbed that this otherwise healthy young girl they'd lavished so much therapeutic wisdom on was only content wandering in graveyards and talking to the sky. What had they done?

But what was vaguely freakish in high school was

vaguely erotic in college. Sara would wear knee-high boots that laced up the front and long skirts, fostering the image of a sweetly brooding, tortured girl with smoky Eastern European eyes. It was enough to make her young male counterparts put down their secondhand copies of Kafka or Camus, gaze across the student café, and seriously consider finally getting down to reading de Beauvoir or Duras or— good God, was sex really this worth it?—Charlotte Brontë.

The loved one is always appointed the custodian of one's romantic illusions, and in this, Paul was well cast— he had a face one could easily imagine frozen on the heath, which rated highly with Sara. Not that Paul was perfect. He could be flippant almost to the point of psychosis, pushing jokes beyond their natural breaking point. Last Thanksgiving when Meredith and her then-boyfriend, Hugh, the Irish poet, came for dinner, Paul insisted on toasting Oliver Cromwell.

"Bleedin' hell you want to toast 'im for?" Hugh wanted to know.

"For criminalizing musical theater," Paul said.

"He banned all theater, Paul," Sara added in a conciliatory tone.

"More power to him." Paul wouldn't let it go.

"Right, and while we're at it, for killin' the innocent men, women, and children of Waterford, Wexford, and Wicklow."

"I've got three words that trump all your dead micks. Andrew Lloyd Webber."

Hugh threw down his napkin and walked to the door, finally eliciting a lame explanation from Paul.

"That was three hundred years ago!" Paul yelled at the door as it slammed shut. Meredith looked woefully across the table as she gathered her things.

"Lesson one, Paul," Meredith said. "Never tell an Irishman, 'That was three hundred years ago.'"

"Paul and Claire seem to be getting along," Meredith pronounced with the proud chill of someone whose disillusion had been confirmed once again. Meredith was trained to find people disappointing on the smallest evidence.

"Please." Sara waved with exaggerated indifference. "He thinks she's a moron. He'll probably have a good story later on." Meredith smirked. Sara felt a sudden wave of nausea.

"So where's the honeymoon?" Meredith asked pointedly.

"Paris." Sara's focus was still trained on Paul and Claire. "I thought she was a lesbian."

"Oh, that's just on book tours," Meredith explained. "Anyway, she's ambisexual, didn't she tell you? Know how much her advance on *Amazon* was?"

"Five hundred."

"And for what? *Diana* Studies?"

"She is a pioneer in the field," Sara added dryly.

Sara watched Claire flick the edge of her bustier with her thumb again and toss her hair back with practiced nonchalance. Claire's hair was constantly being described in magazines as a "tousled mane"—she had wavy, long red hair that really was a marvel, and had Sara been in a more charitable mood, she would have found it just as admirable.

But she was still nauseous. She remembered she hadn't eaten anything. Nothing besides the bad cheese and the occasional fig tart before the wave of free hard liquor.

"I have to find a bathroom," Sara said, already heading downstairs.

If upstairs was Rome, downstairs was Morocco, and the bathrooms seemed to have something to do with Japan. The bathroom was all slate and mirrors with no sign of either toilet or sink. It was a land of all flat surfaces, and Sara realized it was too much to expect a place with such confused geography to deliver a recognizably bathroom-like bathroom. Sara felt something like a panic attack—she was no longer nauseous, now she was dizzy and everything was flat.

She hurried outside, worried now that something terrible was happening, she wasn't sure what, but felt certain it had something to do with the instability of love and inscrutably flat bathrooms and a godless, mean little world. She saw a man tucked into an alcove talking on a cell phone. He looked up at her strangely. "Nykki?" he asked. The word seemed to reverberate, as though the sound had been electronically manipulated.

She felt a great whoosh and then felt herself falling. Had she slipped? She felt strangely in control, as though her descent were taking hours instead of seconds.

Sara blinked. She opened her eyes.

"Are you all right? Here," the man on the phone said. A Roman slave handed her a goblet of water. Sara wondered what a Roman slave was doing here in Morocco and then remembered that her sense of history and the trade routes had always been a little fuzzy.

"What happened?"

"You fainted." The man on the phone was now bending over her. In any crisis there is someone who appoints himself the guardian of the crisis, barking out orders and dispensing water goblets, and here he was—Sara felt a rush of appreciation. But where was Paul, her putative, lifelong crisis guardian, where was he? Upstairs in Rome, no doubt.

"Why don't you try to sit up? Do you remember me?" This seemed like a test of sorts, one that Sara instinctively felt was very important to pass.

"Of course," she lied.

"I heard about, you know, and want to say, more power to you, you know what I'm saying?" Sara nodded. Did she know him? "I've been there and it changed my life, getting clean," he explained. Sara wanted to confess her ignorance, but after her fainting spell she wasn't entirely sure that he didn't know more about her than she did.

"I'm sorry, here—why don't you try to sit up?" The man helped her to one of the sofas that lined the small alcoves, each canopied by heavy fabric. Sara wondered if they were about to reveal state secrets.

"There. Better?" he asked.

Sara nodded.

"I'm fine. Sorry for all the drama."

"Probably just need some food, huh?"

"Probably," Sara agreed.

"What are you working on these days?" he asked casually, sliding in next to her.

"Same stuff," she offered vaguely. That was it—she had met him at a conference. Possibly.

"Which was what?" he pressed.

"The Brontë letters." She wasn't sure how much or how little he already knew. He shook his head to indicate he knew nothing of the project and might be interested. Objects in Sara's sight had returned to their proper alignment; she felt strangely relaxed. Food appeared. Sara nodded her head gratefully, pulling off a piece of bread and stuffing it in her mouth.

"Well, there was this period in Charlotte Brontë's life," she said between bites, "when she left her hometown in Northern England and went to Brussels to study. Now, this period refined her writing skills and gave her her subject."

"Uh-huh." This was usually about the time when the listener's eyes would glaze over. But this listener had an air of active interest.

"She becomes slowly obsessed with her professor, who, recognizing her genius, sort of takes her under his wing. When she returns home, for instance, he writes to her father, requesting that she return as a teacher. He becomes something of a model for the romantic heroes in her fiction, including Mr. Rochester."

"Mmm."

"But his wife—"

"A wife?"

"Madame Heger. Noticing Charlotte's affection probably even before her husband, starts acting a little chilly."

"Uh-huh."

"The professor starts distancing himself. Charlotte grows miserable. She hates Belgium, has no friends. Finally she decides to leave. She returns home and writes a series of emotional letters to her professor."

"Does he answer?"

"Rarely, and a few he tears up. But his wife fishes them out of the garbage and pieces them back together. They're chilling really because they're literally stitched together—his wife pieced the letters together and sewed them up. Anyway, Charlotte's very upset—her life is dull, her father is ill, her brother an alcoholic—so she pours all her sadness into these letters and they're never answered. Then she suddenly shifts her attention to fiction, transforming her experience into art, which you might say can be read as one long, unanswered love letter."

Sara studied her companion, who seemed a little too affable and well-dressed for the usual scholarly ranks. Maybe he was the Kafka scholar she met last year in Toronto.

"Sort of like Kafka," she offered cryptically, testing her mystery man.

"How so?" he asked innocently. Not the Kafka scholar.

"Kafka told his father that everything he'd ever written was what he could not cry upon his father's breast."

"Wow."

"How do you know Claire?"

"Everyone knows Claire."

"Right. Yeah, well." Sara shrugged.

"So did they ever . . . ?"

"Who?"

"The professor and—"

"No—though we don't have all the letters. That's what I'm doing."

"Looking for letters?"

"One in particular. Charlotte mentions a prior letter—she apologizes that it was 'less than reasonable.' There were several letters, but only four are known to exist and three of those were torn up and then stitched back together. None of the letters to Charlotte are known to exist—"

"Why don't you take my card—I definitely want to take a look at this when you feel you're ready. Who else are you showing it to?"

"Um . . ." Sara fumbled for an answer but her companion just gave a knowing nod, as if he admired her calculating evasions.

"I understand," he said. "Just keep me in the loop—I'm a big fan."

Sara wrote down her e-mail address on the back of a napkin, making a mental note that she should really get some cards made.

"You teaching?" he asked, noticing the "edu."

"This semester's sort of a light load while I do research," she said as she glanced down at his card: *Green Light Films, Byrne Emmons*.

Sara fingered the card apprehensively, not sure what to make of it. She definitely didn't know him—but how could she explain pretending to know him now?

"Is this supposed to be the green light at the end of Daisy's dock in *Gatsby*?" Sara asked.

Mr. Emmons smiled. "You know, all these years you're the first person to get that—everyone thinks it's just wishful thinking. But actually I was a lit major as an undergrad."

This was safe ground; Sara ventured a little further. "Where did you go?"

"I went to school in Boston."

Sara smiled. "I hear MIT's very good."

Mr. Emmons straightened in his seat slightly, smoothing the fold in his tie.

"Harvard," he corrected.

"I know."

He gave a kind of smile to acknowledge that he was being teased and was able to be a good sport about it.

"I actually had to lie about it the first couple years in L.A.—everyone was from Harvard or Yale, but it worked against you. Hell, the kid who gets my coffee is a Rhodes scholar."

"Really?"

"Oh, yeah, he's teaching me Sanskrit. Listen, I gotta make a few more calls while people are still in their offices. Are you going to be all right?"

"Oh, yes, fine. I'm more embarrassed than anything."

"Oh, please. It's been a real pleasure."

Sara stood and shook his hand. "Me, too."

Meredith sat curled into a banquette talking to a dark-haired man Sara had never seen.

"Have you seen Paul?" Sara asked.

"He was looking for you," Meredith answered.

"Paul is dead! Isn't that a Beatles song?" the man added without prompting. He spoke with a French accent and gestured wildly.

"Only when you play it backwards. This is Denis—"

"Deh-nee," he corrected loudly.

"Deh-nee," Meredith repeated with fake humility. "He's from France."

"This is Meredith, she's a poet," Denis explained.

"Yes, we know each other," Sara reminded him.

"Yes, but so what?"

"Denis is a poet," Meredith added.

"*Non*, I am a *poem*," he corrected.

"Have you published?" Sara asked.

"*Non*. I never write anything down, that way anything can be in my poem. You can, she can. I write it down and suddenly there are all these things not in my poem—why would I want that? I write it down, now people will give me their stinking opinions. I don't want opinions, I have enough of my own. But now you see they say, 'Oh, that Denis, he's such a clever fellow,' or else they think, What a stupid man that Denis—why have I wasted my time on him? You see? If I don't write down my poem, I save people from making their stinking opinions and we are all happy."

"That's true," Sara answered, scanning the room for Paul.

"But here in America is good because you say one thing one day, it's true, and another the next day, it's true, too. But that's not our question."

"Oh, right," Meredith remembered.

"What do you think? I don't know your name."

"Sara."

"Sara, good. You are in my poem. We want to know if God controls for the psychological variables in testing goodness."

"Assuming you believe in God," Meredith added.

"For the purposes of the moment," Denis continued, "you must suspend disbelief. When I come to New York I load my pockets with change because people are always asking for it. I give it away. But sometimes I don't feel like it—I don't give. I go to a cash machine, someone opens the door and jingles his cup at me. If there are twenty other people there, maybe I don't give. If I am the only one, I feel more responsible, I go out of my way to give. So now if God sends down an angel to pretend to be a bum and I give because of the added pressure of being alone, I am saved. But if I don't give—maybe I'm angry because my wife has left me or my dog has cancer—whatever the reason, now I am damned, yes? Even if I give all those other times. So you see God is a behavioral scientist, but does He control for the other factors?"

"What if you do something wrong but nobody sees?" Sara asked.

"Ah," Denis quickly dismissed, "that's a different game completely."

"What do you think?" Sara asked.

"I think if God exists, He is a sloppy scientist," Denis declared, his attention shifting upward.

"Where've you been?" Paul asked. Sara looked over to see Paul clutching both of their coats expectantly. Denis raised his arms merrily.

"Ah, Paul, you are not dead! Congratulations."

"Bathroom," Sara said, taking her coat from Paul and tucking Byrne Emmons's card into her pocket.

une grande passion

I hope you will not have the romantic folly to wait
for the awakening of what the French call '*Une grande
passion*'—My good girl 'une grande passion' is '*une
grande folie.*'

Charlotte Brontë, to Ellen Nussey, 1840

The cab ride home passed in silence. Sara, already sensing
trouble, decided to forgo the usual postmortems on the
evening. Paul had been gloomy and depressed for weeks
until tonight, until Claire. That couldn't be good. As they
reached their apartment, Paul blurted, "I think I should go
after all."

"Going" meant a year in France. Paul had been offered a fellowship to pursue his thesis on the impermanence of language with a famous and reclusive professor
outside Paris, but Sara still had her first research grant
from the Keane Foundation. The Keanes were a family
whose wealth dated back to copper mines and railroads
and who now generously sponsored new discoveries in the

world of arts and sciences. Her grant was due for renewal in December, but Sara needed to believe it would be renewed. This would keep her in New York for at least another year, covering her living expenses and travel as she searched for lost letters and taught literature courses for little pay. The two contemplated the prospects of a long-distance relationship and a year's separation, but on one drunken evening of mad declarations and marriage proposals, this was deemed unthinkable. Sara had already agreed to teach for the year; it was an offer she couldn't pass up. France would have to wait until next year. Paul agreed, only to wake the next morning with a powerful hangover and a burning sense of regret.

"Is this Claire's idea?" she asked, turning on the lights in their apartment, her nausea returning.

"You know I want to go."

"Okay," Sara said, heading to the bathroom.

"Sara. I live in a corner," Paul explained, standing fixed in the middle of the living room.

"So what?" Sara asked casually, already brushing her teeth: If I behave normally, things will remain the same, some instinct told her.

"In a corner."

"What?"

"That's what Claire and I were talking about, if you want to know," Paul said, now standing in the doorway of the bathroom.

"She said you live on a corner. So what? We do."

"No. Not *on* a corner, *in* a corner. There's this whole world and I live in a corner," he explained evenly.

"Five hours ago Claire was a moron. Now she's your personal adviser?" Sara asked, spitting toothpaste into the sink.

"You don't understand."

"True. I don't understand. I don't understand how we're getting married in a few months if you've chosen to live apart."

"Please, Sara," he pleaded with the tortured eyes he used on her when he was going to do something that would really displease her. "Maybe we could postpone it. Just for a—"

"Postpone?" Sara felt weak; a rush of emotion swelled in her stomach.

"Sara, I don't know—I just need more time."

"More time than living together for six years?"

Paul nodded; she had a point. "Don't you ever wonder?" he asked cautiously.

"About what?"

"Nothing."

Claire was good, Sara thought. She'd gone right to the heart of Paul's greatest fear—that he'd missed out, he'd lived his life on a narrow strip, and somewhere out there somebody was supping fully at the table of life in his place. The thought haunted him. He hadn't wasted his youth chatting up ladies in bustiers, and now they exerted an unreal hold on his imagination.

"What?" Sara pressed.

"I just . . ." Paul was at a loss. Anything he said would reflect badly on him. "I just want some certainty," he finally said.

"About what?" Sara asked tentatively.

"Us. I just don't know . . ."

Accelerated heart rate, chest pain, stomach pain, strange abdominal shifts—Sara felt every little symptom that presages doom. The ways our bodies shift and rock through this life, she thought just as Paul dealt his fatal blow:

"I just don't feel there's any passion. I don't know if you're the one. It's like we're just . . . friends."

Sara stared at him blankly, stunned. "You what?" she finally managed.

"I'm confused. I don't know what I want. Maybe I'll feel differently in a year. I just want a year. Give me one year and you can have all the rest. Then I'll know for sure I'm in love and we're meant to be together." It was a crude way of putting things, unintentionally crude. Paul had meant to sound conciliatory, to strike a fair bargain, create a win-win situation. But there are statements that act like a switch in the whole system and Paul had inadvertently tripped it.

"So what have all these years been if you're not really in love? A lie?" Sara asked quietly with the weird calm that descends after grave disappointment.

"No, of course not, I love you. It's just— I don't know . . . I mean, I *do* love you. I just don't feel that this is 'it' for me somehow. I think I've been trying to persuade myself that it is with the engagement and everything."

"What?" Sara asked. She stormed into the bedroom, slamming the door shut. Now what? She looked around at the artifacts of their life together—the posters, the letters, the guitar that never got played, the copy of Swinburne he used to read out loud in bed to her in the early days of their passionless friendship.

"Sara, I'm sorry," Paul said through the door. "But isn't it better this way? To know now?"

"Oh, yes, this is totally better, Paul," Sara snapped. Oh God, she thought, we're saying all those things that people say at the end. How did this happen?

"Sara . . ." Paul pleaded helplessly. The pleas through the closed door in the middle of the night. This was Sara's first real broken heart but already the signs and symptoms felt rehearsed, sadly familiar.

"You know when's a good time to tell a woman you don't really love her?" Sara asked haltingly through the door. "How about before you say 'I love you' or you move in together or ask her to marry you? How about before then? Women tend to read into those things. I felt passion. I felt real love! I guess I'm glad at least one of us was honest. . . ." That last word stuck in her throat and she started to cry.

Paul opened the door and sat next to Sara on the bed, putting his arms around her. Sara folded into him, clutching him, scared. Goddamned Claire, she thought, this is all her damned fault. Sara had thought Paul's love was stronger than bustiers and foolish overpaid authors. Think again, stupid girl, she thought as she wept into his shoulder.

"Maybe I just need some time away," Paul offered. "Just a little break. Maybe I'll feel differently in a year."

A year's separation. It was a common literary conceit.

Sara racked her brain for examples. *Love's Labour's Lost.* The heroines insist on a year before marriage to test the devotion of their male suitors. *The Tenant of Wildfell Hall* (by Anne Brontë!). Again the heroine insists on a year before marriage to test the man's devotion. A year's separation was always imposed by women to test men. There was no literary precedent for a year's separation to test a woman's devotion to a man's need to be free of devotion. This was a perverse misappropriation of romantic convention.

Sara searched his eyes. She realized there were two types of people: those who, upon hearing that they are unloved, storm out the door, asking that the betrayer never darken their doorstep again, and those who say simply, hopefully, "Okay."

Sara clearly belonged in the second category. Over the next few days, the pact produced a cordial détente. While Paul made his arrangements and Sara watched, they treated each other like lawyers dissolving a firm, politely waiting for the other to do something worthy of litigation. Then, as the day of departure grew closer, the emotions began to fly. Paul suddenly began to weep over his oatmeal one morning.

"I'm such a jerk," he whispered.

"No, you're not," Sara whispered back, taking his hand gently in hers. Yes, you are, she thought. But she wanted to be the kind, understanding woman—the woman men return to on bended knee when sense has come back. She was trying, anyway.

"I wouldn't want you to stay if you're going to resent

it," Sara said. "I want you to be happy. I want us both to be happy."

To himself, Paul would rationalize his situation, his rash desire to flee. It was unfair that Providence had thrust domesticated love on him so young. Unfair that he hadn't tasted the hedonistic pleasures of bad love before sinking into the comfort of the real thing. His friends had affairs. His friends had wild stories. His friends would shake their heads in awe, believing Paul to be above it all. But in fact Paul was jealous. And yet Paul also wanted to be honorable, to be good. He loved Sara, after all. He was committed to being good, had been good for years, and would be good again. But first he had to live his life—wasn't he at least entitled to that much? He wanted to wander the streets of Paris, drunk and alone. He could seduce sweet young things and frighten them with his melancholy.

"Please don't go," Sara asked, turning to him in bed on their last night together. "Please. Stay?" she asked, eyes full of tears. Paul sighed. This was the worst. The pain he caused. Sara could see he was actually going to go, could finally feel it in her body. The bottom was falling out, the sturdy foundation she always thought lay under them buckled and swayed—there was nothing left. Sara wasn't going to sob, she decided, too pathetic. She'd be the sad woman who doesn't understand. Her body vibrated with unshed tears.

"I'm sorry," Paul said.

Sara even helped him to the cab with his bags the next morning. What kind of idiot does that? she wondered, even as she was doing it. Doormats, women who love too much, women whom men leave—that's who.

"Here," she said, helpfully foisting a duffel bag off the curb.

"Thanks."

"Call me when you get in," Sara said mechanically, then realized even this familiar ritual was lost to them now.

"Sure."

"Bye."

"Bye."

"I love you," Sara said. Lame bag-carrying doormat! They kissed awkwardly.

"Me, too," he said, and got into his cab.

Sara strode back across the street, careful not to watch his cab drive off. It all seemed so inconceivable, life without Paul. And she had always assumed Paul felt the same way. But apparently life without Sara was not only conceivable but highly desirable as well. Their year of separation had now begun, though it seemed obvious to Sara, even in the early stages of denial, that the year was simply a face-saving intermediary step—like trade sanctions before a war—on the way to a total break. She turned around, against her better judgment. The cab was already gone.

no desirable feeling

. . . as to intense passion, I am convinced that it is no
desirable feeling. In the first place, it seldom or never
meets with a requital, and, in the second place, if it
did, the feeling would be only temporary: it would last
the honeymoon, and then, perhaps give place to disgust or indifference. . . . . Certainly this would be the
case on the man's part; and on the woman's—God
help her if she is left to love passionately and alone.

Charlotte Brontë, to Ellen Nussey, 1840

Charlotte Brontë was twenty-eight when she first experienced a broken heart. So was Sara Frost, she noted glumly,
staring out the window from her bed, their bed, now her
bed. On the first morning after Paul's departure, Sara
watched a crew of workers assemble an entire water tower
on the roof across from her building before she summoned
the energy to get out of bed. How could people build?
Didn't they know Paul had gone? How was it that the earth
could still spin on its axis without Paul and Sara together in
their apartment? How quickly it all unraveled, she thought,
how easily everything fell apart. What was it Lacan said
about love? That it was giving something you didn't have to

someone who didn't exist. Fucking poststructuralists were never much help during times like these.

Classes wouldn't start for a few more days, and while there were plenty of things she *could* be doing, there was nothing that required her immediate attention. Thus her diminished spirits were freely available to the full experience of misery and despair. She'd decided to make a study of herself. Here was her grand opportunity to be both expert and subject. She expected there to be something like the seven stages of death but found by the second day that there were only alternating visits from Hopelessness and Lethargy.

Sara sat down to do some preliminary lesson plans. This was her first real year as a lecturer—not just a teaching assistant—and she wanted to do it right. She'd been handed an easy assignment, Nineteenth-Century Romantic Literature. Easy, she'd thought. Easy until she'd been appointed Love's Number One Victim, consigned to a life of weeping on the sofa watching cooking programs on cable. Sara normally had a tireless patience for these books. But now she realized resentfully that these people she was reading about simply lacked cable television. Get over it, she found herself thinking about yet another governess suffering from an unquenchable longing. Get over it and get cable. This was hardly the state of mind in which to bestow upon the next generation of literary scholars the riches of the nineteenth century. She set about rereading, with the full responsibilities of her office in mind, Charlotte Brontë's *Villette* and discovered . . . it was *awful*.

It was beyond losing a taste for something, it was a

violent loathing for all the Brontës wrote or ever stood for. Even more it was the loss of a whole family. She'd always secretly regarded it an accident of fate that she hadn't been born into their family, her feeling of identification had been so strong.

As children the Brontës formed intricate, interlocking stories, complete with heroic characters, strange lands, and civil wars. They spun elaborate narratives for several years, merging material from their imaginations with adventures stolen from Sir Walter Scott and the Duke of Wellington. Charlotte and Branwell created the world of Angria, Anne and Emily had Gondol.

This was an ideal childhood, Sara thought, so much better than the therapeutic normalcy of her own. Child safety caps, time-outs, songs and stories that stressed the importance of cooperation and sharing. Helmets. Knee pads. These things had ruined childhood. The best of intentions had wrested the native, grubby weirdness of childhood and ironed it out into a series of "natural stages of development." No matter what Sara said or did as a child, her parents always told her it was "perfectly natural." It drove her crazy.

At the age of nine she'd calmly explained to her P.E. teacher that she was underweight because her parents were missionaries who'd been martyred in Zimbabwe and she'd been left to the charge of a cruel aunt who fed her only half a piece of bread soaked in milk once a fortnight. Her parents, recovering quickly from the news, delivered by an earnest and suspicious social worker, assured everyone involved that her behavior was simply a necessary stage in the preadolescent path of individuation. Just testing boundaries, integrating identity, expressing the normal hostility of a girl toward her parents as she stretches the limits of her childhood dependence. Sara stomped up to her room, firm in the conviction that there was nothing worse than an unshockable parent.

Her real family had always seemed the disappointment. At ten her parents' marriage had briefly dissolved. Sara had no real idea why but inferred that it had something to do with the proper cleansing of a Teflon pan and her mother's inability to act like a romantic heroine. Sara's mother was modern and demanding. She screamed about the state of the kitchen and how it wasn't her sole responsibility and who, who! on earth cleaned the Teflon pan with a scouring pad, permanently ruining it? In fact, Sara had ruined it. But her father either didn't know or care or simply felt so emasculated by the sponge-sensitive edict that he refused to obey.

"Why not just replace the pan?" he'd asked.

"Replace it every week?" she said.

"Why not?"

"Fine. Let's just replace everything every week. Sara doesn't need to go to college."

"That's a different argument. Live a little. Jesus. It's just a fucking pan."

"It's not just a pan. This is about compromise. All life is compromise!"

Sara didn't have much experience in the romance department at the time, but based on her extensive reading, she felt reasonably certain that standing at the top of the stairs shrieking that all life was compromise was no way to keep it alive.

The Brontë family grew up next to a cemetery, it was part of the parsonage, and ten-year-old Sara longed for one, too. No argument could last too long in the shadow of a graveyard, she'd reasoned. Certainly not one about a pan. So she buried the pan in the backyard along with the hamsters and salamanders who'd already found their final resting place there. Sara hadn't told anyone. The pan just disappeared. Her father replaced it. Her parents argued. To a ten-year-old they seemed to be speaking a foreign language, with loud accusations of "invalidation" and "projection" and later hushed and tearful talk of a "transitional object." Her father moved out.

When Sara finally confessed her role in the drama of the Teflon pan to a carefully selected child therapist, she was warned of her tendency to bend to the will of others, to furtively avoid conflict through a policy of silence and stoicism and secrecy. Hadn't this woman read anything? Sara wondered. This was how things were done: under cover of night, preferably with a shovel.

"Be careful you don't do that in the future in your relationships with men. Or women if that's your preference."

Sara nodded blankly. That seemed like a lot to lay on a ten-year-old, but from the looks of the therapist's waiting room, she wasn't alone.

Her parents reconciled. More technologically advanced sponges were invented. Happiness was restored. For her part, ten-year-old Sara made a note to herself: Don't get worked up over stupid, small stuff. Adult Sara did precisely that. For years she swallowed protests. Paul made one mistake after another: He bought broken-down used cars and secondhand computers, purchased over-priced first editions of books with a credit card while the phone bill remained unpaid, cleaned the floor with the sponge meant for the dishes while Sara remained calm. Certainly she voiced an opinion, she was no simp. She registered her opinions—they were polite, quiet, and ignored. But what was the point really? Putting up a fight seemed useless. Arguments with Paul simply looped back in on themselves, leading from minor disagreements to half-remembered and vague rehashes of former arguments. The day Sara found herself in tears over a dirty sponge, she retreated completely. It wasn't worth it.

Then Sara discovered too late the fundamental lesson of cohabitation, that the small bends into the large so imperceptibly that before you know it, you've given away huge chunks of your life. She made this realization while soaking a sponge in a bleach-and-water mix, contemplating passing up a long-coveted teaching position in New York to follow Paul to France and his fellowship. How did he get priority? It was time to take a stand. She'd given away sponges and somehow lost New York in the bargain.

So she made her stand. He agreed. He respected her needs. Miracle of miracles. Next they were engaged. And then, somehow, he misheard something Claire said about living in a corner and everything fell apart. Just like that. This is what love is—getting worked up over nothing and then regretting it. Sara wondered if she'd made a fuss over the wrong thing. Was it enough to lose love? The job now seemed pale and dreary. Maybe she should have followed him to France?

And now, somehow it seemed her phantom family had led her astray as well, had taught her to make romance of what was simply misery. Now that she was in the thick stew of misery, she knew better. What fever of the mind had persuaded her at such a young age to place three celibate consumptives at the forefront of her understanding of not just love but life itself? It seemed quite obvious what her real problem was: Literature had ruined her life. And the authors themselves?

"Two of them, Anne and Emily, never even really *dated*," Sara explained, exasperated, on the phone to Meredith at four A.M. How was it Meredith was her closest female friend? That was another thing about being in a couple for so long: You lost track of friends, had no idea which were your "best" friends anymore, and consequently, ended up with Merediths.

"And Charlotte? Two silly crushes and then she finally settles on some guy, who according to her letters she used to not even like, and then in less than a year she's dead with his baby. Why did I think these women were role models?"

Meredith smoked silently on the other end of the phone before offering any advice. "You should watch Bette Davis movies."

"Bette Davis?"

"*She's* a role model."

"This is ridiculous. I'm just being melodramatic. He just needed some time to himself, to sort things out."

"Hmm," Meredith intoned with the detached interest of a doctor finding a lump. "That's where you are."

"What do you mean?"

"Bargaining."

"Meredith. Stop. I don't even know if we're broken up."

"Did he take his first editions?" Meredith asked.

"Why?"

"Did he?" Meredith pressed.

Sara thought about it. Meredith was the sort of friend who seemed to blossom when a friend's life fell into crisis. She was an expert on crisis.

"No, he left them," Sara answered.

"Then you're not officially broken up."

"What do you mean?"

"If Paul was going to do something that would upset you, he'd have taken his first editions."

"Why?"

"Because you'd destroy them."

"No, I wouldn't." Sara protested, insulted by the suggestion. She could hear the smile in Meredith's voice.

"Yes, you would."

a little interest

... you once showed me a little interest when I was
your pupil in Brussels—and I cling on to preserving
that little interest—I cling on to it as I cling on to
life . . .

Charlotte Brontë, to Professor Heger, 1845

Sara slogged through the first week of classes, aided by the
general wave of indifference that swept over the student
body. The second was harder. The inane pleasantries of
daily life felt like an unbearable burden. She felt weak,
heartsick. She wanted to go home and watch television
and so did most of her students. She was momentarily
tempted to cut a secret bargain with them: *No papers, no
tests, we all watch TV and nobody says a word.*

But this was her first year, she reminded herself. If
she wanted to ask a great nation's best and brightest youth
to fork over thousands of dollars to watch cooking shows,
she'd have to wait at least until she had tenure.

She was walking away from campus when she spotted Claire, who rushed to stop her.

"I want us to do a panel together."

"What? Why?"

Claire pulled a flyer out of her bag.

"Well, they're doing a series of lectures on the 'Image.' *Très* 1989, but whatever, I should do it, don't you think? So I'm thinking Princess Diana and Charlotte Brontë, the construction of the romantic heroine, performative aspects of gender and sexual identity, iconicity, blah, blah, blah. You know the drill."

The drill? Sara had noticed Claire had started incorporating idiosyncratic American expressions into her speech. Just yesterday she'd overheard Claire saying to someone that her decorator was going "the whole nine yards." Claire's cell phone rang. Sara stood blinking down at the flyer as though it could reveal the mysteries of Claire.

"*Merde!* That's not going to work, hang on. Can you teach my class?"

Sara looked up, realizing Claire was talking to her.

"What?"

"My class. It's in an hour. *Romeo and Juliet*—there's a whole chapter in my book—just discuss that." Claire returned to her phone. "That's fine. Tell Courtney I'm in a cab now."

"Claire, I can't teach your class."

"Haven't you read *Romeo and Juliet?*"

"Of course I've *read* it."

"I know it's the second week, but Courtney's schedule is *totally wack,* and when you think about it, I'm really doing this for the students as well."

"Doing what?"

"Interviewing Courtney for *Labia.*"

"Courtney who?"

Claire stared at her. *"Love."* She stashed her phone in her bag. "Thank you so much."

"Can't you ask someone—"

"Like who? That woman that thinks brown is a color?"

"Meredith?"

"Just read my chapter, you'll do fine."

"Brown's a color."

"Thank you, darling."

Claire hailed a cab as Sara turned back toward campus. That morning Sara had found herself tearing up over the lyrics to an REO Speedwagon song while waiting on line to buy coffee, some nonsense about keeping on loving, *'cause it's the only thing I wanna do.* This, she discovered, was one of the unreported tragic side effects of a broken heart. You were cut off from irony. No more the luxury of sneering dismissively at whatever banal crap flowed over the airwaves. You were no longer immune from the easy emotionalism of pop. You were its unwilling victim.

Never had she realized the sheer pervasiveness of bad love songs. In a taxi, buying groceries, getting coffee, they were everywhere. *I just wanna keep on lovin' you.* My God, these men were troubadours, sweet poets of love's mystery. Such simplicity, such ardor. How had she missed, all these years, the undiscovered emotional powerhouse that was REO Speedwagon? Sara rushed out of the shop, her coffee still steaming on the counter.

She dreaded what could possibly happen while discussing Romeo and Juliet.

Sara reentered the building reluctantly.

"What the hell are you doing here?"

Sara lost her breath, turning suddenly to face Meredith.

"Just kidding," Meredith assured her. "Come with me," she ordered, leading Sara out the back door into an alley between buildings. Meredith lit a cigarette, an unfiltered Camel.

"They still make those?" Sara asked. Meredith nodded, offering her one. Sara shook her head.

"You really should take up smoking, it's your best friend during times like these," Meredith advised.

"Thanks, no."

"I just wanted you to know, before Grimes gets it all over the place—"

"What?"

"Paul—he's seeing someone."

"Well . . ." Sara felt the life drain out of her. It was too much. How did people do this? It seemed impossible. Just a few weeks ago everything had been fine—BC— Before Claire. Now there was some undoubtedly attractive French woman Sara had never met cheerfully dismantling her last line on hope.

"Grimes says she's a swimsuit model. With a Fulbright. Grimes has a friend at the Sorbonne who saw them together."

Sara quickly pressed forefinger and thumb forcefully into the corners of her eyes, preventing tears—*Hurry, hurry!*—stifling the small, hollow yelp she knew could follow. Rushing to prevent the spontaneous crying jag had become a familiar routine these last few days, and she'd become very good at it. She could teach a class in it.

"Oh," Sara said. The idea of Paul with anyone else split her in half. Meredith offered the pack, a petty pleasure registering in her eyes: *Life is shit and people are worse. Told you.* There had been a willful avoidance of the subject that is typically known as "other people," which invariably meant that whoever made the first move determined the nature and course of the separation. What's more, there was an unspoken assumption that the "first move" would be Paul's and that the larger purpose of the year in France had less to do with the impermanence of language than with Paul, as Meredith so reassuringly put it, "fucking like a monkey on crack."

"Her name's Therese," Meredith said blankly.

A name! Sara grieved.

"I thought you smoked menthol," Sara managed finally.

"Just when I have a cold," Meredith said, a smirk behind a cloud of smoke.

"Meredith, could you at least pretend you're not enjoying this?"

"What? I told you—you should move on. Screw him.

I'm saying this *as a friend*." She said this last bit with such manufactured concern that Sara felt limp with disgust. Meredith was so much less offensive in her natural, cynical mode.

This was another unreported side effect of a broken heart: the endless unsolicited advice. Married people, single people, the drunk, the broken, the confused and bitter all now got a say. Friends who once stared vacantly at the bottom of a glass saying things like, "I look at him and just want to beat him with a brick—is that weird?" now got to give you a nugget from their own personal brain box. Hurray.

"I have class," Sara said as she rushed inside. In five minutes she would have to explicate the redemptive power of love in Shakespearean verse. She passed Ed Grimes, the drunken medievalist, who was singularly capable of turning a look of sympathy into a leer. She couldn't think about that now.

A nineteen-year-old with glassy Sissy Spacek eyes, stringy magenta-dyed hair, and a navel ring still proudly on view in mid-September sat curled impossibly in her chair reading in monotone:

"Take him and cut him out in little stars,
And he will make the face of heaven so fine
That all the world will be in love with night,
And pay no worship to the garish sun."

Sara gripped the arms of her chair and tried to fix her audience with an unfaltering "What did you think?" look. The class stared back mercilessly.

The class was mainly female undergraduates. The dozen or so men who had signed up on the strength of Claire's book jacket photo and her commitment to "explore the erotic in teaching" had by now slunk away. One earnest young man had announced on the first day of class that he wished to be "whipped into shape" and Claire coolly replied that she didn't whip *boys*.

Claire's effect on the young women was already apparent. Some had adopted her style of dress; some, perhaps unconsciously, had absorbed her tilted head and satirically coquettish style of listening.

"Comments?" Sara asked, trying not to sound pleading. "What's your name?" she inquired of the magenta-haired girl.

"Magenta," the girl answered blankly.

Sara smiled. "Any thoughts?"

A woman in the back row raised her hand. She was a little bit older than the other students, maybe in her early twenties, and she hadn't yet adopted Claire's ironic femme fatale look, opting instead for an ironic butch look of her own. Sara smiled, supposing this woman probably gave Claire a hard time.

"Yes?" Sara prompted.

"Is this a castration fantasy?" the woman asked.

"A what?"

"'Cause it seems like Juliet's main emotional bond is with the Nurse, and then Romeo just comes in and throws everything around like he's all that. Juliet harbors this, like, intense resentment. Isn't that why she kills herself? All that internalized rage against Romeo?"

Sara watched as the woman's classmates nodded in assent.

Magenta agreed. "She does say, 'Take him and cut him.' That's really violent imagery."

"Yeah, I got that," said another woman in the front row.

"Any other reactions?" Sara scanned the room, getting only blank looks and nods of agreement. "Is it possible that Juliet loves Romeo and the heightened poetic language is Shakespeare's way—" She heard a snicker in the back. "—of communicating the intensity of that—" A hand shot up. "—emotion. Yes?"

"In Professor Vigee's book she clearly states, 'The images of dismemberment and destruction—' "

"Actually," Sara clarified, "Claire Vigee is a lecturer, not a pro—"

" '—were Shakespeare's secret coda to women entrapped in Elizabethan England's code of sexuality, to which he was especially sensitive due to his role as a homosexual.' "

"Well," Sara began carefully, "it's always dangerous to make assumptions about the personal lives of authors, especially in the case of Shakespeare, when so little is actually known—"

"Is Professor Vigee coming back?" the girl in front asked.

"Yes. She just had an interview today," Sara answered.

"Who with?"

"With whom. Courtney Love," Sara replied.

An audible hush went through the room. Sara looked down at her notes, carefully crossing out *celestial imagery, effect of verse, universe of dualities* . . .

"I think it's a little dangerous to read things through an entirely modern sensibility," Sara cautioned.

"How else are we supposed to read them?" somebody asked. Sara stared down at her shoes, wishing she'd known ahead of time to wear the ones that made her feel powerful. If only she'd known this morning she'd be facing down these girls and this play on this day of all days, this goddamned day.

"How many people think this is about true love thwarted by violence and vengeance?" Sara asked. Nothing.

"How many people think this play's about castration and female rage?" Sara asked. The entire class raised their hands.

When had girls gotten so hard and sure of themselves? No wonder the boys on campus looked so bewildered. Sara admitted she wanted a piece of that hard assurance even if it was based on harebrained literary speculation. Perhaps the young women were right in appointing Claire to usher them into womanhood. Not just girls, women of all ages clutched her books at signings and followed her appearances on TV. Women were drawn to Claire because she preached the simple gospel of self-love. Claire was fearless and people loved her for it. And maybe, Sara thought, wandering the halls after class, avoiding going home, maybe Claire was right.

Maybe it was time to accept that Claire might know a thing or two. Maybe it was time to finally read the glossy magazine profile Sara had been avoiding for fear of its invoking suicidal professional envy. Salvation comes in many forms. Maybe it's something completely nonsensical and eccentric that will save you, Sara reasoned. She felt a need for salvation. She couldn't run out of bodegas in tears for the rest of her life.

Working hard and expecting approval hadn't gotten Sara very far in life or in the department. Self-promotion was the new religion and Claire was its avatar. Sara needed the career boost of doing the panel with Claire, without question, but even more than that, she wanted to align herself with Claire's fierce confidence. She sat down in the office she shared with three other part-time adjuncts and finally read:

CLAIRIFIC!

Claire Vigee arrives late for her interview at a Left Bank café near her Paris home. Her smooth, pale skin makes her seem altogether more fragile than she appears in photographs. Her demeanor is disarmingly girlish. Yet she lights her cigarettes with a studied, postcoital stare no doubt perfected during years of watching Rita Hayworth movies. Vigee smokes constantly. "I should quit, I know, but I just can't convince myself I'm mortal! I lost my French accent watching Gilda. I lost a lot of things watching Gilda. You see, at a very

young age I saw what power she had and I said to
myself, I want that. So I became that."

And indeed she did. At the tender age of twenty-
five, Vigee rocked French Parliament with her
steamy memoirs, *Femina*, in which she documented
her scandalous affair with a married French
Cabinet Minister. In *Femina*, Vigee compared
herself to other great controversial women
throughout history and literature. Now in her
mid-thirties, Vigee has refashioned her image
once again to coincide with the publication of
Amazon, a continuation of her autobiographical
musings on literature, contemporary culture, sex,
and power.

"I'm interested in women's fierceness. The
Amazons fought with their breasts exposed. They
accepted the icons of womanhood as a source of
power. Now women are running away from that,
hiding their breasts, as it were. I am here to
expose the breast, expose myself." But she hastens
to add, "I'm more interested in the spiritual
dimensions of power, in finding a more rooted
place."

"Women are running away from that, hiding
their breasts. . . . I am here to expose the
breast."

But there are those who claim that Vigee's real
interest is self-interest. "She'd sell her mother

for the right price," says one publishing house executive who declined to be identified. "The thinking man's whore," sniffs one French society wife.

"Now, if there's one thing that really irritates me, that's it. I was exploring the erotics of power, and where better to do that than at the seat of government? This wasn't a trashy tell-all. This was an intellectual investigation. I was studying media and power at the *Sorbonne*, don't forget. I used my body as the site of investigation. Yes, I was the lover of a powerful man. Yes, he had a wife. But one has to understand, I'm a brilliant, beautiful, woman, so if I go to state events and I'm dazzling, then great. If I'm beautiful and men— and women, too, by the way—want me, great."

"The thinking man's whore," sniffs one French society wife.

Perhaps feeling the sting of her critics, who claim her literary success is more the result of showmanship than scholarship, Vigee will be teaching college this fall in New York City. "I want to explore the erotic in teaching," Vigee says flirtatiously over her second espresso.

"If I'm beautiful and men—and women, too, by the way—want me, great."

And she hasn't lost her flair for the dramatic. *Amazon* is perhaps the first theoretical exam-

ination of sex and power that depicts its author
au naturel on its cover. "It would have been
dishonest to do anything else," Vigee
claims. "And you'll notice it's not all me—
there's a chair and a cigarette and lots of
shadow. I believe in the power of shadow,
what's not shown and all that." But what's not
shown of Vigee isn't much. Like her accent, which
shifts between clipped boarding-school British
and a sultry chanteuse French, Vigee prides
herself on her ability to change for the sake of
the moment.

"America is the land of reinvention. I love
America. It's an accident of geography I was born
in France. But then, I've lived everywhere. I
exclude nothing from my field of inquiry because
at base I'm a scientist. My science is desire and
power. This is the study of the next century. It's
the collision of the private and the public. I
think our public persona is the person we invent
to explain to ourselves the private person that we
are. This is the paradox."

Which brings Vigee to her real obsession, the
one woman who fascinates her as much as herself,
Princess Diana. Since the princess's tragic death
in 1997, Vigee has been on a personal mission to
legitimize her particular field of academic
authority, "Diana Studies." This year marked the
first "Diana Symposium" organized by Vigee in
Paris.

"To find yourself in the public, that's the
artform of the twenty-first century."

"That's the power of Diana," Vigee explains a
trifle defensively. "At once so vulnerable, skin so
thin you could practically see through it, and yet
so public. This is the triumph of the star—she
produces a dream of reality that seems more real,
more desirable than the actual world. This is the
tragedy of Rita Hayworth slowly dying of
Alzheimer's—the erotic ideal slowly forgetting
herself. It's like the dream stops dreaming—"

"God. You're actually reading that?"

Sara looked up to see Dell, a reedy young graduate
student who was also teaching that semester, as he stirred
a coffee with his index finger. Dell had the haunted, over-
educated intensity of the academic hand-to-mouth corps
and was perpetually working on his Ph.D. thesis, a com-
parative study of meter and lyric in the works of Samuel
Beckett and Tupac Shakur.

"Yeah. Y'know. Just getting a jump on the competi-
tion," Sara said, straining for a tone of indifference.

"That chick is nuts. Hot. But nuts. Sign my petition?"

Dell always had a petition. And brochures.

"What for?" Sara asked tentatively, trying not to
prompt the usual three-hour diatribe about the coral reef
or the condition of chicken farms or a forestation project
in Central America. She cared, of course, just *not today*.

"About Claire," Dell said. "Know how much she's
making? And they're asking the teaching assistants to take

a wage freeze? I mean, I know you're an adjunct now, but this affects you, too," Dell said, still stirring his coffee forcefully.

"Maybe later." Sara nodded. There was too much and not enough to say in defense of her interest in Claire. She packed her bag and left for her empty apartment.

in the world

. . . who ever rose in the world without ambition?

Charlotte Brontë, to Aunt Elizabeth Branwell, 1841

A young, unassuming English girl grows up in a broken
home. Her mother is absent but she has a devoted father,
two sisters, and a brother to whom she is very close.
Weaned on the silly romance novels of her day, she grows
up to fall in love with an older man. She believes in true
love and the workings of fate. In fact, she is so desperate to
believe, she ignores the fact that this man is already in love
with another woman. The girl, on the cusp of maiden-
hood, as they say, is profoundly disillusioned. She withdraws into her own despair, sending desperate letters to
the man, who cannot return her love.

She is shattered to see her romantic illusions so easily
dismantled by the disaffection of one man, who, if she is

truly honest with herself, is not all that handsome, anyway. The girl grows into a woman; the woman is very famous and has many famous friends. She inadvertently becomes a symbol of modern womanhood. She dedicates herself to what she sees as her calling in this world. She suffers a series of setbacks that make her seem all the more noble. What's more, she has become adept at spinning her own legend and constructing her image before the public.

Finally she meets a man who on all evidence returns her love. She is in her thirties, for once seeming relaxed and content with her love life and career. Everyone says she is on the brink of a marvelous new beginning when suddenly, tragically, she dies. She is mourned by a shocked public eager to learn every detail of her death, and her memory is lionized by biographers who portray her as a martyred symbol of modern womanhood.

Princess Diana? Charlotte Brontë? Both. More or less. Sara realized on reflection that there were indeed parallels that would at least salvage Claire's proposed panel from complete disaster.

Sara told one of her favorite Brontë anecdotes about how all three sisters managed to publish a novel under a male pseudonym, each within the space of one year without anyone in the small town of Haworth, much less their own small home, guessing the truth. Finally, fearful that the mail addressed to her pseudonym was being misdirected, Charlotte walked into her father's office, arms loaded with a published manuscript and a number of rave reviews, to acknowledge that she was London's latest literary star.

Quietly over tea, Mr. Brontë informed the family audience (which included, unbeknownst to him, the authors of *Agnes Grey* and *Wuthering Heights*) that "Charlotte has been writing a book—and I think it is a better one than I expected."

This drew a round of appreciative chuckles from Sara's audience. Sara noticed, with an irritated note of self-regard, that the newsmagazine doing a piece on Claire had turned off its cameras during Sara's performance. Suddenly the red "on" light flashed brilliantly.

"I think it was Yeats," Claire said, "who said Charlotte Brontë was 'the flame that longed for the fire.' It reminds me of something Gianni Versace, the designer, said about the princess shortly before they both met their tragic fates." Claire recited from memory: "'There's a kind of serenity. I had a fitting with her last week for new suits and clothing for spring, and she is so serene. It is a moment in her life, I think, when she's found herself—the way she wants to live.'"

This was from the July 1997 edition of *Vanity Fair,* the most inadvertently tragic issue of a magazine ever, according to Claire. It contained quotes from the soon-to-be-dead Versace about the soon-to-be-dead Diana, but even beyond that, the magazine was saturated with premature death. There was the photo of art stars of the eighties, a single photo containing Keith Haring, Robert Mapplethorpe, and Jean-Michel Basquiat—the floor must have heaved under the weight of so much future mythmaking.

According to Claire, the temperature at the center of the flora that overflowed the lawn of Buckingham Palace during the days that followed Diana's death reached 180 degrees. This was the temperature of fame, Claire pointed out. The white heat of the princess's enduring appeal. For her part, Sara wondered who felt obliged to obtain this nugget of wisdom. Met with a sea of flowers, Sara couldn't imagine in a million years thinking to take its temperature.

"Popular culture is a kind of dream, a lucid dream, in which the participants know they are acting in a kind of dumb show of the collective unconscious," Claire opined. Dumb show was right, Sara thought. This was the uneasy bargain: the legitimacy of Brontë for the sexiness of Diana. Here was the tradition of literature reduced to its most discrete unit of exchange.

"For instance," Claire continued, "Donald Trump writes in his memoirs—" Memoirs! Sara marveled. Donald Trump? "—that his one regret in 'the women department' was that he never 'courted Lady Diana Spencer.'"

Sara really regretted the reporting of this fact. Now she had the phrase "women department" and the image of Donald Trump pressed indelibly in her mind. She imagined some elaborate, gold-plated department store built just for Donald Trump in which the captain of industry, maker of the deal, shopped for his future, plucking the course of his destiny like ripe fruit from a tree. "Floor Seven—Women Department," she imagined the elevator boy, Robin Leach, announcing. "Champagne wishes and caviar dreams!"

If only he had taken a right at the Lady Diana Spencer aisle instead of a left at the Georgia Peach Marla Maples aisle. Life was funny that way, he would think, shaking his head, wistfully recalling that ethereal princess with the low self-esteem. He could have helped, could have saved her from herself. He would have taken her to fine New York restaurants and taught her the Art of the Deal. Her self-esteem would no doubt have improved under the Donald's watchful gaze. Making a wrong turn in the Women Department could really cost you. And more than just moneywise.

There were bizarre divisions created by Diana's death. There were the people who mourned hysterically and there were the people who stood on the sidelines shaking their heads and wondering what all the fuss was about. There were those who said it was just because she was good-looking that she garnered so much press, then there was the backlash, among comedians and male authors mostly, claiming that she was, when all was said and done, really not that good-looking. Howard Stern made this assertion to Donald, and Donald countered that there were times when Diana was "supermodel beautiful." Like a brand name: Supermodel Beautiful. This convinced Howard and seemed to put the issue to rest. Donald owned the Miss Universe pageant after all, he ought to know.

During the question-and-answer portion, a young woman asked Claire if she didn't think that the massive media attention lavished on Diana's death wasn't at least partly due to the fact that she died over Labor Day weekend on an especially slow news day. Claire visibly winced before pointing out that Yeltsin had said he wouldn't run for president that same day.

"But everyone knew he couldn't run for another

term," the woman pressed. "So it wasn't really news, not in the classic sense."

"The term 'news in the classic sense' sounds elitist to me," Claire said, finally dismissing the woman. Another young woman stood up and asked Sara about the place of madness and women in the works of the Brontës. Sara looked out at her audience, gathering a confidence she hadn't felt in weeks.

"Obviously, emotional states, even telepathy, were elevated to a place of prime significance in the works of all the Brontës," she said. "There is a kind of psychological intensity that was particularly disturbing and exciting to audiences of that time and today as well, I think. What's more, even though their works were dismissed as 'unladylike,' they did focus a lot of literary attention on those aspects that have been stereotypically associated with the feminine—intuition, emotions, affairs of the heart—and made them central and, in fact, the elements that defined a life more acutely than the day-to-day reality that existed on the surface.

"Women's mental states have always been, right or wrong, associated with their sex. What the Brontës did was to very subtly co-opt this misogynist tradition and turn it into a narrative strategy of involvement and identification. Likewise, I think Diana called a lot of attention to these same things—in today's parlance, self-esteem, bulimia, whatever. She really was continuing the tradition that the Brontës pioneered of accepting and using her emotional life as the point of engagement with the rest of the world. She was criticized for that tendency, and I think there might be residual sexism in that—the feminization of the world culture, if you will, which is really about the valuation of those aspects that were formerly dismissed as trivial or girlish."

The young woman nodded and sat down. Sara turned to see Claire giving her a look of pride. Sara smiled back.

Then Dell raised his hand and asked Claire what real value Princess Diana Studies had to academia. A few people giggled nervously. His friends clapped. Claire narrowed her eyes and flicked back a mass of red curls.

"Well, my research is sometimes very esoteric and beyond certain people, but I don't see how that invalidates it. For instance, not everyone understands what Stephen Hawking is doing—maybe only two or three or four people really understand it and its significance at any given time. But I don't think anyone would suggest that's a reason for him to stop doing it. In the same way, not everyone understands that when I talk about my breasts I'm not talking about the breasts *qua* breasts but about my power as a woman."

Dell nodded, clearly unconvinced. Claire edged forward in her seat, ready to meet the challenge of any unbeliever.

"Now, what I'm talking about is Diana as warrior, as a symbol of Woman not willing to be a victim anymore, and that's why the monarchy had to get rid of her. I have no doubt she was rubbed out. Why? Because she was dangerous—she was a rebel with a great wardrobe, and let's face it, that's a threatening combination. She was a tremendous pioneer, which is what many fail to realize in acknowledging her power. They'd rather be superior, but okay, what did she pioneer? The commodification of the self, definitely, but more to the point, enjoying it, *controlling* it. She took the power back from her husband, the future king of England, by posing sadly in front of the Taj Mahal. The media ate out of her hand and she played them. She instinctively understood that every battle from the twentieth century on would be waged in the field of the Image. Genius! The whole British monarchy was out of their depth when they took her on, PR-wise."

Dell shook his head. "I find your logic reductive," he said, invoking the quintessential smack-down of any scholarly debate. Claire nodded sympathetically as if concerned for his soul.

"Let me explain," she offered with a lilt Sara recognized as pure Claire, equal parts condescension and seduction. "Every century has had its form of voyage, discovery, and marketing. But now all the lands are discovered, if you will, unless you count outer space, which I don't, because, well, the outfits are terrible. So okay. What's left? The journey inward. Start portioning off pieces of the self and sell them! Diana took her low self-esteem and sold it. She took her new discovery of herself and sold it. People hold that against her, but I say, Look! Marco Polo, Columbus, Vespucci, de León, Diana! She belongs in that company because she looked for undiscovered country and struck gold."

Dell gave an innocent shrug, instinctively aware he was about to be dubbed a misogynist. Sara felt sorry for him, but he should have known better than to openly challenge Claire. In front of cameras, no less.

"Now, not to get too personal, but okay, I'm a woman, I'm brilliant and powerful, I make a lot of money, and I don't apologize for any of it. I dress the way I do to foreground the constructedness of my sexuality and also because I look great. That frightens some men, little men"—Claire fixed her crosshairs on him—"but what can I do if they're pathetic?

"You see," she continued, "here in America all you teach young women is how to be victims and consumers— you want to medicate them, institutionalize them, encourage them to cry and blame Daddy. Instead of being the passionate creators of their own destiny, women today are simply led from one consumer moment to the next; success is the progression from boyfriend to husband, hatchback to SUV, IKEA to Pottery Barn."

Sara noticed herself nodding in agreement, guiltily remembering her dog-eared copy of the Pottery Barn catalog in her bathroom.

"I say 'No more.' No more passive consumer! You are a passionate creator of your own destiny!" Claire announced.

Yes, that is what I am, Sara thought. Or would like to be.

"The first day of class," Claire continued, running a hand through her hair, "I walked in and asked my students, 'Who here is on Serenitol?' and do you know three-quarters of them raised their hands? I said, 'Throw it out! From now on you will be taking Claire Vigee!'" Claire threw the camera a flirtatious smile. "Or should I say, 'Claire Vigee will be taking you'?"

Claire paused, careful not to step on her audience's appreciative laughter. "Then I said, 'Did you know that at your age Jeanne d'Arc had conversed with God and three saints, faced down a British monarch, led her country to military victory, confounded gender stereotypes, challenged religious persecution, and still found time to be dead for four years? She was a passionate creator!"

Claire flashed them a movie star smile—the cameras had gotten it all.

At the reception, Claire's attention was dominated by the film crew, but in Claire's reflected glory, Sara enjoyed a slightly elevated position within the department. The dean of the school finally remembered her name instead of mistaking her for one of the caterers. Even her adviser said, "Great twist on the madwoman in the attic vis-à-vis Diana. Talk to me on Monday."

As the film crew put away their cameras and started rolling up the cables, Sara approached Claire. Claire was reapplying her lipstick.

"I really navy-blued them," Claire remarked to her compact.

"Sorry?"

"Navy blue is a major power color for me. I think of it now as a verb. I'm always inventing new uses for words, I'm just that way." Claire shrugged her acceptance of her own powers.

"That quote from Yeats—"

"That was good, wasn't it?"

"What's that from?"

"Who knows?" Claire lit a cigarette, surveying the crowd with coy evasiveness.

"You made it up," Sara realized.

"Yeats was always talking about something or other. I'm sure he said something to that effect."

Sara shook her head, stunned. How much her life turned on Claire's blithely manufactured trivia! Sara quickly figured Claire made easily about ten times what Sara did—where was Dell's petition now? Sara took a deep breath; she had to stay focused.

"Claire, I have to ask you, did you tell Paul he lived 'in a corner' or 'on a corner'? I've just been wondering . . . it's taken on this sort of ridiculous significance," Sara said lamely, realizing how foolish the question made her look.

Claire effortlessly twisted her hair up into a stylish chignon. "Can you believe that guy?"

"Paul?"

"No. That asshole—the grad student. How rude. And I was going to help him, put him in touch with a record company maybe to help fund his research."

"Dell?"

Claire brushed a crease from her skirt. "I think every suit I buy this year will be navy blue." She zipped up a black leather knapsack and tossed it over her shoulder. Lester was waiting outside in the car.

"It went great tonight, didn't it? I was thinking tonight maybe you should cut your hair. Short. I mean, Jean Seberg short. You have gamine energy—has anyone ever told you that? My silent Victorian is finding her voice. You excite me.

I'm trying to find ways to be more quiet, like you. I think that's an asset in this day and age. Too much noise."

"Right," Sara agreed, but Claire was already gone. Sara walked out of the lecture hall and into the night. The cabs on Broadway were empty and available at this hour, pining for company like drunken lovers. Sara let them pass. She'd planned to treat herself to one but now she liked the cold. It made more sense than anything this evening.

Taking the familiar walk home, Sara felt her resolve to be a passionate creator weakening. She tightened her scarf against the wind. It's all stories, she thought, the pull of nostalgia working through each tree or bodega or restaurant she had passed so many times with Paul. Already she was becoming someone else's story. Somewhere across the black Atlantic Paul was explaining himself to some sympathetic Therese. Or maybe he'd found a Marie by now. Or a Solange. It didn't matter. He'd wrestle with the language, that thing he didn't trust, to explain away the mysterious turns of the heart.

Breaking up with Sara would become the story of how he came to France. Of how he met Therese. It was the story he would someday tell their indifferent, yawning grandchildren at picnics. He'd have a little too much wine and then the picture of Sara would inexplicably surface in his mind, her image yellowing at the edges but still vivid. Still vivid at the center. Sara could feel herself becoming someone's wrong turn in the Woman Department. All those years of being the right turn, the happy discovery, that blessed, happy ending, and then . . .

But worse, she felt Paul becoming a story, a story to

dine out on, a story to impress others with her powers of wry observation. This is how love is, ha, ha, ha. "What's the difference between an English professor and a pizza?" she imagined some wizened and leathery version of her older self asking between puffs on a menthol cigarette. "A pizza can feed a family of four. Ha, ha, ha."

The loss of love made every story you told yourself about how you got to be where you are—why you were with this person and not another, why you lived on this corner, in this city, and worked in that building, and felt the way you did about all those things—the loss made all these stories suddenly untrue. It ripped the narrative. Suddenly you had to invent a new story—a story to make sense of what happened to you—on the fly, without rest or professional consultation. You made do, you made things up and hoped for the best. There was no time for reflection. Reflection made the bottom fall out all over again, it made you stare vacantly at the cars streaming past you on Broadway wondering where your tidy little life went.

Sara cut over to Riverside, walking past the large statue of a Buddhist missionary that had survived atomic blasts in Japan, the statue that always gave her comfort. There were bigger things in the world than a broken heart, she tried to remind herself. But she just as quickly noticed the bench in Riverside Park where she and Paul shared their first kiss. They had escaped a boring department holiday party held at the Vice Dean's apartment on Riverside. It was the first year of graduate school for both of them. They had been aware of each other socially and had even been in a study group together for a class on the modern

British novel when Sara first noted his resemblance to Laurence Olivier in *Wuthering Heights* and developed a strong infatuation. Paul was all the more desirable for being unattainable; he had a girlfriend, a wealthy and angular young woman named Sofie who wore African beads and spoke often of joining the Peace Corps but never actually got around to it.

"You look bored," he had said to Sara in the kitchen. They had both come to this event solo and had both silently noted it. Sara smiled sadly—what could one do at a boring but politically necessary gathering? Before she could really think, he had grabbed their coats and a bottle of champagne, and escorted her to a frigid bench on a freezing December night.

"This is your idea of escape?" Sara had asked, her teeth chattering as she sipped champagne out of a paper cup.

"Isn't it yours?"

In fact, it was and that was all she needed to know about him. They had the same idea of escape. What's more, they were both in the difficult process of ending relationships. Sara had grown weary of her then-boyfriend, Dan, who skipped the better part of an Ivy League education, lived on a trust fund, and spent his days getting stoned and teaching himself Bob Dylan songs on the guitar. For a while she had quietly resigned herself to Dan's mopey indifference, fearing she could do no better, but she had recently made an effort to break away from him. Paul's interest confirmed her hope that life had better things to offer.

They commiserated over the fact that their financially privileged mates seemed never to actually appreciate their luck while poor fools like Paul and Sara had to scrape and claw for every student loan or foundation grant they could find. They consoled each other as they recounted the emotional scenes in restaurants and subway cars that marked the delicate process of parting. This was destiny, no doubt about it, Sara had thought. Paul even spoke in fateful terms, explaining wistfully that there was some advanced field in the study of photons he'd heard about on the radio called the science of "entanglement," in which photons "knew" about one another's movements. This conversation quickly devolved, as most conversations about science between nonscientists generally do, into vague and abstract notions of love. Paul confessed he had long felt "entangled" with Sara just admiring her from afar, he had a feeling he always would.

He told Sara he was the only son among five children, a large family of women, all of them witty and intelligent. He had always believed women were superior beings, especially the smart ones, and in his life, there were *only* smart ones. They fascinated and intimidated him, and in the deepest part of his soul he believed it was their approval that kept him breathing. He was a compulsive chatterer out of nervousness, he explained, especially in the company of intelligent women like Sara.

"In fact, if you don't kiss me," he'd said, "I may never stop talking." Sara had smiled and then leaned over and kissed him.

Several years later Sara stood staring at the same bench. Paul's large family of women who had welcomed her so warmly into the fold hadn't bothered to reach out to her when Paul left. They were like him, intense but abrupt in their affections; when they dropped you, you were gone. She wondered if Paul's photons "knew" her photons now spent the better part of each day composing letters in her head that began something like, "Lenny Bruce once said that there's nothing sadder than an aging hipster—this statement makes me think of you," or the more direct, "Dear Asshole, How's your French whore? Just swell, I hope."

It was an undeniable fact, they were entangled, though the word now had a more ominous, less romantic ring to it. Maybe it was true, Sara thought, rushing away from the bench and its memories, what a philosopher once said: Some people would never fall in love if they hadn't read about it in books. Maybe Sara and Paul had simply read too much. Or maybe it would turn out that she *was* someone's right turn in the Woman Department after all—maybe she was Paul's, maybe she would die before she found out. It didn't matter, she told herself. It was only the story, the snail's trail that life left behind, the cover of *Vanity Fair,* the beautiful corpse in Paris's Alma Tunnel that anyone cared about. It was clear in that moment, the chill of Manhattan frosting her breath for what seemed like an eternity: What happens doesn't really matter, only the story.

without hope

If my master withdraws his friendship entirely from me I will be completely without hope—if he gives me a little—very little—I will be content—happy. I will have a reason for living—for working—

Charlotte Brontë, to Professor Heger, 1845

---

sara—

could you please send my first editions? first class, insured? i had a flu the past couple days but am feeling much better now. hope classes are going well.

sincerely,
paul

The e-mail from Paul stared mercilessly back at Sara as she sat at her computer. That "Sincerely" was at least as revealing as the request. From "Love" to "Sincerely"— here was the sad path of rejected lovers. Sara stared at the books on the bottom shelf as though they were Betrayal itself. Meredith was right. She did want to burn them. She wanted to break their spines and feed their glue to the roaches. She wanted to find a kingdom of silverfish and watch them steadily devour the books, page by page, as the books slowly, sadly forgot themselves. But she was above that. She would confine herself to the violence of the imagination. She was grieved to realize that books were so simply designed that within two hours she'd run out of ways of imagining their violent end. And she'd run out of wine. She would have to insult the books themselves and break out the hard liquor.

Down and Out in Paris and London by Paul's hero, George Orwell. Sara had bought a first edition for Paul for his twenty-fifth birthday. She had taken out an extra student loan just to buy it. He'd been moved to tears by the gesture. He wept and said no one had ever gotten him such a thoughtful gift. No one had ever known him like Sara, he'd said. He's probably using the same line on Therese right now, Sara thought bitterly as she poured some brandy into a coffee mug. Paul had never seemed the type to work the ladies with smooth lines, but now Sara wasn't so sure. She now often found herself rereading the relationship backward with an eye fixed on cynical reappraisals.

Down and Out in Paris and London. Now, *that* is a stupid and romantic book, Sara thought. George wandered around being poor and ponderous and unappreciated in Paris and had to wash dishes. In fact, the whole essay had about it the strapping romance of being a young, undiscovered genius, which only revealed that men were far more romantic than women. Leave it to a man to romanticize washing dishes.

At least women romanticized important things like sex and death and, by extension, gossip and clothes. But men? What a wretched waste of romantic anguish was laid at the feet of dishwashers and women named Brett or Slim who in a million years would never sleep with you. And that was another thing, Paul was always looking down his nose at the Brontës, at the foofy girliness of all those "books with corsets." Here was an irony he could discuss with his swimsuit model: In their day, the Brontës were constantly criticized for being too masculine. Writing under male pseudonyms, the women were chastised for the strange passions of their female characters, the crude realism of their depictions of the male-female relationship, the outright impropriety that these authors actually seemed to endorse! Women were actively warned not to read them.

When it was finally discovered that the authors were authoresses, it was assumed that the harsh countryside, the strangeness of an isolated, backward community had warped the imaginations of these sweet, motherless girls, the daughters of a parson, no less. The Brontës were too masculine for women to read. Perhaps Therese could deconstruct that.

And what about that pansy Orwell, weeping into his shirtsleeves about shooting an elephant? The Brontës were looking better all the time. Even dreamy, fantasy-riddled, consumptive Emily, when bitten by a strange dog, took it upon herself to cauterize the bite with a fire iron and never even mentioned it to her family until the fear of infection had passed. It was odd, wispy Emily who clung to life, managing the household, planning her next novel, referring to the cough that would take her as a "dry uninteresting wind" and denying she was dying until her final breath at twenty-nine.

Emily Brontë could kick George Orwell's ass any day of the week, Sara noted as she drifted off into a thick and boozy sleep.

Of course, she woke up at four o'clock in the morning. Four to seven was the new contemplation hour. Sara rubbed her temples, trying to think of something therapeutic to do with this unfortunate window of time. Naturally her thoughts turned to the past and to Paul. She remembered a paper they had often joked about coauthoring together on the inherent falseness of biography. They already knew the title: "Mongoloid on a Pogo Stick." They had only been in the apartment for a few weeks when they began to wake up to the sound of rhythmic thunking on the ceiling above them.

At first it started at seven. It was Sara who presumed it was a pogo stick—it had the same rhythm, the whip and pop she'd remembered distinctly from childhood. Paul supposed it was a mongoloid for no real reason other than he liked the sound of the word. This produced an endless debate about the etymology of *mongoloid*. Why were people with Down's syndrome called that and why were they offended?

Finally they broke out the books. Anthropologically, the term refers to the people of central and eastern Asia and is no longer in use. Offensively, the term was a scientific classification of mental retardation devised by nineteenth-century British physician John L. H. Down. Dr. Down invented his classifications along ethnic lines. Hence the confusion. Now nobody wants to be called mongoloid, but for the boy on the pogo stick upstairs, the name stuck.

The times of pogo-playing progressively moved back earlier and earlier so that finally at three A.M., Paul raced upstairs and demanded silence. The old man who lived in the apartment had no idea what Paul was talking about. He lived alone. He'd been sleeping peacefully. He didn't hear any noise.

This, they resolved, was the fundamental problem of biography, in fact, of history in general. Once the idea of the mongoloid on the pogo stick was created, the image was indelible. All future suppositions would be predicated in relation to the mongoloid on the pogo stick, a ridiculous but too vivid image to forget. Reimagining the past always presupposed your ability to dispense with the image you began with, and no matter how many facts rush to contradict your initial impression, you can never forget that mongoloid. Down through the ages that familiar whip and pop will sound like what you want to hear.

Anybody with a passing claim to fame has an instinctual insight into this fact. Charlotte Brontë's husband, Arthur, was horrified at the detailed character descriptions contained in her letters to friends, claimed they were "as dangerous as lucifer matches." He gave Charlotte an ultimatum: She could stop writing her letters altogether or she would allow him to censor them. In addition, he demanded that her best friend and correspondent, Ellen Nussey, burn all of Charlotte's letters to her—a correspondence of twenty years. "He says women are most rash in letter-writing— they think only of the trustworthiness of their immediate friend—and do not look to contingencies—a letter may fall into any hand." Charlotte dutifully burned all her letters. Ellen agreed to burn hers as well. Yet here was another great tradition of literature: the friend who lies. Ellen Nussey never burned those letters.

Patrick Brontë, Charlotte's father, however, cut up many of her letters to appease her fans who wrote to him after her death asking for a piece of her handwriting. Mr. Brontë obliged, sending off one-line snippets of her letters. Thank God for Madame Heger, the unlikeliest of literary saviors. Charlotte's passionate, pleading letters to Professor Heger were torn up and thrown away. Madame Heger collected them, stitched them back together, and gave them to their daughter for safe keeping. When the daughter reproduced the letters on Professor Heger's deathbed, he again refused them. Again they were saved, this time by the daughter. Something in the imagined scene of Professor Heger again and again turning away from these letters until his dying breath captivated Sara. Maybe Charlotte's passion could be denied, but the letters themselves took on a strange, indestructible life—miraculously, the letters survived to this day.

This was the world that intrigued Sara, the unwritten history that never saw the light of day, that was killed early on by its creator or receiver, or was perhaps wandering the globe like an orphaned child, slyly hiding in the strongboxes and attics of depressed Belgian widows. Maybe they would show themselves, finally step into the light. But you had to find them. You had to stop hearing that noise as the thunk of a pogo stick, had to reimagine it completely. But you were always wrong. No matter what you assumed, no matter how you pieced together the fragments of lost lives, you never got it right. You could grab ahold of them, tighten your grasp, and they would turn to vapor and laugh at you while you stared at your empty hand. They would just vanish and all you'd be left with was the absurd image of a mongoloid on a pogo stick waking you up in the middle of the night.

the only revenge

I have the vague feeling that there are cold and rational people who would say on reading this—'she is raving'—The only revenge I would wish on such people is a single day of the torments I have suffered for eight months—we would see then if they did not rave too.

Charlotte Brontë, to Professor Heger, 1845

"Oh."

Sara could hear the sharp intake of breath on the other end of the phone as her mother considered her response. Sara knew she'd be disappointed. Her parents loved Paul; in fact, he made Sara seem more approachable to them. But her mother would have to reconfigure it in a positive light.

"Maybe you should look on this as a terrific opportunity to get organized!"

And she meant it. Sara's mother had given up her therapy practice and opened a design and consulting firm called SPACE (Stimulating Peace Arranging Closets Efficiently). She did people's closets. But she didn't just "do" them, she arranged for a special consultation, ordered necessary dividers and organizers, and eliminated all unnecessary items of clothing. The combined practice of assessment, organization, and "letting go" was a profoundly individual, though universal, therapeutic process. This, she discovered, was indeed a form of therapy, and a very effective one at that.

Her favorite success story concerned a middle-aged woman, an alcoholic whose husband beat her regularly. Years of therapy hadn't helped this woman, who continually returned to her husband only to have another rib broken, another tooth knocked across the kitchen floor.

But after having her closets done, a miraculous transformation occurred: The woman kicked her husband out and stopped drinking. Countless therapy sessions had failed to breathe courage into this woman as the daily sight of neatly folded merino wool sweaters tucked away in see-through acrylic boxes had.

"There's just something about an ordered closet that says, 'I can!'" Sara's mother explained. "What's the first thing you think of when you wake up in the morning? 'What am I going to wear?' But what does your closet reflect back to you? 'I'm a sloppy loser—I have no control over my life.' A well-ordered closet reflects a well-ordered sense of self and well-being. A clean closet says, 'I matter.'"

"No, thanks, Mom."

"You'll feel worlds better."

"No, I'm swamped right now, anyway."

"If you invest the time now, you'll be saving it in the future."

"No, thanks. Really."

It was no use explaining the therapeutic benefits of self-pity and reckless drinking to a therapist. It was something understood intuitively or not at all.

"You are coming out for the weekend, though."

"I don't think I have time, Mom."

"It's only an hour train ride. At least come for Friday night. I'll cook lamb shanks." This was exactly what Sara had hoped to avoid, a weekend of her parents, therapists no less, tending to Her Feelings.

"Oh, come on. What do you have to do Friday? Are you seeing anyone yet?"

"Mom! I'm just busy is all."

"Come for Friday. What else are you going to do?" *I do have cable television,* Sara wanted to protest.

"I'll take the four-thirty train."

"Focus on what you can change, not what you can't," Sara's father said as he handed her a plate.

"Thanks, Dad. I am."

Her father smiled wistfully. All those damned books. Romanticism belonged in certain German operas and nowhere else. His training had taught him that suffering was a choice, and he'd watched his daughter choose one hair shirt of a boyfriend after another. At least Paul had seemed a bit more practical, more energetic and optimistic. He'd made his daughter happy. Or so he'd thought.

"Taped something for you. An interview."

"Really?" Sara asked between bites of lamb. Her father was famous for his obliquely relevant videotapes of any old thing he caught on television he thought you might like. Once Paul had offhandedly expressed a desire to learn about mushroom hunting, really just making conversation, and a week later a three-hour nature documentary on mycology appeared on their doorstep in a bubble-wrapped envelope.

Oh, the Evening of Mycology, Sara recalled sadly. They sent for Chinese and opened champagne and laughed at the ridiculously serious English narrator's lisp. *Most mushwooms awe supwrisingly vigowous.* Tears welled in Sara's eyes. Not another spontaneous crying jag, she worried. She bit hard into the lamb, but it was soft and barely even needed chewing; the sweet ginger tang against the sharp cumin spread through her, calming her.

"This lamb is perfect, honey," her father said.

"Thank you. It really is, isn't it?" Sara's mother agreed. "Falls right off the bone. I'm surprised. We lost our butcher—as if we need another one-hour photo. This is just from the supermarket. But it's good, isn't it?"

Relaxing with a glass of wine after her parents had gone to bed, Sara watched her father's therapeutic tape. It was a talk show featuring a famous young actress who'd recently weathered a very public marital breakup in which she was clearly the Injured Party. Instead of playing the victim, the famous actress had opted to rise from the ashes promoting her new film. She seemed chatty and amiable in a soberly mature way. She obliquely referenced her recent troubles with grace and humor, allowing the interviewer's hamhanded questions to throw her briefly before answering with serene equanimity. Life was full of surprises, she remarked wisely. Like the handsome Australian actor she'd begun seeing? the interviewer asked with a wink. She only smiled and said her latest film was her deepest, her most personal work. Some people are mentioning "Oscar," the interviewer said. The actress looked humbled by this news as well.

Sara watched in startled amazement. What on earth was her father thinking? But then she realized, the actress had it figured out. Somewhere out there the actress's estranged husband was weeping over a Four Seasons minibar, kicking himself—at least briefly—for giving her up. Actress knew how to play this scene.

What about that producer she'd met the night Paul decided to leave? There were no accidents. It was kismet. Perhaps he was just the man to make Paul weep over the minibar. Already Sara was shopping for furniture for her restored farmhouse in Vermont with her Hollywood producer. . . .

"Sweetie." Sara looked up to see her mother standing in the doorway smiling sadly. "You're thinking about Paul, aren't you?"

"No, Mom. Really, I'm not."

Her mother nodded gently. "Let's see about doing your closets soon."

"I'm fine, really."

"Well. Good night."

Sara watched her mother climb the stairs up to bed. Maybe it could all be worked out. Weren't her parents a testament to that? Somehow lovers argued over sponges and pans, shed tears and said too much and still somehow got back to *I love you, I love you, too.*

Perhaps it was the wine doing the thinking. Or the spurious reasoning of the depressed. Or perhaps the pan had magical properties that, grail-like, could restore a misguided and confused destiny. In any case, Sara ignored the lightly falling rain, ignored the dark, damp chill of the earth under her fingers and started digging. *Why didn't she follow Paul to France? Her passion could remind him of his own—maybe he's afraid of the depths of his true feelings. Or perhaps it wasn't a lack of passion so much as the threat of it. Her emotional bravery would prove a stirring inspiration for him!* Surely there were worse fates—rooting around in your parents' backyard in the dark, in the rain, trying to avoid the skeletal remains of hamsters while unearthing an ancient Teflon pan, for instance.

Sara dug deeper, mud under her fingernails as she felt a bit of what? Plastic? The handle. The handle! She dug faster, pushing the mud aside in great, wide swipes. She felt superhuman, the way mothers can allegedly lift semis to procure a wounded baby. Sara pressed the earth back mightily, producing with three massive shoves a sad and broken pan. But it was still there. Like her parents' marriage. Still there. Like Paul would be when he finally came to his senses. Still there.

"Sara?"

Her mother stood shivering under an umbrella, the rain drizzling onto the shoulders of her flannel bathrobe.

With a look of horror and pity, she pointed a flashlight into Sara's eyes.

"Remember? I buried this," Sara said.

"Honey . . ."

Her mother looked frightened. I've frightened my mother, Sara thought. This is what love is: making a fuss and then regretting it.

faculties unexercised

. . . such a strong wish for wings—wings such as wealth can furnish—such an urgent thirst to see—to know—to learn—something internal seemed to expand boldly for a minute—I was tantalized with the consciousness of faculties unexercised . . .

Charlotte Brontë, to Ellen Nussey, 1841

Sara knew it would be a while before she could live down the episode of the Teflon pan in the garden. A clean sweep of her closet with her mother was now an unavoidable certainty. But Sara had appeased her parents somewhat by vaguely mentioning their separation, Paul's departure, healing, the pan, and closure all in one scattered monologue. And true to its possible grail-like qualities, the pan, now cleaned and hanging in Sara's kitchen, ushered in an Era of Intriguing Possibilities via e-mail:

Nykki—

Brontë project a (very) possible go. The weirdest things
happening—on plane back to L.A. two women are sitting
behind me talking about Brontë. Then I'm at a meeting, I
notice the receptionist is reading *Jane Eyre*—this is
getting weird, so then I hear a certain A-level actress
(I can't say who but probably who you're thinking) is
scouting for her next project, which she's hoping to be a
"prestige, period costume drama with a lot of class—
possibly a classic." !!! Then I hear—on good authority—
that a certain producer who's soon to be an executive at
(I shouldn't say—but one of the ones that actually
matters) is a huge Brontë fan. Soon as you have it done,
I can have it on her desk the next morning. In the
meantime please send me enough info to pitch and
bullshit over drinks—I've been able to download some
stuff from the Internet, but I specifically need your angle
on the material. This could be very hot. Write fast (but,
of course, as long as it takes).

Regards,
Byrne Emmons

Dear Mr. Emmons,

You seem to be the victim of a serious misunderstand-
ing. I recall meeting you at Claire's book party and
vaguely suspected what is now obvious, you have
mistaken me for somebody else.

I apologize for any oversight on my part that led you to your confusion. Please rest assured that your confidences are safe with me, as I've fortunately no clue to whom or what you alluded in your e-mail. I would be more than happy to provide information for bullshitting or other purposes, but as far as angles are concerned, I am simply a scholar.

However, I must say I'm intrigued and would welcome the chance to talk further. I would be quite interested in meeting again, as I enjoyed our brief conversation and have always been fascinated with the world of film. If you're ever in New York again, please feel free to look me up.

My sincere apologies,
Sara Frost

Sara . . .
There's a party you must go to this Saturday. Call my assistant for details.
—C.

Sara was surprised to find Claire's party in full swing by the time she arrived at ten. She didn't see Claire anywhere, but the loft seemed to belong to her: an enviably spacious apartment dimly lit by candlelight. She had wall-size photographs on opposing walls that Sara overheard someone (possibly the artist) explain were something microscopic blown up to outsized dimension.

"They're so small in reality and yet in consequence

so large, when you think about it. It's eroticizing biology," the possible artist explained.

"I would think it's the other way around," a man in vinyl pants responded.

"Hmm?"

"Isn't it biologizing the erotic?"

"Um. Well . . . it's *big*," the artist concluded thoughtfully.

Sara gazed up at the ceiling where white muslin curtains billowed tastefully. The apartment had been decorated sparingly, favoring bold navy blue furniture and the abundance of candles one would naturally expect of a self-described ambisexualist. Sara noticed a man in his thirties dressed like a teenager, baggy jeans and a striped T-shirt. He picked unashamedly at a bowl of mixed nuts, ferreting out the cashews. She was surprised by the mixed nuts. They seemed like such a banal offering from an ambisexualist. The man produced a massive Brazil nut.

"Who eats these?" he asked Sara, brandishing the nut menacingly. Sara shook her head. The man tossed the nut back in the bowl and walked away. This is stupid, I should leave, Sara thought. There aren't even any cashews left—

"I saw her gazing at the heavens. Something about the way she folded her arms like so said, 'Pry me open!' "

"Denis."

"Sara. You are in my poem."

"How's it coming?" she asked uncomfortably, sorry now that she hadn't left when she had the chance.

Denis shrugged his indifference. "Some days I am brilliant. Some days less so. It's like life."

"Right."

Denis stared at her, smiling.

"How do you know Claire?" Sara asked, unnerved by his smiling.

"She's in my poem."

"Of course." Denis continued to stare, smiling that smile.

"Do you do illicit drugs?" he asked finally.

"What? No."

Sara looked around the room hoping she might see someone she knew.

"I only ask for my poem. I must control for everything."

"What do you mean?"

"Paul is dead?"

"No. He's in France."

"I'm from France!"

"He's fine."

"Good for Paul."

"I'm going to get a drink," Sara said, looking for an out.

"Let's you and I get drunk."

"No, I just—"

"You see, when there is a mystery standing in front of me with her arms folded, I must investigate. I must unpeel what I do not understand. I am French."

"Well, I'm American and we destroy what we don't understand."

Denis laughed. "I like a witty woman, too," he said as he led her by the arm into the kitchen, where Dell was lecturing an actress Sara recognized.

"Coral reef, *completely gone!*" Dell told the actress. "I saw it myself."

"Dell?" Sara asked, stunned to see him of all people.

"Hey, Sara." Dell waved casually. Sara had to hand it to her, Claire had a way of co-opting her dissenters.

"Is there a producer here?" Sara asked Denis.

"Everyone."

"No, I mean I got this letter—"

"A letter!"

"From a producer I met at Claire's last party. I thought—"

"Love letter?"

"No, e-mail—"

"E-mail!" Denis waved dismissively, as though clearing the air of a bad smell. "I leave the Internet to the children and the pedophiles."

There are opportune illnesses that attack the body when its defenses are down and preoccupied with greater catastrophe. Likewise there are friendships that grow in the wake of a larger misery, and Denis, he explained, specialized in this brand of opportunistic friendship.

"I collect people who are in the midst of one crisis or another, on their way to becoming someone else, because that's when people are most interesting, don't you think? When they are between characters? I come to New York and the women—oh! they are terrifying, beautiful cold creatures, they'll knock you in the stomach. They have big shoes and big coats and then you see them on the subway and what are they reading? These hard women are reading silly romance! I think, Ahh, they are such little girls— tenderhearted little schoolgirls who want to be swept away, but agh, they'll never become anything. Not till their silly hearts are broken. Then maybe they'll be interesting."

Sara checked her watch.

"Time passed. Remarkable!" Denis threw up his arms in delight.

They were drinking from a bottle of liqueur—something bitter and heavy that Sara had slowly grown used to to such a degree that she had become very drunk.

"This is what I wonder about America—why she is so fascinated with the penetration of children?" Denis asked. Sara shook her head.

"Every time I come to your country, there is something on the news about getting a shot for something—"

"Vaccinations?"

"Yes, okay, vaccinations. So every time, every chance they get, they show a child getting a shot."

"So?"

"They are obsessed with penetrating a child!"

Sara gave him a dubious look. Denis looked heavenward, preparing himself, yet again, to explain something to an American. "You see," he began, "they show a close-up, they linger on the needle going in, the look of agony on the child's face. The child is completely sexualized and yet you Americans cannot cope with this reality, so you make it about vaccinations."

"We want children?"

"Children are very erotic and yet only the French appreciate that eroticism pervades every aspect of life. We do not have to hide behind needles."

"You copulate in the streets?" Sara asked pointedly.

Denis sighed. "I am only saying we do not fear the sexual. You give something power by fearing it. This is why you have child molesters—"

Sara rolled her eyes. "France has no child molesters?"

"We do." Denis smiled. "But they all come from America." Sara laughed, striking an agreeable détente between their two nations. She was reassured by the party, that she still had the ability to have fun, that the fog that haunted her could lift ever so slightly. She looked around, realizing she still hadn't seen Claire.

"Where is Claire?" Sara asked.

"What I love about Claire," Denis said, ignoring Sara's question, "is that she is always becoming—that's her power. But you. She fears you a little, this is your power. You see, as her rival you possess an erotic power over her—in you she sees everything she denies in herself. A person is as much defined by what they don't become—either by chance or by choice. Don't you think?"

"I'm not her rival," Sara assured him.

"You are here."

"She talks about me?" Sara searched the room for Claire, flush with pride—oh, the simple joys of being visible, being envied.

"On you, she is silent. You see, your influence already. A smart person who rarely talks terrifies people—in her mind she's forming judgments. What does she think? It's a kind of power and Claire collects power. Did she tell you she's trying to be quieter?"

Sara stared off thoughtfully, feeling the weight of the liqueur on her thoughts. She looked at Denis and smiled mysteriously. If silence was her power, so be it. She took the bottle from him and poured herself another shot.

"She says nothing!" Denis exclaimed.

a moment's interest

I felt as if I did not care what I did, provided it was not absolutely wrong, and that it served to vary life and yield a moment's interest.

Charlotte Brontë, to Emily Brontë, 1843

Sara had once noted in an article she wrote that nowhere in the history of the world had the notion of romantic love taken root with such force as in America. Its songs, its movies, the collective force of popular culture indicated the primacy of romantic love. In many cultures the idea of marriage and romantic love coinciding was naive and foolish. Romantic love undermined social harmony, it led couples into exclusive alliances that denied the bonds of society. It was childish.

Romantic love preached destiny and fate. And yet America was founded on the philosophy of the Enlightenment: the notion of free will, the sovereignty of the individual. The freedom to choose one's partner in love seems the logical extension of this philosophy. And yet what do people want to turn this act of choosing into? Fate. Destiny.

A strong sense of destiny has a chastening effect, so much so that at the age of twenty-eight Sara had had only one other lover, and he didn't really count because she and Paul were fated soul mates, Enlightenment be damned. However, the contradictory nature of the Age of Reason and the philosophy of Romanticism came to considerable blows when Sara awoke the next afternoon next to Denis.

To the mix of this heady debate was added the unhelpful presence of a crushing hangover. Sara turned onto her back, staring up at the white curtains on the ceiling. Did the loft belong to Denis?

"G'morning."

Sara turned her head to see Claire across the apartment in the kitchen making espresso. She walked over to Sara and sat on the foot of the bed, handing her a cup of coffee.

"Thanks," Sara managed in her confusion, propping herself up on an elbow.

"I guess you've met Denis."

"I'm sorry—where—" Sara whispered, still piecing together the night.

"Don't worry, you won't wake him—he's an incredibly sound sleeper. Once when we were children there was a bomb—some terrorist something or other. Anyway, it was blocks away—this was Paris—but close enough that the whole apartment building shook, rafters came down, Denis slept through it all."

"I'm not—" Sara shook her head, still confused.

"What?"

"You're not—"

"Lovers? Not since I found out he was my brother. I do respect some taboos."

Sara blinked her eyes, hoping she was still asleep.

"I'm kidding!" Claire announced merrily.

"I didn't see you last night."

"I was on the roof most of the time."

"I didn't know there was a roof."

"There's always a roof."

Sara stared down at her espresso. She felt Denis stirring next to her. Sara looked under the covers—they were both still dressed. That had to be a good sign.

"Ah, she is wondering if she has deflowered me in the night," Denis said, rolling over onto his back. "Or if I am a vampire and have robbed her soul." He stared up at the ceiling. "I've never understood why people should fear the vampire. Are they afraid of him or are they afraid of becoming vampires? What's the problem? They never die, they sleep all day, they're always meeting new people. Sounds good."

"It's a metaphor for erotic possession," Claire reminded him tersely.

"That sounds good, too, but then, I am French—"

"We know you're French, Denis. Do you have to remind us every other minute?"

"Oh, Miss Proper British Boarding School, I apologize for our origins," Denis taunted with a posh English accent.

Claire stormed off into the bathroom. Denis looked at Sara with a bashful smile.

"She's mad at me."

"What for?"

"She likes to keep her discoveries to herself."

Sara looked out the window, wondering now how to leave gracefully. Denis got up and sat on the edge of the bed as Sara searched for her bag. He pulled it out from under the bed, offering it to her.

"Thanks."

Denis leaned in to kiss her forehead. "You were a perfect gentleman. I am almost offended."

Sara smiled.

"But then," he added with a knowing smile, "I am French."

In spite of, or maybe because of her stand-off with Denis, Claire insisted that Sara join them for dinner. And as much as Sara wanted to go home, she couldn't resist when Claire mentioned dinner would be at the Burke-Iveses'. Mr. Burke and Mr. Ives were wealthy New York eccentrics who lived entirely in the nineteenth century. Sara remembered reading about them in the back pages of some magazine, a puff piece on New York oddities. Life après Paul had become strange, it was true, but also a little more intriguing.

Wedged between Denis and Claire in the cab, Sara felt it was her responsibility to repair the rift between them.

"What do they do in the winter for heat?" she asked cheerfully. Dull silence.

"Who has cash?" Claire demanded as the cab pulled up in front of a brownstone in the West Village. Sara rummaged for the ten-dollar bill she remembered stuffing in her coat pocket. Denis shrugged.

"No, of course, Denis, why would you ever have money?" Claire snapped, handing Sara's ten dollars to the cabbie and dashing out before getting change.

Claire reached the door first and rapped at it. A man in nineteenth-century period dress answered the door, smiling warmly. Denis and then Sara were ushered into the foyer by the smiling man. Sara took in her historically accurate surroundings and felt uncomfortably as though she'd wandered into a lavishly produced piece of performance art.

"This is the Miss Frost I've been telling you about," Claire announced.

"Brilliant." Burke took her hand.

"She also lives in the nineteenth century. She's the Brontë scholar."

"Ah, yes," Burke said, taking their coats. "Odd bucket of fish. Whatever became of them?" he said as though wistfully recalling some old neighbors.

"Um, they died," Sara explained warily. True eccentrics are disarming, she realized, because their oddness is so complete, so constant.

"Oh, what a shame." Burke smiled sympathetically. "Well. Let's get you warmed up with some drinks."

They moved into a common room lit only by candle and gaslight. The town house was decorated in grand style with antiques and velvet wall-hangings, creating an effect that hovered uncomfortably between Edith Wharton and Vincent Price.

Ives had pale skin and nervous hands that seemed to fidget in unison with the flicker of the gaslight. The smaller of the two, Ives had blond hair and pale green eyes, while Burke had large dark eyes and a bad habit of staring.

The sheer oddness of the last twenty-four hours was beginning to wear on Sara. She felt a pang of homesickness, a mad urge to run to a pay phone and tell Paul all about her strange encounters. He would love these guys, she thought sadly. Too bad he's not here. Too bad he's a heartless jerk, she reminded herself.

"You have a beautiful home," she said, unnerved by Burke's incessant gaze, his unblinking smile.

"It keeps the rain out," he said, still smiling.

"You missed a fine party last night," Claire reprimanded them.

"We're both in bed so early. What could we do?"

"What book are you working on now?"

"We're not allowed to discuss. But expect a certain marriage of a royal nature in the next year," Ives answered, clearly wanting to reveal more. Burke handed out glasses of wine.

"Really?"

"Without a doubt."

"Who?"

"Can't say."

"Can't you tell me the country?"

"Not without dying. But I may be able to whisper the colors of the flag in your ear." Ives leaned into Claire, provoking excited laughter.

Sara swallowed her wine quickly, trying to approach a state of benumbed social confidence. She was suddenly aware of her silence.

"You're a writer?" she asked Burke.

"No."

"But your book—"

"Oh, no. We make books. Literally. By hand."

"You'll have to show her your workroom after dinner. It's so da Vinci," Claire added.

"Of course. We're working on a wedding album, you see. Something of this nature could take months. Denis, you're unnaturally subdued."

"He's unhappy because I'm ignoring him," Claire explained.

"That is tragic," Ives offered diplomatically. "You won't spoil dinner, I hope. The caterer has even been kind enough to remove her nose ring for the occasion."

Dinner was roasted pheasant with quince cheese and something involving pears. Sara picked at her food nervously, aware of Burke's intense stare.

"Mostly I teach to the disinterested and search for nonexistent letters. And it's still not as glamorous as it sounds," Sara explained.

"I would think there's more to it than that," Burke insisted.

"No—well, there is this very odd man. A film producer, I guess," Sara said, searching for something provocative she could pretend to be indifferent about.

"That is odd."

"He thinks I'm someone involved with films or something. He keeps writing me about some sort of Brontë movie, and I have no idea what he's talking about."

"Take the money. Those people have buckets of it. We made a nursery book for—who's that actress?" Ives asked Burke. Burke shrugged.

"I forget. Anyway, they've plenty to throw about, that's for sure."

"Maybe you should look into *that*, Denis," Claire suggested. "Denis loves to be around scads of money."

"I'm a poem," Denis reminded her through clenched teeth.

"Oh, right, you must be exhausted."

Noting the decline in civility, Burke turned to Ives. "Mr. Ives, please, talk about Florence."

"Mr. Burke and I were in Florence last week, sort of a medieval bookmakers' convention—very odd sorts, as you can imagine," Ives continued unironically. Denis pouted at his pheasant.

"We were staying in this very old villa—a converted convent run by this old, old woman. Very, how to put it, mystical seeming, she was."

"She had crone energy," Claire explained, warming up to her subject, "which is an archetype I believe deeply in—the power of the woman who is beyond sex intrigues me."

Ives cleared his throat. "Anyway, she guides us to the

room and she tells us the story of a young novitiate who was brought to the convent because she was in love with a young man her parents disapproved of. So she's sent to this convent to spend the rest of her days. But she and the young man plot her escape and on the appointed evening she waits and waits. No young man."

Ives took a sip of wine. "So. She waits another night and then another. Weeks pass. Finally, she overhears that the young man has married someone else—a girl with a dowry and more agreeable parents. So. The young woman goes to her bed heartbroken but otherwise perfectly healthy . . . and is found dead the next morning. Died in her sleep. Now everyone who sleeps in this room has the same dream, as though the girl's dream has continued without interruption, only the dream is specific to each dreamer. In this bed, one sees the love of their life, their grand passion, but they also witness its passing—either through rejection . . . or death. Of course, I can't sleep at all. Mr. Burke sleeps like a log. So the next morning I say, 'Mr. Burke, what did you dream?' And he says he doesn't remember. Just like that.

"So I tell the old woman and she says that's the problem: If you believe, you can't sleep; if you don't, you don't dream. 'So how do you know the story's true?' I ask her. She just shrugs and says that's how the story was told to her."

"Now, that's the power of celebrity, isn't it?" Claire asked.

"No. Is the dream that keeps dreaming itself," Denis corrected.

"That's what I said!" Claire continued enthusiastically.

Burke and Ives smiled. The story had had its intended effect of returning everyone to their pet theories.

"Where is this?" Sara asked Burke quietly.

He turned to her, interested in her interest. "Just outside of Florence. Twenty kilometers maybe. Why? Will you try it?"

"I don't sleep as it is," Sara answered, feebly trying to hide her interest. "How could you sleep?"

"I don't remember. It wasn't a normal sleep, though. It was more like a lack of consciousness. I simply ceased to be aware of being awake. It is, I imagine, how it must feel to be dead." Burke turned to realize everyone was now listening intently.

"Who wants dessert?" Ives asked cheerfully.

"What do you think?" Burke asked.

"It's beautiful," Sara replied.

Burke was showing her the papers, the press, the ancient drawings that served as inspiration for their new book designs. A sea turtle, a curled fish, the murky shape of a maenad, a Roman statue, page after page tacked to their walls. Collections of shells, butterflies, and pieces of colored Venetian glass lined one wall while the other was taken up by large windows that opened onto a garden.

"No. I meant Denis and Claire."

"They're fine," Sara said, unsure of the nature of his interest. She was uncomfortable being alone with him.

"Do you think they're lovers? Ives and I can never figure them out."

"They're half brother and sister," Sara reminded him.

"I know. As you can imagine, this gets lots of sunlight in the afternoon," Burke added, gesturing to the windows.

"I don't really know that much about Claire," Sara said.

"That's an accomplishment. She talks of little else." Burke smiled warmly, his gaze resting a little too pointedly on Sara. She walked to one of the shelves, where piles of colorful paper lay.

"Do you have to import all your paper?" she turned to ask, but was startled to realize Burke was no more than two inches from her face.

"I know I've been staring," he explained.

"Have you?"

"I— How can I say this without sounding foolish?"

"Maybe you shouldn't say anything."

"It was you I saw."

"Where?" Sara asked, eyeing the door.

"In my dream."

Sara laughed nervously. I want to go home, she thought. I want my normal life back. I want my nights in front of the TV with my fiancé.

"I'm not kidding," he said. "That's why I haven't been able to take my eyes off you."

"You said you didn't dream anything," Sara reminded him, feeling foolish.

"I lied. It's Ives. He's obsessed with me. How could I tell him I'd dreamed of someone else?"

"I don't—I don't know. I should—"

Sara turned to go upstairs, then noticed his grip on her wrist.

"Please—" Sara said.

"I'm sorry," Burke said gently, letting go of her. "I didn't mean to frighten you."

"I'm not—I'm just very tired."

Burke nodded, studying her eyes, assessing her carefully.

"Someone has broken your heart. I knew there was something about you. That's it, isn't it?"

"A little," Sara said, suddenly self-conscious.

"I'm sorry."

"It happens." She shrugged, straining for nonchalance.

"Maybe," he said. "But if it's your destiny, what can you do but accept it?"

She turned to him and then realized Denis was standing at the top of the stairs, about to intervene on her behalf. Impulsively, she leaned into Burke and kissed him. If he was her destiny, who was she to argue, her fate having changed so many times in the course of the past twenty-four hours? Besides, he had proof, or at least a murky story to back it up, and in the imagination of a romantic, the murkier the better.

But the kiss had as much to do with passionately creating her own destiny as knowing Denis was watching. In the delicate measure of betrayal, kissing two possibly demented men within the space of a day certainly added up to one swimsuit model with a Fulbright. Perhaps she hadn't hit her intended target, but she'd hit something. A door slammed at the top of the stairs.

Sara looked up at the closed door and then kissed him again, realizing for once that a perfectly viable philosophy of life was to take pleasure whenever the opportunity presented itself. She had always connected sex with love and love with destiny, and so literal was her interpretation that she had failed to realize that people could be attractive *because* of their fleeting presence. Having spent her life kissing men on the basis of an elaborate network of predestination, she realized there was a certain animal satisfaction in kissing men on the slimmest of pretexts. This was the thing itself, Sara discovered. She was a passive consumer no more, she was a passionate creator.

"We should go back upstairs now," Sara decided. And Burke agreed, following her lead.

Sara took her seat in the salon. Claire and Ives were already on their second glass of port.

"Of course I would watch it," Claire announced.

"How could you?" Ives demanded.

"Watch what?" Sara asked, noticing Denis sulking in the corner.

"Dodi and Diana."

"What?"

"Having sex."

"According to rumor, and we know how reliable that is," Ives explained with a sarcastic drawl, "Dodi had his yacht rigged to tape their assignations."

"You would watch that?" Sara reflexively asked Claire.

"Absolutely. I am a scholar, after all. I exclude nothing from my sphere of inquiry."

"But that's private," Sara reminded her. She was ready to go home.

"Privacy is my subject!" Claire answered.

"But Claire," Ives intervened, "isn't part of your study the line at which the public crosses into the private?"

"Not at all. I believe the line does not exist. Privacy has never really existed. It's a quaint artifact. You Americans—" Burke quietly took a seat on the sofa next to Ives, eyeing Sara.

"You think privacy is in the Constitution," Claire continued. "It's not. The pursuit of happiness is. The pursuit of privacy is not. It's an artifact, a collective illusion, this valuation of nondisclosure. It's never existed. You people have an insatiable lust, which you cannot ever accept, hence the gnawing appetite. Of course I would watch Dodi and Diana having sex. Wouldn't you want to see Charlotte Brontë having sex, if such a tape existed?" she asked Sara.

"I don't think such a tape could exist," Sara explained rationally.

"But if it did?" Claire insisted.

"No, I wouldn't want to see it."

"Of course you would," Claire pressed. "You use her letters. How is that really any less of a violation? Aren't the letters, in a sense, just as intimate?"

Sara couldn't answer.

"Aha. Our superior privacy-loving American is struck dumb!" Claire announced.

"Sara doesn't share your pleasure of voyeurism," Denis remarked, pointedly looking at Sara.

"No, you're right," Sara agreed. "I would say that private acts belong to the people participating." She looked over to see Burke staring at her again. Oh, the legions of odd people, Sara thought—so charming and tiring at the same time.

"It's not about voyeurism," Claire added. "It's about full knowledge. Everyone's curious, so why not accept it and go the next step and actually see it? Curiosity is the road we take outside of ourselves to understand another's experience. It actually protects us from self-absorption."

"Yes, Claire, but when does that turn into prurient exploitation?" Burke asked. "Does the public have a right to see Diana in bed? Does that serve some sort of moral purpose or common good?"

"Absolutely."

"Would you want a video of you having sex distributed?" Ives inquired.

"If people were that interested in me, I'd be flattered," Claire asserted.

"You would not," Burke countered.

"I would."

"What about the time I sold your letters to *Paris Match*?" Denis asked, angling to hurt someone, anyone. Claire looked surprised, then quickly regained her composure.

"You *sold* her letters?" Sara asked. Denis shrugged.

"It wasn't the selling of the letters I objected to, Denis. We've discussed this before," Claire said in a tone that inferred she didn't wish to discuss it again. "This was when *Femina* first came out and Denis wanted to buy a car—"

"An *Audi*," Denis clarified.

"Well, Denis has always been in the habit of selling

whatever was lying around. He once sold my mother's bracelet. Another time he rented out our father's country home when we weren't there. So he looked around and there were some old love letters. Such as they were." Claire shrugged.

"You sold them?" Sara asked again.

"You were angry," Denis reminded Claire.

"I objected to the timing. *Femina* had just been published and was already getting plenty of publicity. And Denis just threw them out there in the midst of that. He's never had any sense of timing. It was a waste to publish them then."

"How could I know?" Denis asked defensively.

"Read the field, you have to *read the field!*"

"All right," Denis said with finality. Claire turned away from him, bored with an argument in which she was so obviously right.

"You would watch it," she said, returning to Sara.

"What?" Sara asked.

"Brontë and that what's-his-name."

"Maybe they didn't even have sex," Ives offered.

"She died pregnant," Sara said.

"Just like Diana!" Claire reminded everyone.

"That was never proven," Ives pointed out.

"It was never not proven," Claire hastily added.

"What do you think?" Claire asked Sara as they walked away from the Burke-Iveses' home.

"What do you mean?"

"Are they lovers?" Claire asked, teasingly aware that the question made Sara uncomfortable and Denis miserable. "We can't figure them out."

"They're nice."

"I'm afraid Denis's poem has taken a turn for the tragic," Claire announced. Denis glared at her contemptuously.

"I thought it might be rude to ask them, but why do they live in the nineteenth century exactly?" Sara asked.

"Some notion about all times existing at once, the past being present in all times and being free to choose the one you like—something very Zen or whatnot. Plus, you've noticed, they're utterly mad."

Sara nodded. Claire seemed to be in a bit of a glass house on that front, but Sara didn't care to point it out.

"Nightcap, anyone?" Claire asked, as they passed a bar.

Sara shook her head; the combined effects of alcohol and philosophical reversals had settled in for the night right between her temples, and she longed for a quiet, Claire-less night. She scrambled down the subway steps, leaving Denis and Claire to negotiate the fallout on their own.

a man of power

There is one individual of whom I have not yet spoken
Monsieur Heger the husband of Madame—he is professor of Rhetoric, a man of power as to mind but very
choleric & irritable in temperament . . .

Charlotte Brontë, to Ellen Nussey, 1842

---

hey sara,
hope everything's going well—just wanted to check and
see how everything's going. things are good here (so far,
that is). i also wondered if you'd had a chance to send
my first editions? not a huge issue but i wondered if
there's a problem or a reason you haven't sent them
yet? i'll reimburse you, of course—whenever you can get
to it . . . pls let me know—thanks and hope your
semester's going really well,
paul

Sara—

I don't care who the hell you are, my ass is in the wringer
on this—I've already pitched it and there's interest and I
don't know what the hell I'm talking about. Didn't you
tell me there was some sort of extramarital affair or
something juicy of that nature?

Maybe we can toss some events together, more of an
"events inspired by the life of" type of thing—though
obviously enough to keep the name and the "true love
story" type thing. I'm in New York day after tomorrow.
Let's meet. I want to get moving on this.

Sara, I don't know about you but I sensed a real
connection during our conversation and my acupuncturist
has been encouraging me to follow through on my
intuitions. I have a great feeling about this. Do you? Do
you believe in intuition? I think you do.

Let me please at least buy you dinner. I recall you have
trouble remembering to eat . . . ? I'd like to take care of
that at least for one night.

I'm at the Royalton Hotel Wednesday, please call me. I
look forward to seeing you again.
—B.E.

Dear Mr. Emmons,

Once again I apologize for any inconvenience I've caused
and hope you realize it was the work of my confusion and
not deliberate. Yes, I do believe in intuition, and yes, I do
forget to eat at times, so I'd be happy to take you up on
your very kind offer.

For a quick rundown: Emily wrote *Wuthering Heights*. Anne, the youngest, wrote *Agnes Grey* and *The Tenant of Wildfell Hall*. Charlotte, the oldest, wrote *The Professor, Jane Eyre, Shirley*, and *Villette*. The Brontës' father, Patrick Brontë, was widowed when his children were very young. A parson in Northern England, he sent the children to boarding schools, where his two eldest daughters promptly died. Not too surprisingly, he withdrew the children from boarding school and decided homeschooling might be a more attractive option. He encouraged his children's imaginations and the four remaining—Charlotte, Anne, Emily, and Branwell (the son)— developed elaborate stories with interlocking narratives and characters, which they continued to develop into adulthood.

Charlotte and Emily were sent to Belgium for more advanced studies. Charlotte did develop a crush on her (married) professor in Belgium and stayed on briefly as a teacher. Anne and Branwell worked as a governess and a tutor, respectively. When Branwell was suddenly fired from his job, the rumor was that he'd had an affair with his employer's wife. Around this time Charlotte and Emily began writing their first novels—all of which were published under male pseudonyms (Currer, Acton, and Ellis Bell). Branwell rather violently drank himself to death, and it's believed he brought the tuberculosis into the house that killed Emily and Anne. A few months after he died, Emily developed tuberculosis and died. And a few months after that, Anne also died. Having lost all her siblings in one year, Charlotte is understandably depressed. But she continues to write, and years later, marries the parsonage's curate Arthur Nicholls. She dies from complications due to pregnancy (it's generally believed,

though also a bit of a mystery) that same year at the age
of thirty-eight. Rather depressing stuff, I'm afraid, and a
cinematic translation may be difficult, but I hope this helps!

Sincerely,
Sara Frost

P.S. This may be presumptuous but may I suggest a few
titles?
   —*Une Grande Passion*
   —*Madame Charlotte*
   —*Rue d'Isabelle* (the street on which the Pensionnat
where Charlotte studied with Professor Heger is located in
Brussels)

Sara,
You're right. I'm afraid. The story as is is depressing and
(this is the industry talking, not me) a little too female.
You can have one or the other in this business (given
there's a bankable star), but certainly not both. However,
like I said, there's this actress who now has the seed
planted and an executive keen on making a film with the
actress, so now all we need is a story. Details . . .
—B.E.

P.S. I like that you're thinking of titles already. However,
I'm afraid the ones you suggested won't work for the
following reasons.
   —French
   —French
   —Belgian—Keep thinking!

Sara didn't know much about the movie business, but she recalled one colleague who had done some consulting work sneering that everyone was stupid but well dressed. She deduced that this meant she should hide her intelligence and buy a new outfit. A cursory glance at her closet revealed a truth she could no longer avoid: Her mother was right. Which was how she found herself standing in front of her closet with her mother staring anxiously at a never-worn navy blue dress three days later.

"Say it."

"Oh, Mom."

"It helps."

"I'm letting go of you."

"No, say it to the dress."

"You're joking."

"Say it."

"Oh my God."

"Honey, I'm trying to help you."

Sara sighed. "I'm letting go of you."

"Because . . ."

"Because I don't need material things to feel good about myself."

"That was great." Sara's mother proudly whisked the dress out of her hands, carefully checking the price tag before setting it in the reject pile.

"Oh, honey, you spent way too much on this."

"I know. I'm taking it back."

"You could get this same dress at half that much at—"

"They cut out the labels."

"Who needs labels?"

"I do."

"That's why you never have any money."

"I don't have any money 'cause I don't make any money."

"Okay. Let's let this conversation go. It's not helping either of us."

Sara held up a green sweater, squinting at its pattern before tossing it out.

"You're angry."

"No, I'm not."

"When people either throw everything out or hang on to everything, I know they're not expressing anger."

"You said it was healthy throwing things out."

"Not a pretty sweater like this."

"All right, I'll keep it."

"Now you're patronizing."

"Mom."

Sara rolled her eyes resolutely as they finally fell into a calm routine of disposal and organization. As much as she hated to admit it, her mother was right. Waking up to a well-ordered closet would be enormously invigorating. Her shoes, stacked neatly in acrylic boxes, sighed with pleasure in their airtight security. Sweaters lay in neat stacks under the tidy vigilance of moth-deflecting cedar blocks. There was even a bittersweet moment of closure as the last of Paul's clothing was entombed in a vacuum-sealed storage bag and shoved under the bed.

"What's this?" her mother asked, noticing the small cardboard box of Paul's first editions.

"Paul's. Haven't gotten around to sending it," Sara admitted sheepishly.

"That would be a great end to our day! Let's take that to the post office."

Sara smiled in agreement, weak with worry. Wasn't the closet enough? The first editions meant things were really over, over in ways that Sara couldn't fully comprehend yet. But her mother stood expectantly, hands on her hips, asking for more movement in the mental health department. What else could Sara do? She nodded, and while her mother was in the bathroom, she was able to steal the copy of *Down and Out in Paris and London* from the box and hide it in her bedroom. She was never one to pull the bandage off quickly.

"Can I just make an observation?" her mother ventured as they waited in line at the post office. Sara nodded.

"The whole—I don't know—Brontë *thing*, the long hair—so many dark sweaters! Wear a bright color once in a while, sweetie. You've got such a pretty face—those cheekbones—and a nice, little figure—why not flaunt it? You hide behind all these bruisy colors—they weigh you down. Maybe time for a change? It could be cleansing. Just a thought. Did I say too much?"

Sara shook her head and smiled sadly, hoisting the package up at the post office window. The clerk flew indifferently through the motions of first-class insured until Sara told her how much insurance the package required.

"Dang, girl." The woman behind the counter whistled. "What you got in here?"

"Books," Sara answered.

"Damn," the woman said, "those must be some books." Sara just nodded and smiled.

"You know what I'm thinking?" her mother asked, a dangerous hint of inspiration in her voice.

"Lunch?" asked Sara.

"A haircut," her mother suggested. The clean closet had worked Sara's mother into a frenzy of efficiency-based healing; she was now full of ideas. "Let's lighten the load some more!"

Sara smiled hesitantly, then realized, Why not? The closet had been truly transforming—why argue with a professional?

Later that evening, feeling (she had to admit it) lighter than she had in a decade, Sara met with Mr. Emmons for drinks.

"As I see it, our main problem now is there's no story."

"Yes." Sara nodded in agreement. Mr. Emmons was shorter than she remembered, reduced from her heroic memory of him. But she remembered the focused stare as he studied her intently. Everything about him was clean, crisp, and intense, from his white oxford shirt to the nervous tapping of his foot, which made Sara wonder if he needed a cigarette.

"You look different," Mr. Emmons finally decided.

"I got my hair cut," Sara explained, running a hand through her newly short hair, mussing it self-consciously. It was short, Jean Seberg short, just like Claire had recommended, and it looked good, Sara knew. The only draw-back was Claire would undoubtedly take credit for it.

"But that doesn't have to be a problem."

"The haircut?"

"No, the lack of story. Well, it's a problem, but not in-surmountable. The haircut is great."

"This is obviously more your field," Sara demurred.

"But your subject," Mr. Emmons added graciously. "Nice shirt—that's a great color on you."

"You think?" Sara asked with studied casualness about the green Armani blouse she'd just spent a week's wages on.

"Y'know, Sara, I'll admit this is the most unorthodox way of setting up a project, but I'm getting a really power-ful feeling about this."

"And your acupuncturist told you to follow through on it?" Sara asked.

"God, that sounds so L.A., doesn't it?" Mr. Emmons said, rolling his eyes in self-deprecation.

"There are acupuncturists here, too," Sara offered gently.

"It's not the same thing. But thank you," Mr. Em-mons said with a wink. "You're a good sport. And you call me on my crap. I like that."

Sara nodded, unsure of herself as she sank into an outsize white chair in the Royalton's bar. She surveyed the room, noticing a leather-clad German couple poring over the movie section of the *Times*. Mr. Emmons followed her gaze, leaning in confidentially.

"Next year they'll be sitting there looking for our

movie," he said conspiratorially. He smiled warmly, putting Sara at ease.

"If we can just come up with a story," she reminded him.

"Details."

A waitress with a bare midriff set their drinks down in front of them.

"You're welcome," she said icily before being thanked. Mr. Emmons smiled admiringly.

"I love that about New York," he said as she went to take the Germans' order.

"What's that?"

"The way nobody bothers to hide their resentment. Everybody resents somebody else's money, job, apartment, whatever, and they make no effort to hide it."

"I'm not sure that's a good thing," Sara said.

"Why not? What's the alternative, L.A.? Where everyone pretends things are going great, things are right on track, acting peaceful and content while their latest project's down the toilet? That's why there's road rage. People crack up being so goddamned positive."

"New York has road rage," Sara protested.

"Not like L.A."

Mr. Emmons leaned forward, resting his chin on the tips of his fingers, which were joined in a thoughtful, prayer-like composition. Sara noticed his gray-blue eyes focus on something in the middle distance. A wisp of hair escaped from its brushed-back station and Mr. Emmons pushed it away, irritated that it had interfered with his train of thought. His manner was earnest, verging on ecclesiastic.

"I want to tell a love story," he said.

Sara bit her lip. "All right."

"No, I mean in the film. I want to tell a love story."

"Oh," Sara said, laughing slightly.

"I mean it. I had this skiing accident recently," he added significantly.

"I'm sorry."

"No, it was great. I mean, it changed my life. I'm lying on the side of this mountain, my leg is bent in this way that is not encouraging, and I'm wondering, you know, are they ever going to find me? And then, I swear to God, this is going to sound so corny, but I swear, I heard the voice of my ancestors, I heard them calling me."

Sara nodded.

"I swear it happened. And then I started thinking: Great, well, that's it—when your dead relatives start calling you, *good night, Vienna*, you know? But then I started worrying about my memorial—you know, who's going to talk—and I admit it"—he smiled sheepishly—"I worried about turnout."

Sara laughed.

"But then, I'm thinking past that, I'm thinking ten, twenty, a hundred years in the future what will they think of me, what will be my 'legacy,' if I could use such a pretentious word? What will people know of me?"

Sara didn't have the heart to point out that it was still present day, he was buying her a drink, and even she didn't really know who he was.

"Anyway, that's what got the ball rolling. I mean, I'm

very grateful for my success—I've made a very nice living blowing things up and getting the good guy to save the world but . . . you know, you can only spend so long building a better mousetrap before you start wondering who is the mouse, who is the trap, right?"

Sara nodded unsurely.

"Love is all there is," he summed up. "I want to do something honest, simple, and true. I want to tell a love story. Just to have done something like that would make it seem worthwhile. It's such a cynical world—you just yearn for it, don't you? One honest, tender story. Because when it comes down to it, love is all there is. Right?"

Sara was suddenly a little worried. The Brontës lived respectable lives and died early deaths. Wouldn't a film demand more of them? Sex, incest, suicide, at the very least adultery? Certainly Branwell got into some trouble, but even Sara knew no studio would finance the story of a failed, drunken writer whose name reminded people of breakfast cereal. She had to tell Mr. Emmons. Now. It was her duty to herself, the Brontës, world cinema, and Byrne Emmons's ancestors.

"There's no story," she admitted shakily.

"The Brontës must have done something interesting."

"Well, they were interesting, but they didn't really do anything except write and die."

"That is a problem. So Charlotte almost had an affair?"

"Not even almost. She was a decent pastor's daughter, after all. And he was a married man. He's interesting,

I think, only insofar as he's a sort of Rosetta stone for all her romantic fiction, her creating the modern romantic hero, a basically decent man with a past—a very modern construction actually, the romance of the flawed man—"

"Like film noir!"

"Well, no, more like a good man in a bad situation—"

"But that is *film noir*," Mr. Emmons announced excitedly. "Very modern!"

"—the story of a man trapped in a loveless marriage saved by the love of a young governess. But in real life nothing ever actually happened. Not in the way you mean."

"What about the others?"

"Emily lived pretty much in her imagination—quiet, shy, odd. Anne, interesting writer but her life was fairly uneventful. There was an episode where she was a governess and left very suddenly, supposedly because her brother, Branwell, who was working as a tutor, had an affair with the wife of the family they taught."

"That's good!"

"So they both leave. The wife dumps Branwell, her husband dies, and she marries a rich widower."

"So what does Branwell do?"

"Drinks himself to death."

"We need something a little more upbeat."

"Branwell dies, three months later Emily dies, and three months after that, Anne dies, too."

"I thought there was a stronger love angle." Mr. Emmons stared at his drink accusingly.

"No, I'm sorry," Sara answered guiltily. The color drained from his cheeks.

"Sorry," she said again and shrugged lamely, feeling suddenly the full weight of responsibility for the Brontës' depressing, uncinematic lives.

Mr. Emmons took a deep breath and then did something that astonished her. He dismissed the thought with a wave.

"The concept's very strong. The names are familiar."

"Is that all that counts?" she asked, relieved.

Mr. Emmons launched into a tirade about the elaborate constellation of busy schedules that had miraculously opened up from mid-May to the end of June. The Actress had been scheduled to do a techno-medical thriller, but when her role as a brilliant neurosurgeon was deemed not complex enough by her advisers, she backed out of the picture. She was interested, more than interested, fascinated with the Brontës, with the nineteenth century, with finally showing her real skills as an actress.

The Director had just had a third child and his wife was threatening to leave him if he did another film that involved a year holed up in a water tank in Mexico. And then there was the Executive at the studio, a big Brontë fan, who during the brief time she could expect to survive as an executive had the power to greenlight the project, and most certainly would on the strength of the Actress's enthusiasm.

Things usually fell together very slowly, he explained. Projects languished in development for years, and even when they finally appeared to be well on their way to existence, one ever so slight realignment could send them back into purgatory. It was also the reason that every now and again lightning struck—elements fell into place, usually in the wake of other doomed projects, and voilà! But one had to act fast.

All that was needed was a story, and if the subjects of the story failed to comply by being cinematic, well, then, what was his obligation to them? Fuck them. Who were the Brontës, these silly celibates, to stand in his way when all the other elements had aligned with such cosmic efficiency? If their lives weren't interesting, he would make them interesting.

"I know!" he said, pulling a phone from his breast pocket with superhero conviction. He flew into action, punching numbers, leaving messages, breaking through the firewall of assistants with just the right tone of condescending self-importance and just-between-you-and-me bonhomie. The phone had been invented for Byrne Emmons in the same way opera had been invented for Mozart and physics had been just waiting around for Einstein. Mr. Emmons was a virtuoso, a coloratura of the push button, and if he had to admit it, he would have to say that these moments on the phone, these blessed, rare moments when the elements miraculously started falling into place, were the happiest of his life. It was like ground control—you pushed the right buttons, knew the right things, said them in the right order, and every now and then, when luck was also on your side, you watched a rocket land gently on the moon.

"Yes!" Mr. Emmons beamed as he tucked his cell phone back into his breast pocket. "Nykki's out of rehab."

"Who's Nykki?"

"Writer. Excellent. She's the woman I thought was

you at first. Does women's angle on stuff—you know, witty, sensitive. She just got out of rehab and nobody's willing to take a chance on her, so I can get her for a song." He chuckled gleefully, then took out his phone again, looking up only briefly to ask, "Spanish food okay?"

"Fine," Sara assured him.

Dinner was at a small tapas lounge in Chelsea that Mr. Emmons always went to when he was in New York. Conversation was an excited blur of non sequiturs and contradictions from Mr. Emmons—his upbringing and how it was both awful and wonderful; Los Angeles, which was full of phonies and yet some of the most genuine people you could hope to meet; anecdotes about what a really great guy Mel Gibson is. Sara found his patter touching, poignant even, in its insistent need to win, cajole, impress. She was warming to him. And to the Brontë project.

They were seated next to a large party—tourists from a country whose language Sara didn't recognize. As they got louder, the restaurant seemed to rock with their laughter and their random whoops of joy over nothing more extraordinary than the arrival of a plate of shrimp.

Sara and Mr. Emmons shared an exasperated smile, a smile that lingered too long. A splash of sangria from the noisy neighbors broke the tender spell, as Sara looked down to see that the shirt that cost her a week's wages was ruined.

"Sorry!" the woman at the next table practically screamed with a combination of embarrassment and indifference. A waitress rushed to Sara's side, sprinkling her shirt with salt.

"No, really. *Eet works!*" she assured them.

"That's an Armani, not a bag of popcorn," Mr. Emmons said wearily.

"Just try to help," the waitress explained, backing away.

"I'm sorry, Sara. I hope you'll let me get that cleaned for you," he said as he fumbled for his wallet. He paid the bill quickly, then led her out of the restaurant.

"I'll see about that shirt tomorrow," he reassured her in the cab home.

"It's no big deal. It's old," she lied.

Mr. Emmons had insisted on escorting her home. She wasn't sure if he was expecting to be invited up and was already fearing an awkward moment. But he wasn't.

"Good night, then," he said as the cab stopped in front of her building.

"It was great to meet you. Again," Sara said. "When do you leave?"

"Tomorrow. Early. I'll call you soon as I get back. I want to set you and Nykki up ASAP. We'll get her writing with you and then we'll make us a movie. How does that sound?"

Sara smiled, trying to look like someone who discussed these things regularly.

"I'd like that," she said.

Mr. Emmons returned the smile and then waited gallantly for her to unlock the door to her building and go inside.

In the morning she woke to find that a bouquet of flowers and an identical new shirt had been delivered. Sara was a little embarrassed to discover tears of happiness sliding down her cheeks.

talking to you

When I pronounce French words, I seem to be talking
to you.

Charlotte Brontë, to Professor Heger, 1845

Dear Miss Frost:
I am responding to your advertisement. I may have
a letter that could be of interest to you from a C. Brontë.
Is it worth anything? You can reach me at the number
below to schedule a time to look at it.

Yours sincerely,
Mrs. Evelyn Wright

Dear Mrs. Wright,
I would be very interested in the letter you mention. If
genuine, it could be quite valuable to my research and

other Brontë scholars. I will call you to arrange a time to
meet at your earliest convenience. I am very eager to
see the letter and am so grateful for your response.

Sincerely,
Sara Frost

"Did you have any problems with the gangs?" the woman
who answered the door asked.

"Excuse me?" Sara followed her in. A radio call-in
program blared in the kitchen, competing with a TV in another room.

"I'm Mrs. Wright."

"Sara Frost. Thank you so much for making the time."

"There's a lot of crack addiction going on," Mrs.
Wright added significantly while leading her into the
kitchen. Mrs. Wright wore a pink twinset that was pilling
at the hips and a bright smear of crooked lipstick.

"Is Mr. Wright here?" Sara asked, gesturing to the
noise in the living room down a long hallway and hoping it
would prompt a request to turn it down.

"Certainly hope not. Been dead for eight years. You
shouldn't be walking around alone, pretty girl like you, not
in this neighborhood."

Sara nodded. Mrs. Wright lived in the East Eighties, a
neighborhood as removed from gangland warfare as one
could possibly imagine. But there was nothing to be gained
by contradicting her worldview.

"Would you mind?" Mrs. Wright offered a bottle of
white wine, unable to manage a corkscrew with her arthritic
hands.

"Sure."

They sat in the living room, with the large-screen TV screaming in the corner. A talk show was on, concerning the sexual exploits of a man and his wife and the woman's sister, who would periodically sleep with the man because his wife had gotten too fat. The program was aptly titled "Help! My Wife's So Fat I Had to Sleep with My Sister-in-Law." As Sara and Mrs. Wright settled into wicker chairs beside a sun-drenched bay window, a woman in the audience on TV was remarking upon the general sluttiness of the panel.

"Girl, you's a ho. And you, you's a fat ho. That's the only difference I can tell." The crowd hollered their approval. Mrs. Wright took a big gulp of her wine, seemingly indifferent. Sara couldn't decide if she was deaf, nuts, or a handy combination of the two.

"Have some cookies, I made them myself." A bizarre claim, as just moments ago she'd had Sara help transfer them onto a plate from their Entenmann's box. Nuts.

"Please. Drink." Mrs. Wright had already polished off half her glass, and out of some sense of decorum Sara felt obligated to keep up. She took a sip. It was horribly sweet, almost a syrup.

"Good, isn't it? I don't care about price. I tell those wine snobs, 'Give me something that goes down nice.'"

Sara nodded weakly as Mrs. Wright refilled her own glass and topped off Sara's.

"My daughter's on crack."

"I'm sorry."

"She never visits. That's fine. Don't want to see her, anyway."

Here it was. Payment. This was what Sara paid to look at the forgotten letters of forgotten widows. She was good at it, too. Her natural quietness drew them out, much to Sara's dismay. Her reticence they read as a sign of integrity, proof of her unwillingness to pry. Entire family stories came tumbling forth: widowhood, crackhead daughters, impotent suitors. It all came out eventually.

The truth was she did feel sorry for Mrs. Wright, she did want to help these widows. But she was never sure where her pity left off and her fear of someday being one of them began. They all read the actuarial tables, they must've known statistics leaned heavily in favor of widowhood. But they all seemed so surprised by it even as they passed into a state of resignation, serenely keeping the once-a-week hair appointments and cutting off the crusts of sandwiches for no one in particular.

". . . so I told her, 'I don't want you coming in here with your dirty men.' And do you know what she called me?" Mrs. Wright's voice fell into a hush. "A *bitch*."

Mrs. Wright straightened in her chair as though she'd just delivered the most damning evidence at Nuremberg.

"Let me see if I've got another bottle," Mrs. Wright said brightly. Sara looked to see that Mrs. Wright had polished off the wine with very little help from her.

"Actually, I think I'd better—"

"Of course. I suppose you'd like to see the letter?"

"Well, yes. Thank you."

"Let me get you the gloves."

Sara was encouraged that Mrs. Wright knew enough

to use gloves to handle old documents. Perhaps she was the real thing in spite of her craziness. You never knew.

"Here you go." Mrs. Wright handed her a pair of woolen mittens that looked suspiciously like two aborted attempts at tea cozies.

"The gangs stole my other ones." She shook her head and walked into the other room. Sara's heart sank. Another day lost listening to the complaints of a paranoid lush on the Upper East Side. At least, she reasoned, she didn't have to travel all the way to Belgium for her disappointment.

"Now, this I got from a cousin of mine in Cork," Mrs. Wright said, returning to the living room and setting a strongbox on the table between them. "That's in Ireland."

"I know."

"Well, I didn't. Didn't even know I had a cousin there till she was dead. Oh, well." Mrs. Wright sifted through photos and letters, the last effects of a woman she never knew. "Don't know why they thought I'd want it, but . . ." She pulled out a small manila envelope, sliding out the contents into her bare hand. "Don't understand it myself. It's in French. But when I saw your ad, I thought maybe you'd be interested. Maybe it's worth something?"

On the television one sister had broken down weeping. She was overweight, she said, because her husband didn't love her. And now he didn't love her because she was overweight. Life was awful, it was. Just awful. The audience sighed, dabbing their eyes. The host who had been baiting the woman for a full thirty-five minutes walked onstage and enclosed the sister in a tender, maternal embrace.

Sara's hand trembled as she took the letter. French. From Ireland. The letters to Professor Heger were always in French. Charlotte Brontë's husband, Arthur Nicholls, moved to Ireland after her death to avoid the legions of fans who'd begun pilgrimages to the Brontë home. But he'd made special efforts to destroy her letters.

Sara gingerly unfolded the tiny letter, dangerous work with the tea cozies on her hands. It was one page only, an ancient-looking page with the distinctively cramped, tiny writing that was Charlotte's. If this was a forgery, it was a very good one. She held her breath. She scanned the page, translating quickly. The date was the first indication of something special—December 1845 was a full month after the last known, existing letter. This was something nobody even supposed existed . . .

December, 1845
It has been only a month since my last letter. I know already you are scolding me for my impatience. But as I wrote you before your letters are my life.

At the bottom the letter trailed off:
. . . each day that passes sends me deeper into misery without notice of you. I say I try to forget you. The days occupy my mind and I tell myself—

Why did she leave off? Had she been distracted and then thought better of the letter altogether? Ever mindful of Charlotte's posthumous reputation, surely Arthur Nicholls would have destroyed an early love letter written to a married man. Unless he didn't know French. And why would it be in her possession? Unless she never sent it.

"Is it worth anything?" Mrs. Wright asked, turning her attention away from the television.

"Possibly."

"What do you know! Almost threw it away. Think I can get some money for it?"

"If it's authentic, and I think it could be, it would be enormously valuable academically."

"And financially?"

"Yes. I think it would be worth something. Quite a lot actually."

"How much?"

"Well, a letter, one not nearly as valuable as this, came before Sotheby's recently for nearly forty thousand."

"Dollars?" Mrs. Wright asked, stunned. She gave a little yelp of happiness. "Good thing I cut that daughter of mine out—she'd be out there selling this for crack in a second."

"I don't know that it actually has a street value, but there is a thriving market for literary memorabilia. Of course, I'm not sure it's authentic. It would have to be verified. But by virtue of the date and the nature of the letter and its significance to her work and personal life, I'd say this is very valuable. Of course, the other option would be to donate it—"

"Donate?"

"To a university or museum, perhaps. I could put you in touch with the Brontë Museum in—"

"Why would I want to donate it?"

"Like I said, it has—if authentic—it has great value to research institutions like my own and to many other—"

"I see," she said, frowning cynically.

"I'm just saying—"

Mrs. Wright took back the letter and stuffed it into the pocket of her sweater.

"I would recommend keeping it in a sealed—"

"I think I should talk to a lawyer," Mrs. Wright affirmed proudly. She might be a little tipsy, but she knew how to protect her goods from some little operator from a fancy university. "Now, you seem very nice," she allowed, "but I got to look out for myself."

"Of course. If you'd like to get it appraised, I could recommend—"

"I'll find my own."

"Certainly. I wonder if you might at least let me copy the letter?"

"Why?" Mrs. Wright asked, gripping the letter more tightly in her pocket.

"It's important for my research. I don't want to take it. I just—"

"I think I should talk to a lawyer first."

Sara was so elated by the discovery, she treated herself to a cab home. Certainly in time Mrs. Wright would realize the necessity of sharing the letter. Sara knew she was an idiot for telling her its possible value. Why was she always so damned honest? It was enormously important to Sara, perhaps her most important—all right, her only—discovery—why did she have to go telling that old nut its value? If it was real, she reminded herself. Maybe she could procure the money herself. Maybe Mr. Emmons would pay her forty thousand dollars as a consultant on the film. If the letter was real.

How could Charlotte have left off, suddenly abandon such a letter? Her correspondence with Professor Heger showed a shocking emotional rawness—especially shocking in one so reserved. Trying to dampen her passions, the professor had put her on a strict diet of one letter every six months to which he rarely replied. Mrs. Wright's letter confirmed an open rebellion against this policy—Charlotte had written it only weeks after her last surviving letter. But it was unfinished and unsent, implying somehow that she thought better of it, put it away and forgot about it. What caused such a change, what cooling of the emotions occurred perhaps in the middle of that very last sentence?

Branwell had just been fired at the time of Mrs. Wright's letter, Sara calculated. He had returned home in disgrace after carrying on his open affair with the wife of his employer. Charlotte was appalled by his behavior and judged him harshly, perhaps because she felt herself indulging the same desires. Perhaps watching Branwell's descent into self-pity and despair caused an awakening of sorts—maybe she saw her own future somewhere at the end of that self-destructive path. In November 1845 Charlotte wrote the professor:

> *I have forbidden myself completely the pleasure of speaking about you . . . but I cannot conquer either my regrets or my impatience—and that is humiliating—not to be master of one's own thoughts, to be slave to a regret, a*

> *memory, slave to a dominant fixed idea which tyrannises*
> *the spirit.*

It is humiliating to be a slave to memory, ensnared between the irretrievable past and an impossible future. This was the sad fate Branwell pursued and Charlotte saw herself increasingly unable to escape. What's more, the object of Branwell's affections wasn't worth it—Charlotte knew the woman lied to Branwell, and his love for her was misplaced at best. She could see with an outsider's eye how ridiculous he and his love really were. The fact was that one could be pulled under the tide of an overwhelming passion or one could find a project to throw oneself into.

This was also the time during which Charlotte found Emily's poetry—"they had also a peculiar music—wild, melancholy, and elevating." She decided the sisters should all pursue writing careers. Charlotte stopped writing letters to the professor and began writing a first novel, entitled, perhaps not coincidentally, *The Professor*. Mrs. Wright's letter maybe represented the exact moment of that shift into the cool intelligence of self-preservation. What happened in that moment? Did Branwell walk into the room? Did she look up and see yet another huge invoice from the local pub for his unpaid tab? Did she hear the *chip chip* of the headstones being carved for the cemetery just outside the parsonage and remember with startling clarity, *this is the only life I have*? Survival was a choice; she became her own project. As she later wrote after the death of her siblings, *Labour is the only radical cure for rooted sorrow. . . .*

Sara looked out the window and realized the cab had passed her apartment several blocks earlier.

"Oh! Stop!"

Sara walked into her bedroom to find Denis lying on a mess of pillows and magazines on her bed.

"Some fascist's been at your closets," he said.

"How'd you get in?"

"I don't know how you can go on living with this closet staring you in the face every morning." Denis stubbed out a Gauloise in a Pepsi can.

"Did you pick my lock?"

"What are locks?" Denis asked with a shrug. "They mean nothing."

"Denis, what are you doing here?"

"I was lonely. I thought we could make love. You have terrible magazines." He lit another cigarette.

"I want you to go."

"Claire doesn't know I'm here."

"Denis—" Sara wanted to be with someone who appreciated her discovery of the letter or she wanted to be with no one.

"You don't even remember it. Neither do I."

"You don't remember what?"

"That night. It's in my poem, but the truth is, I don't remember."

"You said nothing happened," Sara said, confused.

"The truth is I don't know. I was drunk."

"Well, so was I."

"How many lovers get to make love for the first time twice?"

"None."

"That man is a homosexual."

"Who?" Sara asked, then remembered. Burke. "Oh."

"And he's a drug addict."

"Denis—"

"Claire and I are only half brother and sister, you know."

"I don't care."

"Byron made love to his half sister." Denis stared at a fashion layout, looking fatigued. "But then he was a drug addict, too. I think."

"It doesn't matter, Denis."

"Isn't that why you won't see me? What did the homosexual tell you?"

Sara felt a wave of nostalgia rush through her and started to cry.

"*Cherie*, what did he tell you?"

"Nothing," Sara managed.

It was nothing to do with that, she wanted to say. She was happy. Happy to have found a Brontë letter. If it was real, she reminded herself, if it was real. She wanted to call Byrne Emmons to tell him the happy news, but he probably wouldn't understand the significance, either. After all, it didn't exactly juice up the story. The only person who would understand was Paul, and Paul was with a swimsuit model with a Fulbright and Sara was with a Frenchman flicking ashes on their bed and it was all just so sad. So they made love.

Denis thought she cried during sex because of her tender little schoolgirl heart. These American girls, he thought appreciatively, it all means so much.

As his fingers wandered her body, Sara wondered if Claire and Denis really were lovers. What sort of lover was Claire? She'd read somewhere that people who make great claims for sexual prowess were notoriously lackluster in bed. Denis must have sensed her attention drifting because he looked at her, a look hovering somewhere between hurt and irritation.

People are either charming or tedious. Oscar Wilde. That would have to be Denis's motto. Sara was being tedious. Denis moved away from her, searching for his cigarettes on the floor.

"In France," he explained to the ceiling, blowing out a gust of smoke, "we make love with our whole bodies, our whole minds." Sara felt foolish, wiping her silly American tears from her eyes, feeling the full weight of her failure to be charming. They lay silently at opposite sides of the bed.

"You are what"—Denis shrugged—"on antidepressants?"

"What? No," Sara said. "This is just the first time— Paul and I were together for— Never mind. I probably should be on antidepressants."

"Claire thinks you need several lovers. I think you just need me."

"She does?" Claire and Denis discussed her love life? Sara wanted more than anything to be rid of them all right now. . . .

"Why does that boy keep playing the pogo stick?" he asked finally.

"You think it's a pogo stick?"

"What else could it be?" he said, shrugging his shoulders. Sara smiled.

"Why is the American girl unhappy with sex but happy because of a pogo stick? This is the problem with your country." Denis shook his head, flicking an ash from his chest.

"Tell me your first erotic memory," he demanded, in his usual random fashion, as if he were hiring Sara to be a salesclerk.

"What? You mean my first—"

"No, not that. That's always boring. Tell me the experience that marked you. Before all that. Or after."

"Well, I don't know," Sara offered haltingly. Denis smiled reassuringly.

Sara searched her memory, offering, finally, "When I was sixteen a man in an art museum touched me."

"Is that all?"

"I let him."

"Why not?"

"It was completely out of character."

"All the better."

"I shouldn't have let him."

"You should have enjoyed it."

"I was scared."

"You should have been scared. You weren't yourself."

"He told me he could only feel aroused in the presence of great art. And then he said that he could only feel aroused in the presence of underage girls. He responded only to jailbait and watercolors. He gave me twenty dollars and told me not to tell anyone—he was on the board for the museum or something very important. And I was just a volunteer."

"So what did you do?"

"I asked for fifty."

Denis stared at her and, noticing a brief flicker in her eyes, said, "You're lying."

Sara laughed. Denis continued to stare at her, appalled and delighted.

"Part of it's true."

"Which part?"

Sara gave an evasive shrug. Denis kissed her. She hadn't realized until now how much she missed human contact—the warm comfort of skin against skin. He moved his hand down her side, sliding a finger inside her—touching her expertly, too expertly, Sara thought fleetingly.

"What are you thinking?" he asked.

"That's nice."

"But what do you think? What do women think when a man touches her?"

"You need to know for your poem?" Sara asked glibly. What was with all the talking? Paul never talked.

"I need to know for everything."

Sara thought about what she was thinking. She wanted a sexy reply. She searched desperately for a sexy reply.

"I don't know. I feel like I'm supposed to say . . ."

"What?" He moved his hand deeper . . . *still talking*, Sara thought.

"Uh. Something sexy."

"The truth is sexy. What do women think?" Sex for Denis was just another form of talking, Sara realized. There was no separation between sex and conversation, no neat partitions like she and Paul traditionally had that signaled the ends and beginnings, just constant, curious *flow*.

"I guess we're thinking we need to hurry up. Women, I mean. We take forever."

Denis sighed. These efficient Americans and their speedy lovemaking. Sex was wasted on them. And his sigh triggered something in Sara and she relaxed. Finally.

"I want to make love," he whispered, "to the woman who takes too long and makes too much noise."

And he did.

The next morning Sara awoke to the sound of the pogo stick. Denis was already awake, keeping to his strict schedule of smoking five cigarettes before noon. She noticed cigarette butts, squashed into fetal positions, along the windowsill. Somehow the butts confirmed the experience of Denis more soundly than his body between her sheets. The habit of monogamy died hard within Sara and she watched Denis guiltily. Sex with someone else felt alien, adulterous. Sara felt the weight of her disloyalty, all the while thinking: Paul beat me to it by weeks—why should I be the one feeling guilt?

How easy it must be to be Denis, Sara thought. Or Claire. This must be what it's like. Waking up to strange things and thinking, simply, This is lovely. Such luxury, such genius for finding plain wonder in everything. Experiences passed through them and they would throw up their arms and say, "Remarkable!" No predestination, no neat network or unraveling of a divine plan. Just one remarkable thing after another.

"What do we do now?" she asked. Denis shrugged, unconcerned.

"If we were in a movie," he said, "there would be a montage right now. We would engage in all sorts of frivolous crap that would make us grin like idiots and kiss each other a lot."

"We're not in a movie."

"No. We'll have to experience our bliss in real time," he concluded, exhaling a gale of smoke. "In any case, we should eat."

Denis picked one of the most expensive restaurants in New York for lunch. Sara had read about it in a magazine. Its chef was French, and Denis made a point of ordering all the dishes on the menu that involved lymph nodes or digestive tracts or any of the other dishes the French had devised to antagonize the rest of the world. With each dish he would either say "Just like France!" or "Not the same as France!" and finish it just the same. Finally when the bill came he offered up Claire's credit card and ordered more dessert.

"Of course, Claire is a narcissist. Why not?" Denis explained. "So is a cat. It is in its nature to be so, so how can you blame it? It is in Claire's nature to be like Claire."

"Yes, but don't you find she doesn't— I don't know."

"What?"

"She has no . . . morality."

"Ah, yes, America loves morals."

"No, not that way. I mean she doesn't believe in any standards—"

"Except the ones she creates. Perfect! In that sense she is more moral than you or me. She is consistently Claire, she is whatever serves Claire at any moment. That's very honest. She is always interested in what interests her. That has a fundamental morality. The real sin in life is failure to be what? Curious!" Denis stopped abruptly, noticing the empty restaurant and his equally empty wineglass.

"Now I think we walk around in a park or get a puppy," he announced, throwing down his napkin with finality.

Sara suggested that they walk around in a park first and then think about a puppy and Denis was agreeable. They walked in Central Park—a sufficiently cinematic setting. Walking past Sheep Meadow, Sara watched a young Indian couple rearranging their son in a stroller. The boy looked delighted, throwing Cheerios at the greedy pigeons who flocked around him. As the pigeons drew closer, he would scream with pleasure and they would back away.

Sara was reminded of a man she knew in college from Bengal whose marriage had been arranged for him when he graduated. Sara had been appalled.

"But what about love?" she'd asked. He smiled a patient Third World smile, as if Sara had just asked if his people still swung around the jungle on vines or sucked the brains out of monkey skulls with a straw. He flicked his wrists so that his palms were outstretched, a gesture meant to indicate that he was the sanest man in the world. "You grow to love each other," he explained.

Sara watched the Indian couple, wondering if they had grown to love each other or were in love when they married. Or maybe they thought they would grow to love each other but actually hated each other, and the only thing that kept them together was their pigeon-loving baby and these walks in the park. Maybe she would grow to love Denis. He was attractive and had access to Claire's credit cards; surely there were many a contented Indian couple who had started with far less.

"Okay, now we buy a puppy?" Denis asked.

"I don't think so. I have a meeting this afternoon," Sara said. She had to meet with her adviser at school about her still-unfinished Ph.D. thesis. And then she hoped to call Mrs. Wright before the cocktail hour. . . . She had a full afternoon, no time for an affair, if that's what this was. Sara suddenly felt very Continental—lovers and meetings. What a world!

"Every time someone says, 'I have a meeting,' an angel in heaven dies. Did you know that? Heaven is empty because so many meetings."

"I didn't know that." Sara laughed.

Denis gave a Gallic shrug. Of course she didn't know that. He was funny, Sara thought. Maybe a fling was just what she needed. Maybe she would go home and put Paul's remaining first edition in the mail. She was a haver of affairs, not a carrier of torches.

"So what's your week like?" Sara asked, supposing that this was standard repartee in the love affair world.

"No. We will not have those kinds of conversations," Denis said, waving the idea away with his hands.

"Oh. All right."

"We won't talk about weeks, or plans. We will be in a poem. Together. And when we meet in the poem again is when we are supposed to meet."

Sara smiled. "Does this work on all the women you sleep with?" she asked slyly. She might be a little inexperienced with this affair business, but she'd seen movies.

"What is this 'work'?" Denis asked, confused.

"Nothing," Sara replied shakily, the pendulum from independence swinging back wildly, unexpectedly, to wistfulness, infantile dependence, the ache of separation— Sara felt a pang. She kissed him good-bye—it was in the poem, after all—and made her way to the subway.

what blame, what sympathy

Do you—who have so many friends, so large a circle of acquaintance—find it easy, when you sit down to write—to isolate yourself from all those ties and their sweet associations—as to be quite your own woman— uninfluenced, unswayed by the consciousness of how your work may affect other minds—what blame, what sympathy it may call forth?

Charlotte Brontë, to Mrs. Gaskell, 1853

By the end of the semester, Sara had witnessed a transformation in the department that she assumed would bode well for her: they were sick of Claire. They were sick of her posturing, her self-promotion, her erosion of academic standards—all things they could withstand in a quieter professor, but Claire had to be so public about it. They would no doubt be well prepared to fund the pursuit of Brontë letters instead of the social history of pasties and G-strings. Sara assumed the renewal of her grant was all but guaranteed.

"What do you mean?" she asked, staring across at her thesis adviser's stony expression. "I would think the department would welcome a bit more traditional research."

Her adviser straightened in her seat. "Sara, you know as well as I that these Keane Foundation grants are highly competitive. There are only so many dollars to go around. You've already had one year, and where has your research gotten you?"

"But I found a letter! It marks her transition to a more pragmatic—"

"What about the Diana/Brontë angle you were developing? I'd assumed that that would be your proposal."

"That was a sound bite, not a thesis," Sara groaned. "But this letter is really something—it could be profoundly significant."

"Where is it?"

"Privately owned. This woman has it. And she's very eager to help," Sara lied. Mrs. Wright never answered her door. Nor had she answered any of Sara's many calls or letters. She'd even sent flowers. Maybe she should've sent wine.

"Well, I guess maybe . . . if you can actually produce a new letter . . ."

"It's not certain. But I've seen it—I know it exists. It's remarkable—if it's real," Sara offered, realizing that her years of research now dangled from the thin thread of Mrs. Wright's generosity. She sighed. Everything was falling out of reach.

"Well, if you can get the letter . . . But without it, honestly? I don't see the significance of pursuing this," her adviser said delicately.

"Significance? Really? This isn't more important than the affairs of Princess Diana?"

"This isn't about Claire Vigee."

Sara gave a short, disbelieving laugh.

"It's about your research. It just isn't . . . very *sexy*."

"The department hasn't had enough sex for one year?"

"Please . . ." her adviser said wearily.

But Sara was right. The department had had its fill of sex. By the end of the semester Claire had been feeling the stress of her educational chores. Teaching meant having to show up regularly somewhere. In addition, there were papers to grade and problems to be heard. The book wasn't doing as well as expected, but then hadn't she warned the publishers to wait until she had more time to do publicity, to establish her image in America? These things took time.

The prospect of grading dozens of final papers was daunting, especially during the Christmas season when she could be out promoting her book. Certainly she was a pioneer in Diana Studies, and that was important to her, but she was so much more than that. She was an opinion maker, not some grade-dispensing machine—couldn't they see her real value? magenta blue provided the answer.

magenta was one of Claire's students, a senior who felt verbally colonized. She was able to produce a lower-case note from an Upper East Side psychiatrist to attest to this fact. magenta believed capital letters were a form of linguistic oppression that not only encouraged value-based judgments but were the very site of oppression itself. This made the creation of what was once traditionally called a "term paper" into a coercive form of totalitarianism on par with the Weimar Republic. Instead of a paper, magenta would produce a work of art that expressed her inner reaction to the course material.

Happily, this also freed Claire from the arduous tasks that were once traditionally known as "reading" and "analyzing." This was an inspired departure and Claire decided every student should do the same. Students were delighted once they realized "art project" was given the broadest possible definition. One student stuffed a tampon into a bong and got an A. Another made a large-scale brassiere constructed from manhole covers and chain link and called it Womanhole. She got an A and a dealer. But only magenta's work of art was provocative enough to warrant a visit from the Department of Health.

True to her name, magenta's work was colorful. Just in time for the holidays, magenta had been thinking a great deal about the Nativity and what it all meant. *The first coming* was a life-size sculpture of "mary" giving birth to "jesus." The sculpture was a dynamic tableau—the viewer was treated to a "mary" lying back, her face contorted in a fit of blissful agony. But it wasn't the face people noticed first. With her legs spread-eagled, her arms thrown back in divine submission, one first noticed the slash of "mary's" bright pink vagina and the small head barely mottling the shocking color of her genitals.

People didn't know what to think. The first reaction was usually an embarrassed giggle or, for the more sophisticated, a wizened shrug to suggest it'd all been done before. At first it just seemed to produce outraged yawns on campus. Then the story started appearing in the newspaper, first in the back pages of the Metro section, then slowly, like a young starlet finally finding her light, emerging on the front page.

Nobody was sure how the Catholic community first came onto the scene. There were rumors that Claire herself, fearful the story would never heat past a low boil, tipped off the Archdiocese. In any case, the Church was not inclined to accept magenta's assertion that a beaver shot of the Virgin was "a profound and deeply religious meditation on the true nature of 'mary' as vessel, as woman, as creator, as biology, as nature, the ultimate miracle."

This was magenta's central metaphor, the miracle of life. Life pulsed inside "mary." It was a sweetly simple sentiment. For all her posturing, magenta was really a sentimentalist at heart. This was why she had to have real life in her sculpture. This was why she had to have the pig's fetus emerging from "mary's" bright pink nether regions. It wasn't that she equated "jesus" with "pig," as some people later claimed. She simply couldn't procure a human fetus, not even a dead one. And she did try. But even a pig's fetus was more than the Department of Health would allow, and while heated meetings were being held across campus, the fetus was removed and disposed of, leaving a gaping pink crater in "mary" that was just about the saddest thing magenta had ever seen.

Parents withdrew students. Politicians thumped podiums, using magenta's artwork as an object lesson in all that was wrong with publicly funded universities, lack of values, lack of prayer, feminism in general, bright pink vaginas in particular. Claire went on a lot of talk shows.

She also used a photograph of the sculpture as the cover of the Christmas edition of, what else, *Labia*—just in case the story threatened to die down. magenta watched it all, confused and impatient. Why wasn't anyone listening to her? She'd been reduced to a supporting player in her own show, and nobody had even gotten her message.

Just as the Church and the women's groups and freedom-of-expression groups and animal-rights activists were drying the ink on their position statements and sharpening their knives for bloody battle, magenta announced that she would be holding her own press conference. There, in a quiet, halting voice, she described a recent abortion in which "jesus" appeared to her while she underwent the anesthesia. He explained why what she was doing went against his wishes, but when she awoke it was too late—the procedure had been done, but she was now a devout Catholic. The artwork was her way of expressing her regret and her newfound understanding of the mystery and wonder of childbirth, especially the "birth" of "jesus."

To her, the sculpture was deeply religious and entirely sincere. It was neither an ironic deconstruction of ideology nor the flippant publicity seeking of an upstart self-promoter. It was an expression of faith. Pure and simple.

"i mean, what if mary decided to abort baby jesus just because he interfered with her career or something? i think we can all agree that would be bad for all of us, even jews and muslims."

Shocked silence went through the room as each assembled interest reinterpreted this new information in light of their established position. The women's group was disappointed; naturally, they had assumed that magenta was sympathetic to their politics. The Church reversed itself— here was their poster girl for a new generation of Catholics! Young, hip, perhaps a little misguided, but, aw shucks, that's youth for you—it was probably the antidepressants (or lack of them!). Why was science always trying to medicate old-fashioned goodness? The animal-rights people were still annoyed, the freedom-of-expression groups didn't know which side to take, while the Department of Health had already moved on to an E-coli outbreak in upstate New York.

Claire was so adept at spinning, she wasn't at all fazed. She couldn't care less about the American debate over when life begins. As far as she was concerned, life didn't begin until you'd been profiled in the pages of *Vanity Fair*. magenta was simply exploring the erotics of childbirth. Claire, never missing an opportunity for free publicity, showed up at magenta's press conference to defend the girl.

"Why does that terrify everyone so much? It's the mother who is at once maternal and sexual. It's the power of Woman that's being expressed, which is the subject of my new book, *Amazon*. It's the same reason the royals were so threatened by Diana, who was a terrific mother and at the same time unapologetically screwing a Muslim—"

"i just want everyone to know," magenta interrupted, barely audible even with the aid of a microphone, "that i consider myself a christian in the truest, non-oppressing form—with love and charity."

The scandal ultimately caused the department serious trouble, and worse yet, the administration had no one to blame but themselves in hiring Claire. So they blamed Claire. And punished the lower ranks of instructors by limiting fellowships.

"I happen to have a very highly successful film producer interested in my research," Sara told her adviser, the last card in her deck. Sara knew *that* wouldn't make any difference.

"You do?" she asked brightly.

"Now you're interested?" Sara asked in disbelief.

"I think you should have let us know that."

"I spend years researching this and some guy who makes action films suddenly makes all the difference?"

"It's certainly a point of interest," the adviser intoned cheerfully, picturing herself at the premiere.

Sara stared at her adviser in astonishment. This was the most encouragement she'd received in years, and she finally realized how worthless it really was.

"But I still have my classes to teach next term?"

Her adviser played with the cap of her pen. "Parents are taking their kids out of the department's offerings. It's across the board. We're all getting slammed."

"Who's fault is that?"

"Sara, this isn't a time for pointing fingers. We have to support the department. It's only temporary. Maybe summer session?"

Sara stared at her blankly. "Excuse me," she said finally, getting up, "I have a script meeting."

the plain truth

Let me speak the plain truth—my sufferings are very great—my nights indescribable—sickness with scarce a reprieve—I strain until what I vomit is mixed with blood. Medicine I have quite discontinued—

Charlotte Brontë, to Amelia Taylor, 1855

There had to be a moment when it turned. When the realization came, during the life of an illness, that its course was irrevocable. It's said the worst trial a person can endure is to outlive one's child, so it stands to reason that going through it six times would prove unendurable. By the time Charlotte Brontë died, her father, Patrick, should have found the process remarkably familiar. Illness never left the Brontë house empty-handed, usually finding a bounty of fresh young life while exempting the perpetually ailing father.

The letters to friends started optimistically; Charlotte was not feeling well but would soon feel better. Her stomach disagreed with her, she felt nauseous and tired. It was January; maybe the excitement of the holidays had worn down her strength. Finally in March of 1855 he wrote:

> *... hope is now gone, and we have only to look forward to the solemn event with prayer to God that He will give us grace and strength sufficient to our day.*

The realization had dawned. Was it in increments or sudden—a hollowness in the eyes, a flicker of deadness he had seen before? Was he used to it by now or did it still seem strange?

Each child's death seemed to define them. Branwell, defiant, violent, and vainly staring down death in a willful fit of self-destruction. Emily, fiercely denying her illness and any doctor's help, refusing to be bled, acting as though she could overcome her illness through imagination. And Anne, knowing how Emily's death pained her family, accepting all the tortures nineteenth-century medicine had to offer. Now years later, Charlotte—always a strange blend of thwarted passion and dutiful propriety—too weak to maintain her cherished correspondence, pregnant and unable to eat, politely slipped away on the last day of March.

How must he have felt that Saturday morning when his last child left?

```
INT. BRONTË HOUSE—MARCH 31, 1855—MORNING

Patrick stares at a stone wall, a blank, de-
feated look on his face as—
```

"There was this Buddhist monk once who meditated for so long that his eyelids atrophied and fell off," Nykki said, staring blankly at her laptop, where Patrick Brontë sat staring blankly at his stone wall. "That's how I'm starting to feel." They were still stuck at the moment of Charlotte's death—that is, page one.

It would be told in flashbacks, they'd decided. Nykki helpfully explained that the moment screenwriters graduate from film school they immediately start indulging in all the devices they'd been warned off, namely, flashbacks, voice-over narration, and arty dream sequences. She explained that they should employ all three of these dangerous devices and perhaps more. They would resolve story problems with atmosphere, filling the screen with the sort of moody, romantic lushness that permeated Brontë fiction.

There were many Charlottes to choose from. Each biographer had a different version: Charlotte as judgmental neurotic, Charlotte as self-sacrificing, martyred dreamer, Charlotte as brilliant, thwarted feminist icon. This being a movie, they had decided to lean toward romance and legend. They would tell the romantic version of her life—the youthful passion, the thwarted desires, the professional success, the survival of great loss and family tragedy and then the final irony: the attainment of real happiness closely followed by unexpected death.

Sara was well aware of her power in constructing the definitive Brontë. Didn't the movie version always trump the written accounts? People could look down their noses and pretend to be unaffected by the wildly inaccurate Hollywood gloss version of "real events," but it was the visual that stuck. Sara sensed this much was true if only because she was now sitting in a hotel room struggling to forget that Paul looked uncannily like a young Laurence Olivier in *Wuthering Heights* and that losing him felt like the defining tragedy of her life. But what had she lost? The visual that so neatly corresponded with the romantic myth? Or the man who inhabited it?

"Think I'll pop out for a smoke," Nykki announced, throwing her coat over her shoulder and leaving Patrick to stare at his stone wall. "Be right back."

Sara was new to screenwriting, but she'd learned after the first week that it had mostly to do with staring at a computer screen and taking protracted smoking breaks. As the door closed behind Nykki, Sara looked at her watch: ten-thirty. She had taken to timing Nykki's smoke breaks; yesterday's was a new record at three and a half hours.

At first Sara had been afraid to ask that Nykki not smoke during their work sessions in the hotel room. Smokers had become so used to having their rights compromised that each new concession tended to arouse contempt. But Nykki was accommodating to the point of excess, virtually insisting that she smoke in the Royalton lobby, which she soon discovered had banned smoking.

So Nykki went outside in the bitter December air. This apparently took large chunks of time after which Nykki would reappear, animated and happy and ready to stare at the computer again. Through her parents' work Sara knew that the recidivism rate for drug addiction was high, but she always wanted to give people the benefit of the doubt. When Sara first met Nykki she was pleased that people saw a resemblance between the two of them—she was wiry and bright with lively eyes. But within hours, Sara saw a different Nykki, haggard and morose. Which Nykki do people think I resemble? Sara wondered.

By five-thirty that afternoon she was starting to worry. A seven-hour smoke break seemed excessive. Sara had wasted an entire day—Christmas Day, no less—watching the traffic in and out of the Algonquin Hotel across the street and doing the *Times* crossword. She had received a mass e-mail from Paul—a smiling photo of him in front of Versailles—wishing everyone a happy holiday. How touching, Sara thought, stung by the anonymity of the gesture. She'd tried to call Mrs. Wright and wish her a Merry Christmas and, incidentally, inquire after the Brontë letter. But as usual, there was no answer. Meanwhile Patrick Brontë was still staring at a stone wall. Sara watched Claire on CNN discussing the erotics of childbirth with some lady senator from Texas who wasn't buying any of it.

Finally she resolved that she would have to call her parents and ask their advice about what to do for Nykki. She knew they would advocate direct action, which was never Sara's strong suit. She would also have to explain once again why she couldn't spend the day with them in Connecticut. She had told them she and Nykki were under an intense deadline, working night and day, etc. In truth she didn't want to spend the holidays with her therapist parents during her first Christmas alone as they delicately probed and accepted and supported her in Her Feelings at

This Difficult Time. Sara jumped when she heard a violent knock at the door. Nykki always forgot her key card.

"*Merde!* Do you know how long I have been looking for you?" Denis asked accusingly, moving past her into the room. Sara noticed he had bags.

"What are you doing here?" she asked.

"What are *you* doing here?" he replied.

"Why do you have bags?"

"Claire threw me out, can you believe?" Denis lit a cigarette and started rifling through the minibar.

"What happened?" Sara asked.

"Nothing!" Denis swallowed a tiny bottle of whiskey. "This stuff is terrible. D'you have any money?"

"You don't have any money?" Sara asked nervously. Denis threw up his arms in exasperation. Of course not.

"This is a nice place," he said, looking around, assessing cheerfully.

"Denis, you can't stay."

"Why not?"

Disaster on top of disaster, Sara thought. Please don't let this man screw up the one thing that's actually working in my life.

"Because we're working," she said.

"So am I," Denis protested indignantly. "We could make love," he offered charitably, lighting a cigarette.

"I don't think that's a good idea."

"It's always a good idea," he said. *Americans!*

"We're working under a deadline," Sara insisted.

"You think I am not?"

"Are you?"

"Every day! Work, work, work."

Sara heard the door. Nykki entered and without greeting or explanation calmly sat down in a sleek armchair opposite Sara.

"We're just gonna have to make this a smoking room," Nykki concluded, smoke funneling out of her nose.

"This is your sister?" Denis asked, looking at them both in confusion.

"No. Nykki, this is Denis," Sara said.

"Oh, you look so much alike," Denis said.

"No we don't," they both said in unison.

Nykki resumed her place at the computer. She realized Patrick Brontë was still sitting in the same place he'd been sitting for weeks and buried her face in her hands.

"Who is Champagne Charlie?" Denis asked, apropos of nothing.

"It's the nickname the London tabloids gave to Charles Spencer, brother of Diana, Princess of Wales," Sara answered almost by rote. She was astonished at the amount of information she'd acquired just by osmosis from Claire. "Why?"

"Claire called me Champagne Charlie."

"What'd you do?"

"Nothing."

"You must've done something."

"I gotta get some junk," Nykki said. Junk? Sara had thought only Sinatra used that phrase, as in *Sammy, you gotta get off the junk*.

"I don't even like champagne," Denis said wistfully.

"Do you know what a methadone clinic is like during the holidays?" Nykki asked no one in particular.

"Like McDonald's?" Denis asked.

"Yeah, sort of," Nykki agreed. "I'm gonna need something if we're gonna get this thing finished."

"What do you need?" Sara asked, trying to effect a jaded, worldly tone.

"Heroin," Nykki said as though it were obvious. Sara must've lost her jaded, worldly manner because Nykki added defensively, "I only *snort* it."

"Where are you going to get it?" Sara asked cautiously.

"I can't get it," Nykki told her. "I'm on probation. I get caught, I have to do time."

"You're not asking *me* to do it?"

Sara wouldn't begin to know where to get drugs. The only places she could think of were from articles she'd read in the *Times* about areas that no longer trafficked in drugs, places like Tompkins and Union Square that had been spiffed up and were now thriving districts of over-priced bistros doing clever things with fennel and ahi tuna.

"Why don't you just go down to the lobby?" Denis asked.

"They have that in the lobby?" Sara asked, astonished.

"Half the clientele is German," Denis explained, drawing the word *German* out to convey his disapproval.

"So?"

"Germans love needles. It's true, they did a study," Denis said.

"And what do the French love?" Sara asked.

Denis smiled. "Suppositories."

Over the next several days, Denis happily discovered that the hotel's restaurant catered to a long line of magazine editors who would cheerfully spot him the price of lunch in exchange for a few anecdotes about Claire. Real hair color: red. Real sexual orientation: Who knows? First dalliance with a politician: sixteen. Actual experience with prostitution: as an experiment with anarchy when she was nineteen. Current lover: How could you not know? magenta blue.

Denis watched as the long line of editors streamed back to offices, suddenly remembering important business after he dropped his bombshell.

"The sea bass was excellent!" Denis reported back to Sara and Nykki. "I was the only one drinking, though. Those people don't touch anything stronger than Pellegrino. I might have more luck finding drugs during the cocktail hour." Nykki looked at her watch anxiously. Patrick Brontë stared at his wall. Sara gave Denis a reproachful look.

"Is it my fault if I like to eat well? There are certain times in life," Denis said loudly, drunkenly, "when you just have to coast on good looks and charm."

"How could she have slept with her student?" Sara asked aloud, staring down at the late edition of the *Post,* featuring Claire's nude book-jacket photo and the headline PORNO PROF."

"Why? Isn't she attractive?" Denis asked quizzically.

"That's not the point."

"I think it's the point, don't you?"

"Claire can't just seduce whomever she finds attractive."

"Why not?" Denis asked, perplexed.

Later, when he'd returned from the cocktail hour drunk and empty-handed, he slumped in a chair and addressed the heel of his shoe.

"There is one thing we could do to help Nykki. But it would involve proper attire."

"We wondered when we might see you again."

Sara and Denis were both relieved to see Ives answer the door instead of Burke.

"Mr. Burke is just putting on some tea," Ives said as he took their coats and ushered them into the parlor. Sara had wondered what they did in the winter, and apparently the answer was: freeze. They all gravitated to the fireplace, hardly noticing Burke as he entered with a pot of tea.

"We wondered when we might see you again," Burke said with special significance to Nykki. Sara realized his mistake and introduced them.

"Sara, may I speak to you a moment?" Burke asked. "In the kitchen. Would you excuse us?" He led her away from the group.

"This is very embarrassing," Burke started.

"Please, don't—" Sara wanted to avoid another weird scene; she'd had enough of them lately.

"No, I mean, what I said—"

"Let's forget it. We're friends."

"Of course, I wondered why you never responded. You must have known."

"Known?"

"That woman, Nykki. I confused her with you. She's more like my dream. She's my destiny."

"Oh."

"I'm sorry."

"No, well, I suppose in these things there's always a little chance of mistaken identity."

"Yes."

"She'd actually like to see the *Chinese* room," Sara said significantly, offering the code words Denis had instructed her to use.

Burke smiled. "Anything."

While Nykki wrote her opus in longhand on special Florentine watermarked paper at the Burke-Iveses' town house, Sara typed it into the computer at the Royalton, and Denis had remarkable three-hour lunches. On the fifth day, Claire and a reporter with a newsmagazine show found themselves seated next to Denis and his audience of patrons.

"You little pimp!" Claire said, tossing a plate of pumpkin risotto in his lap. "My private life is *mine* to sell."

what it costs a man

Shaking from head to foot, looking deadly pale, speaking low, vehemently yet with difficulty—he made me for the first time feel what it costs a man to declare affection where he doubts response.

Charlotte Brontë, to Margaret Wooler, 1852

"Brilliant! The best first draft I've ever read," Mr. Emmons said, lifting his glass in a toast.

"Really?" Sara asked, genuinely surprised.

"Of course, really."

"Nykki said that when a producer says it's the best first draft he's ever read, it's code for 'You're fired.'"

"You learn fast," Mr. Emmons said with a sardonic wink. "No, seriously, it's dreamy, it's passionate, it's as though it was written in a fever dream, it's eccentric yet beautiful. It's profound. It's love." He gave Sara a significant look that made her wonder where her wine was.

"There was a lot of rain in the Piedmonts in ninety-four," the waiter said without prompting as he set down their glasses. Mr. Emmons waved him and his Piedmonts away.

"You did an amazing job, Sara. It's exactly what we talked about: an honest, tender, true love story."

Sara's cheeks flushed with pleasure—oh! the warmth of admiration, of flirtation. She had been in a panic about his reaction, had seen it as her last hope of validation. Finally!

"Thanks. Well, Nykki mentioned that I should talk to you," Sara managed haltingly, "about compensation. We never really talked and I was wondering if my services were at least worth, maybe, fifty thousand dollars?" Nykki's primary negotiating advice was not to mention a figure. Sara had already screwed up her only instruction.

"Never mention figures, Sara. I'd have said you're worth much more—you created the story with her. You provided all the background. Do you know how many months it would cost to research all that? You wrote this, you monitored the writer's drug levels—hell, that's more than writing, that's *producing!*"

"How did you know?"

"What? Nykki? Well, you know when you read *Alice in Wonderland* you're struck by a lot of things, but one of the main things you think is, This person was on *something really good.*"

"It was all very safe. I mean, we know some opium enthusiasts who live in the nineteenth century."

"Perfect!"

"They're very nice."

"Sara, you ground me. You are so *sane.*"

"Thanks," Sara said, staring at her clever fennel salad.

"Sorry. It's just been two weeks with the folks. My mother just had a bunch of work done and she looks younger than me. It's very disturbing."

"Work?"

"Plastic surgery."

"That is disturbing."

"Anyway," Mr. Emmons began, looking distracted, "I'm known to be a good negotiator, but I just told you you're worth more than the figure you just quoted. Can you guess why I'd make such a rookie mistake?"

Sara shook her head. Mr. Emmons pulled a jewel box from his pocket and handed it to Sara. She opened the box and found a silver pendant with an amethyst.

"It's DNA. Isn't that brilliant?"

"I don't understand."

"I found it for you in England. It has Charlotte Brontë's DNA embedded in the stone. They can do that now."

"Why?" Sara asked, fingering the pendant.

"They do key chains, too."

"Great." She stared at it uncertainly.

"They get it from locks of hair. Mother has a Charles Lindbergh watch."

"Somebody collects famous hair?"

"Great idea, huh?"

Sara didn't know if he was being ironic.

"Yes. Great," she agreed with an arch lilt to her voice.

Mr. Emmons leaned forward, helping her with the clasp and then withdrawing his hands with awkward reluctance.

"Sara." Mr. Emmons cleared his throat in the way that people do before they level with you. "I think it's pretty obvious how I feel about you."

Sara was never sure how that comment was meant to be answered.

"Uh-huh."

"I know I'm moving awfully fast, but sometimes you just feel something's right, don't you?"

"Uh-huh."

"So?"

"What?"

"'Come live with me and be my love, and we will all the pleasures prove.'"

Sara was always a little queasy when grown-ups quoted poetry in conversation. It seemed like a precocious kid thing to do unless you were Richard Burton and could get away with it. Mr. Emmons's confidence seemed to flag and he gave an ironic little shrug to indicate how lightly he took these big moments.

"Christopher Marlowe," he explained.

"I know."

Sara smiled self-consciously, and Mr. Emmons realized he was laying it on a bit thick, even for him.

"The whole long-distance thing? It's bullshit. I know right now I'm in love with you, so come to L.A.—live with me. I know it's sudden, but ever since my accident? I'm just really intuitive. I want you with me. I don't want to be modern."

Now he was speaking her language, the lingua franca of people who die on cold heaths whispering names. . . .

"I don't want to take red-eyes," he continued, "or talk long-distance about our needs and where this is 'going.' That's such sanitized bullshit. So twenty-first century. We both feel it. Let's jump! Let's be romantics. Come away with me. In whatever capacity you choose."

Sara understood that "capacity" was in this case code for "bed." She smiled, flattered and panicked by his certainty.

"Hey! You don't have to decide now. About us. I realize it's . . ." Mr. Emmons waved at the waiter, trying to get another glass of wine. Something about the way he fished for attention, trying to emulate the casual man of business, broke her heart and she longed to tell him what he wanted to hear.

Too fast, too fast, she thought. What did she really know about him? Certainly she was attracted, but for all she knew, he could have a cellar full of lady scholars chained to the wall begging for death. And what about her furniture? There would be change-of-address forms and calls to Con Edison to be made—it was crazy.

"I'd like to say yes, really. It's just— I'm coming out of a relationship and now I'm out of work and there's just a lot sort of overwhelming me. . . ."

Mr. Emmons smiled politely, it was the usual list one grown-up offered to another—the typical barrier adults build to protect their unhappiness.

"It's not that I'm not interested," Sara said. "I am. You're just going to have to slow down for me a bit."

He smiled gently. He could be patient, too, if that was what was required.

"You make me want to be completely honest with you," he said. "I don't get that very often. Not since sobriety."

"How long have you been . . . ?"

"Sober?"

Sara nodded.

"Six months," he said.

"So the skiing accident?"

Sara could see him reaching back in his mind for a bit of spin. He clearly had an official version of this story, but something stopped him. His eyes opened wide and he smiled.

"I was totally wasted," he admitted. "Only my sponsor knows that. And you. Now."

"Thank you."

Mr. Emmons finished his glass of wine.

"But you still drink?" she asked.

"Wine I can handle. My weakness is coke. And meth. And weed. You're now totally scared of me, aren't you?"

Sara laughed self-consciously, about to deny this. "A little," she admitted.

"Thanks for being honest. You're so not L.A."

Sara noticed that he often perceived people via region—*he's so London, she's so not New York*—and she sensed it was high praise to be assessed as "not L.A."

"What does that mean?" she asked.

"You're not spinning all the time. It's relaxing being with you—although you do scare me, too, I suppose," he said, smiling.

"Why?"

"I feel you're testing me. Women test men, don't they?"

"Life tests men. Women just get the front-row seats."

Mr. Emmons grinned. "Wit. I like that."

"Tell me what you're afraid of, then. No spin," Sara said.

Mr. Emmons took a deep breath. More tests! But he was a man for the challenge.

"I'm afraid I'll mess this up somehow. I'm afraid I'll start doing drugs again. I'm afraid this project will fall apart. What about you?"

"I'm afraid my academic career's in the toilet," Sara answered.

"Is that all?" Mr. Emmons asked, teasing.

"There's this rare letter—it could save me—but I can't get it."

"Why not?"

"This lady has it. She got very suspicious when I told her what it might be worth."

Mr. Emmons looked relieved. Saving the day for Sara would be easier than he imagined. God bless the problems that can be solved with money, he thought.

"We'll pay the check, get in a cab, and go get it."

"Oh, no, it could be worth a lot. She hasn't returned any of my thousands of calls—"

"Let's go buy you that letter—my gift to you."

"No, you couldn't. If it's real, it's worth tens of thousands of dollars. Maybe more."

Mr. Emmons waved dismissively as though this was the very least of his troubles.

"Sara, my mother's nose cost more than that!"

❖   ❖   ❖

A younger version of Mrs. Wright answered the door.

"I'm Carolyn Anson, her daughter," she explained. "Can I help you?"

"I met your mother awhile ago. About a letter?" Sara said, still standing in the doorway. Carolyn shook her head, mystified. She was probably the crack addict, Sara thought, though she didn't look like one.

"My mother's in the hospital. She's had a stroke."

"Oh, my God, I'm sorry."

"I'm here just looking after the place. Packing things up. The doctors say she'll need one of those round-the-clock places when she comes out. We all just pray she has the strength."

"I'm sorry."

"She never mentioned—"

"She'd answered an ad I placed in reference to an old letter she had."

"Oh, come in. Sorry—the place is a mess."

Carolyn walked them to the living room. The massive TV was silent and black, hovering like death in the corner. No wonder Mrs. Wright always left it on, Sara thought. In the light Sara could see Carolyn was neither a crack addict nor a purveyor of dirty men but rather a nice, middle-class woman. It hadn't occurred to Sara that Mrs. Wright had made all that up about her daughter. Carolyn lived in Westchester, she explained. She saw her mother frequently—she even found her the day she had the stroke, thank God.

"Did she seem a little out of it—" Carolyn lowered her voice discreetly. "—y'know, tipsy?"

"Um, she seemed fine. Why?"

"Just ever since Dad passed she's been a bit . . . depressed. And she drinks. I mean, just a glass every now and then—don't get the wrong idea, she's no Betty Ford or whatever."

"Now that you mention it, she may have had a glass," Sara offered.

"I knew it," Carolyn said, anxiously lacing and unlacing her fingers in front of her. "She could get a bit paranoid. I hope she wasn't that way with you."

"She was perfectly lovely," Sara said.

"We actually came to see if she'd done anything with the letter," Mr. Emmons asked gently.

Carolyn nodded and went to find her mother's strongbox. When she opened it, it was empty.

"When you found her, was she wearing a pink cardigan?" Sara asked.

"Oh, yeah, that was sad, that was her favorite twinset," Carolyn recalled fondly.

"Sad?"

"I threw it out. I found her in it and, well, she was a mess."

Sara's stomach tightened, remembering the letter stuffed in its pocket. "I see," she said, exhaling slowly, her throat aching with the effort not to cry.

"*I'm so sorry,* Sara," Mr. Emmons consoled her in the cab.

"Ohhh," Sara said. Maybe it wasn't real, she reasoned, not really believing it herself.

"Are there any other letters?"

"That's the closest I ever came to one. Without it, my research is . . . pointless."

"Not to me. We have a project. Right?" He winked, trying to cheer her up. Sara smiled sadly. But he was right. She did have a project and perhaps it was her fate to only glimpse that letter, glean its meaning, and lose it. Survival is a choice. *This is all you get, make use.*

"You're right," Sara announced defiantly. "We'll have a movie instead."

"That's the spirit," Mr. Emmons said as they pulled up to her building.

Sara managed a smile and turned to him. "Would you like to come in?"

real happiness

The destiny which Providence in His goodness and wisdom seems to offer me will not—I am aware—be generally regarded as brilliant—but I trust I see in it some germs of real happiness.

Charlotte Brontë, to Margaret Wooler, 1854

"L.A.? You mean, like, *Los Angeles*? Sara. You are so not L.A.," Meredith said.

"That's what Mr. Emmons said, too," Sara said.

"You call him Mr. Emmons? That's kind of creepy," Meredith said. "What's his first name?"

"Byrne," Sara answered.

"Stick with Mr. Emmons." Meredith scooped the last of the cafeteria's potato salad off her plate and into the garbage. "You were right to turn him down. L.A., really?"

"We're still seeing each other. I just need to take it slow. Besides, I need to be looking for a job."

"Don't remind me," Meredith said as she reached for a cigarette in her bag and fished for matches.

"Is he a Scientologist or something?"

"Close," Sara admitted reluctantly. "AA. Actually, NA. One of those. He can drink."

Meredith smiled and rolled her eyes. "That's a comfort."

Sara looked out across campus, which was always eerily empty during winter break. At the edge of campus she could see the sliver of a group of protesters still finding something to scream about in the wake of *the first coming*. The afternoon sun fell on the protesters in such a way that they looked like a choir singing in a TV Christmas special. The snow had fallen just that morning and still had its crisp, telegenic sheen. The city always looked beautiful in the first few hours of snow, before grime formed an icy layer over the top and people tossed old Christmas trees or mattresses into the banks along the sidewalks.

"Besides . . ." Sara began, pushing tuna salad around her plate with a fork.

"What?"

"Nothing. I'm happy. . . ."

"No you aren't. What?"

"I'm just still . . . damn, I'm still just so . . . hung up on Paul. . . ."

"Shit," Meredith said, realizing: "He hasn't told you?"

"What?" Sara asked nervously.

"He's moving in with that woman—Therese. I can't believe he didn't— Well, he wouldn't. Fucking baby. See? You're better off without him."

Sara felt the now-familiar sensation of the bottom falling out. She stared out the window, stunned.

"God. I'm such a fool. When did this all happen?"

Meredith shrugged; she wasn't sure. At first Sara was angry because all she felt was pain. Then the pain went numb and she felt angry because even the pain was lost to her, creeping in the depths, inaccessible. Like the song says, Sara thought, *good morning heartache, sit down.* She felt pure hatred for Paul and felt the horrid realization that hate wasn't the opposite of love but its cruel extension.

"I'm really sorry." God, things were horrible; even Meredith was being sensitive. Sara nodded and tried to say something intelligible. She desperately wanted to be alone.

"I have to go," she finally managed as she threw her lunch in the garbage. She could hear Meredith calling after her, but sympathy from Meredith only made things worse. Sara sped out of the building, stalking across campus, past the building where she and Paul met, past the courtyard where they shared sack lunches—what a parade of ugliness, how ridiculous to believe in anything, Sara thought. Making her way past the Literature department and through Culture Studies, Sara inadvertently walked smack into the thick of the protesters. Something about them stopped her. She stared at each of them—their mood matched hers: numb, sad, hopelessly let down by the world.

Their numbers had dwindled to about fifteen or fewer, and Sara realized they were watching "mary" being packed up in a crate. The protesters had the disgruntled air of an audience who'd shown up after the show—Claire had been suspended and her "improper relationship" with magenta was under investigation. magenta had dropped out, signed with an agent, and was assembling a series of Christian rock videos.

They stood outside in the fresh snow, the sun bouncing off the windowed room where "mary" lay with a sea of Styrofoam peanuts flowing up her thighs, restoring her modesty. The scene was quiet and in the hush Sara was hard pressed to tell if the assembled crowd was pro or con. She stood next to a woman in a green velvet hat that seemed oddly whimsical sitting on top such a hard, pinched face. The woman was maybe forty-five, Sara guessed.

"They're taking it downtown," she told Sara without being asked, "where it belongs." From the flat way she said this Sara was unsure whether it was intended as a slight against downtown or uptown. Most of the people assembled had the same look of fatigue Sara associated with the perpetually outraged, and she felt out of place, as she hadn't even bothered to form an opinion about *the first coming*. Until now she hadn't even seen it.

But it was too late. *The first coming* was a full-fledged controversy and there was no point joining the conversation now. Rather than exciting debate, controversy seemed to obviate it. Once something was fixed in the firmament as an object of scandal, it was somehow beyond human scale. It was a thing unto itself, like a species of fish or a unit of currency. There was no point in being for or against something once it had achieved this status because it was already beyond you. People would see *the first coming* because they had read about it or they would read about it because they had seen it. There would be preordained schools of pro and con, and one would form one's opinion in reference to these camps. It was its own self-sustaining object and vessel through which pointless opinions would continually flow.

The sun was falling behind the trees, creating a mottled, golden glow around "mary" and the two maintenance men dispatched to crate up the Virgin. One was a small Puerto Rican man who kept chasing the Styrofoam peanuts as they scattered on the ground. The other was a muscular young man with an Elvis pompadour. He seemed preoccupied with "mary's" safety, tenderly hoisting her into her crate with care.

As he lifted her, "mary" slipped from his grasp, sliding swiftly into a halo of light that seemed to suspend her, momentarily, in midair. Sara heard the woman next to her gasp, then heard herself gasp, too. But the boy with the Elvis hair gracefully slung one arm under her hip, seeming almost embarrassed by their propitious intimacy. Once he had a grip, Elvis realized the only secure way of moving "mary" was to enfold her, wrapping his arms over her outstretched posture of ecstasy. They looked like they were performing some seductive modern dance. Then finally, slowly, he eased her into her case. It was a sweet moment; Sara half expected the man to say, "Sorry about that there, Mrs. Christ, ma'am," with the deferential manner of a small-town paperboy.

Sara looked around at her companions, who all seemed to share the same sheepish look of astonishment. For a moment, "mary" was a beauty, a sight to behold. "mary" being cradled and lifted in an unrehearsed gesture of tender and erotic flight was a weird and gorgeous sight— a "mary" and Elvis pieta. The protesters looked at one another a little guiltily, wondering what had just happened.

Sara had momentarily forgotten how confused and heartsick she'd felt, how worn down by disillusion. Then the moment passed. The crowd regrouped as she began planning how to destroy Paul's first-edition Orwell. Fire or water? Water would involve walking it to the river and watching it sink. Too depressing, she thought. Fire could spread easily, it was dangerous, and therefore more exhilarating. Or she could sell it. No, too pragmatic. Sara wanted to exact pain and suffering. But whose? Paul had moved on; his life was impervious now to whatever casual cruelties she could send his way. Destroying his book only exposed her vulnerability, her shaking rage, her inability to cope with life's heartbreaks. It amplified her weakness. She needed a countermove, one that suggested vast reserves of psychological resilience and steely mental health. She needed to move on, and if she couldn't do that, maybe she could at least act like she could. Wasn't that what her parents, therapists no less, often advised? Smile and you'll feel happier! Something like that, Sara remembered.

"After that they're sending it to Los Angeles, where every nut rolls eventually," the woman in the green velvet hat related to Sara.

"I'm going to Los Angeles," Sara decided suddenly, brightly—too brightly, as it aroused the woman's suspicion. She turned away from Sara, fixing her sights again on the efficient dispatch of the Virgin. Sara stayed. They all stayed and they watched as the boy with Elvis hair nailed "mary's" crate firmly shut.

The sun had set by the time Sara started walking home. The shop windows were advertising end-of-the-year savings, inanities to celebrate the New Year. Sara wasn't sure what she'd just decided except that it felt like an intelligent escape.

Here were the things she liked about Mr. Emmons, she thought, listing in her head: He was decisive, he was masculine, he was smart and well-educated, he had a sense of purpose, he owned suits and returned phone calls, he seemed grown up in a way that she had never experienced in a partner. He'd had the maturity to recognize and address an addiction—this was preferable to the relative shallowness of a man who'd never felt the weight of real struggle. He was protective of Sara; she felt watched over, desired in his presence. He was interested in her, truly interested, perhaps even more than she was in him. This was reassuring. His appearance in her life felt almost magical in its timing.

The things that concerned her were: He could be the teensiest bit pretentious—he made a big show of knowing wines and wove foreign phrases into everyday speech with studied self-importance. He had a temper and didn't suffer fools. His sense of humor was a bit snide, but for all her outward politeness, Sara was ultimately of the if-you-can't-say-something-nice-sit-down-next-to-me school. All his faults were seemingly manageable. Sara wasn't perfect, either.

Here are the things I like about Los Angeles, she continued in this vein: It will be good for my career (if the film goes forward), it scares me, and it will put an ocean *and* a continent between Paul and me. *Need more space in the New Year?* a flyer in the entrance of a hardware store asked. Sara stopped and stared at it. Yes, storage space. I'll need storage space if I'm moving. She wrote the number down in her notebook and walked the rest of the way home.

much to forgive

If Lucy marries anybody—it must be the Professor—a man in whom there is much to forgive—much to 'put up with.'

Charlotte Brontë, to George Smith, 1852

It was seventy-two degrees and partly sunny on the January afternoon that Sara arrived in Los Angeles. Mr. Emmons was waiting for her just beyond the security checkpoint with flowers. This struck her as yet another omen that she had made the right decision in coming; no one had actually met Sara inside an airport since she was a child.

"You look beautiful."

"Thank you. Were you waiting long?" Sara asked, kissing him. They were still physically awkward together, still so new, she noted. Hugs lurched clumsily into kisses and vice versa.

"Not at all. Your flight was early."

"So where's this new car I keep hearing about?"

Mr. Emmons smiled and led her out to the parking structure where his newly arrived Facel Vega awaited them. Mr. Emmons had a tough time deciding which he was more excited about: Sara moving to Los Angeles to be with him or the Facel Vega vintage car he had been waiting for for six months to finally arrive from France. Miraculously, they both arrived on the same day, and Mr. Emmons took it as a portent of things to come. Suddenly things just became easy. Surely it was the combination of his dream girl and his dream car arriving on the same day, a perfect day, in Los Angeles.

"So this is it?" Sara asked, taking in the beautiful pale yellow vintage car and its deep red leather interior. It was true; he had exquisite taste, Sara thought, feeling all the more flattered by the fact that Mr. Emmons had chosen *her*.

"Fit for a queen," he said, opening the door for her with a flourish.

"That statue's from Lhasa—I outbid David Geffen for it," Mr. Emmons said, pointing out the large meditating Buddha in his deck garden.

"Who's that?" Sara asked.

"You're funny." He smiled and arranged the picnic he'd prepared. "I used to come out here and sit while I was first in recovery. Dreaming about lines of coke," he explained. "There was one night. I couldn't sleep. All I wanted to do was get in my car and go party. But I'd gone about a month. I was proud of myself. So I came out here and I thought, I need to get out of this town—too many reminders. But then I remembered something they say in

AA about changing geography. You think if you change lo-
cation, your problems will vanish, so you move somewhere
or change something radically in your life and then, well . . .
there you are again. You know?"

Sara nodded.

"So I came out here and sat down—it was probably
three A.M.—and I said, 'Okay. I won't move. I'll be here.
I'll be completely here. I'll cultivate this garden, I'll learn
all the names of the flowers and trees and butterflies and
birds.' . . . It sounds corny, I know."

"No, it doesn't. Not at all."

Mr. Emmons smiled, reassured. "That right there is a
Cabbage White," he said, pointing to a white butterfly hovering over a spray of purple bougainvillea. "So named because they leave their eggs in cabbages, mostly. The orange
one? That's a Gulf Fritillary. I planted this passion flower for
them. They love it. The passion flower, *Passiflora*, was seen
in a vision of St. Francis—he saw it growing on the cross.
So the Jesuits named it," he said, gesturing to a climbing
vine. "The blossoms have ten petals, which are said to rep-
resent the apostles, the crown is the halo or crown of thorns,
depends on your mood—I've seen both—and the stamen
are the five wounds. You think I'm crazy, don't you?"

"No, I don't." Sara laughed.

Sara looked around his garden. All of this should
have unsettled her, yet she felt strangely assured by her
surroundings, by Mr. Emmons himself, who seemed like
a man who knew everything: the names, the origins, the
entire plan. She leaned in to kiss him. It was their first
completely natural kiss and they both felt a little overjoyed

by this new development. Clearly the destroyed letter was a blessing in disguise. How many more years would she have wasted looking for letters, plying sad widows with Chablis, and begging for fellowships?

"Do you know what we have in common?" Mr. Emmons asked.

"What?"

"We're both romantics."

Sara smiled, flattered. "I guess you're right," she said, kissing him lightly.

"Do you want to go inside?" Mr. Emmons asked.

"You mean you don't want to drive around in your new car?" Sara asked, teasing.

Mr. Emmons smiled guiltily. "It's not just a car. It's a nineteen sixty-two Facel II."

"Uh-huh."

"And yes, I'd like to drive it."

"Why don't we drive up the coast a bit, then come back? There's plenty of time."

"I knew there was a reason I love you so much," he said, kissing her again and reaching for the keys.

part two

The spirit of Romance would have indicated another course, far more flowery and inviting; it would have fashioned a paramount hero, kept faithfully with him and made him supremely 'worshipful'—he should have an idol, and not a mute, unresponding idol—either—: but this would have been unlike Real Life, inconsistent with Truth—at variance with Probability.

Charlotte Brontë, to George Smith, 1852

truth

Fate affords some lovers only one opportunity to meet.
Others it allows endless opportunities. Whatever the circumstances, any number of preconditions must gather
around this fortuitous event. In the case of Sara and Mr.
Emmons it was the combination of nausea, the inscrutabil-
ity of a certain bathroom in New York, and the tempera-
mental nature of Mr. Emmons's cell phone. They were
given only one opportunity to meet, but they had so capitalized upon their meager portion that within the space of
a year they were lying next to each other in bed half-
awake, half-asleep, both silently appreciating Mr. Emmons's taste in sheets.

   While it's generally assumed that a romantic has to

part with a great number of illusions to wake up in bed with a film producer, Sara awoke each morning with most of hers still intact. A person could use fate to justify all sorts of things. A person could move across the country to be with someone she hardly knew, someone with a rather checkered past. She might make this decision while she is, herself, in the throes of romantic despair, or, as the doctors might call it, affective situational depression.

She might wake each morning with a pang of recognition, a small voice in her head that says, *I want to go home.* She might stare at her lover and wonder how this person had become more, not less, of a stranger during eight months of cohabitation. And if she has the weakness of a romantic disposition, she will decide that fate led her to this stranger's bed. It is the story she tells to explain her life to herself, and so far, the fate rationale has been stronger than the thinly veiled concern of friends and family.

After months of brief and evasive calls home, she would very probably have late-night conversations on the phone with her mother, punctuated by long silences after which her mother would sigh and say, "Well, honey, you know your father and I are always here for you," implying impending crisis or, more obliquely, "Well, you know what's best," or the practical, "How much longer d'you suppose you'll need to store your stuff in the garage?" Sara was well aware that her mother's theory assumed that she had recovered hastily and incompletely, which was to say, not at all, from her break with Paul and was now engaged in a standard-fare look-at-me-now affair that would end up hurting Sara more than it could ever hurt Paul if it got too serious. If she, for instance, moved in with the man.

So Sara returned fewer phone calls. She made new friends, or at least, acquaintances. She started seeing her earlier passions as immature, silly. She gave up on her thesis and bought new shoes. She wasn't sure if she was happy, but her surroundings, at least, assured her that she should be. Who wouldn't dream of waking up here? Mr. Emmons's home had been featured in a magazine, after all. He collected furniture, artifacts, paintings, and always prided himself on being just ahead of the curve. *Steel apothecary cabinets? Chinese snuffboxes? Midcentury modern? Why, I've been collecting that for years! That writing table? Old-growth wood—you can't get that anymore. I had it salvaged from a warehouse in Pennsylvania. They were going to throw it away, if you can believe it. Word's out, though, every fucker's got someone out there scouting for old-growth.*

Even the sheets were real linen, from Ireland, Mr. Emmons said, and were beaten clean within an inch of their lives by a domestic with a vaguely Irish accent. Everyone Sara met these days seemed to have an accent that had more to do with their aspirations than their origins. Sara was sure she had overheard this woman discussing her childhood in Redondo Beach.

"It's when he thinks he's past love that he finds his last love." Sara's yoga instructor, Jasmyn, had told her to pick a more upbeat mantra. "Something more now. Live in the present." Sara would approximate a look of serenity while sipping ginger and lemongrass tea after their sessions,

guiltily hoarding the secret belief that she was constitution-
ally incapable of inner light. "Inhale warmth and joy, ex-
hale, surrender . . ." Jasmyn demanded. Sara would nod
dutifully, staring out at the soupy haze of Los Angeles.

And her "happy place"? Where she envisioned herself
at peace with her surroundings? Strangely, she fantasized
about being back where she was a year ago, teaching and
heading toward a career of academic oblivion. Just nostalgia for samsara, the ego hanging on to its own drama, Jasmyn would probably say. Mr. Emmons had saved Sara
from all that and she had been happy about it at the time.
Romantics are forever longing for rescue, after all. She
should be grateful, she reminded herself. If only Mr. Emmons wouldn't talk.

"DO YOU KNOW WHAT YOUR SHIT TASTES LIKE?"
Mr. Emmons's voice traveled from his office down the hall.
He was at the telephone early this morning—Sara hadn't
even heard him get up.

"'Cause you better get used to that taste 'cause I am
going to FUCKING BURY YOU IN YOUR OWN FUCKING
EXCREMENT, DO YOU HEAR ME? I don't care if that's
her quote. I'm sorry, but did her last film even make ten
million? No, it didn't, that's bullshit, even Japan stayed
home. No, no, you are screwing me and you are not listening. I am gonna ream your ass, I will kill you, I will
SLAUGHTER you, there will be no survivors, I am talking
GENOCIDE."

Phone calls for Mr. Emmons began directly after a
light breakfast of oatmeal and seasonal fruit and continued until the personal trainer arrived at eleven A.M.

"How does that make me an anti-Semite? I'm Jewish. I'm a self-hating Jew? No, I love myself. I'm a you-hating-Jew, asshole! Don't fucking lecture *me* about *anger management*! I'd say the fact that you're alive right now is a testament to my anger management skills. Oh, please! That was not a threat. Hello? Bastard!"

Sara heard the phone's death rattle as Mr. Emmons winged it against the window. New telephone, new glass.

"Morning, darling, did I wake you?" he asked cheerfully, poking his head in the doorway.

"No, I was already awake." Sara never adjusted to his split-second reversals. She would have to watch him closely. Mr. Emmons flopped on the bed, careful to keep his suede driving shoes from touching the linens.

"She still wants ten million. I told her agent that's practically half our whole budget, this is a prestige project—we already had a verbal agreement. Marty's going to *love* this. This is enough for him to call off the deal—"

Marty was the studio executive who'd been brought in last minute to replace the original executive, the woman who loved Brontë and had spent the last seven months asking for script revisions and had recently been fired. Mr. Emmons was well aware that Marty was hoping to sink the project since he'd inherited it from someone else. Marty not so secretly believed this dog couldn't hunt, but the actors were big names and they had no other prestige projects—the studio still wanted to make it. At least until Marty could find a reason to talk them out of it.

"Maybe he hasn't heard about it yet. There's still time for me to talk her down," he said wistfully.

Sara watched him carefully, noticing the pronounced veins, the blood surging at his temples. He would be in a sour mood all day.

"I didn't know you were Jewish," Sara said finally. This was enough of a non sequitur for Mr. Emmons to stop thinking about how he could get his hands on ten million dollars.

"I'm not. But I'll be damned if that hunchbacked little maggot's going to call me an anti-Semite."

Mr. Emmons stared at the ceiling, thinking the genocide remark was perhaps ill-advised and could someday work against him during some critical moment. He shifted his gaze from the ceiling to Sara.

"Why? Would it make a difference?"

"No, no, of course not," Sara answered, moving next to him on the bed reassuringly. "It's just— I sometimes realize how little I really know about you."

Mr. Emmons's eyes moistened. He pulled her hand to his chest in a self-consciously dramatic gesture. "You know me."

Sara smiled, unsure whether she was moved by the sincerity of the gesture or the degree to which he struggled to make it appear sincere. He kissed her; she pulled him closer and the suede driving shoes came dangerously close to the Irish linen. Mr. Emmons sat up suddenly.

"The trainer'll be here any minute. I'm sorry, darling, I just have to keep my focus today."

"It's all right," Sara replied.

Mr. Emmons looked in the mirror. "*Ten fucking* million," he muttered, unaware that he was even speaking out loud. Sara watched him change into a T-shirt. He shook out its wrinkles, irritated by them.

"You were lovers?" Sara guessed.

"Who?"

"What's-her-name. The actress." Sara's penchant for forgetting the names of the truly famous had gone from charming to annoying. Mr. Emmons gave a short, revealing snort of a laugh.

"You make it sound so romantic." He shrugged his shoulders good-naturedly, adopting a worldly tone. "We messed around a few times. Long time ago—she was still doing bit stuff on TV."

Sara stared at him.

"I might have forgotten to call her or something, I forget." Mr. Emmons was sensitive enough to hear the scratch of a little black mark going next to his name in Sara's mind and realized he was coming across as disappointingly male.

"I could be a real prick," he admitted. "Before I met you," he added, remembering that a woman's belief in her ability to transform cads into princes was primordial and universal and allowed him to get away with a hell of a lot in the bargain.

Sara gave him a smile; she might be willing to believe him but not quite yet.

"It was during my *substance abuse days*," he said. "It's just— I want this to work so badly. You, me, the project."

"I know." Sara smiled. He looked relieved to hear the doorbell ring.

"That'll be Eryk! Ten fucking million," he said to himself as he padded to the living room.

Sara lay back in bed. She could hear the clicking spray of the morning sprinklers. It was the only noise except the ocean, and she listened as the watery duet of the waves joined with the *click-click-spray* of the sprinklers. It was always quiet here. The sprinklers turned off, and the only thing keeping time with the ocean was the clank of barbells as Mr. Emmons did his bench-press with Eryk.

Mr. Emmons appeared in the doorway. "Darling, you're not even dressed. Eryk's waiting. And we have a meeting at one."

"Heaven is empty because so many meetings," Sara said vaguely to herself.

Mr. Emmons stared at her blankly. "Darling, are you all right?"

a paroxysm of anguish

I found him leaning against the garden-door in a parox-
ysm of anguish—sobbing as women never sob. . . . they
all think in Haworth that I have refused him &c. if pity
would do Mr N– any good—he ought to have and I believe has it. They may abuse me, if they will, whether
they do or not—I can't tell.

Charlotte Brontë, to Ellen Nussey, 1853

"Is there any way we could make Charlotte seem like . . .
less of a bitch? Maybe? Especially this scene with Nicholls
here where she rejects his proposal . . . ?"

"Sure, Marty, that's not a problem," Mr. Emmons
weighed in quickly. "She is a little bitchy, I agree."

"Nykki and I felt that was a key moment," said Sara.
"It shows her strength, her pragmatism—she's got that romantic side, but here she's thinking with her head," she reminded them. This apparently wasn't done in a meeting
with a new exec, as Mr. Emmons subtly shook his head
between swigs of Pellegrino.

"Well, I think there's a middle way that keeps
her strong and historically accurate but not bitchy," Mr.

Emmons explained, trying to salvage the moment. "Sara's new to screenwriting. I'm sure the note will make sense to Nykki."

"We need . . . I don't know how to put this . . . more of a *Titanic* moment. Do you know what I mean?" Marty asked. Ever the professional, Marty continued to dole out script notes while furtively trying to sabotage the project.

"I'm not sure I do," Sara hedged.

"Nykki will understand," Mr. Emmons quickly assured him.

Sara and Mr. Emmons sat across from Marty and his assistant, Elyse, in what felt like a bizarre double date.

Sara always felt out of place in these meetings, never knowing just how much "input" she was really supposed to have.

"We need a grand-sweep moment, y'know?" Marty mused.

"Big, right . . ." Mr. Emmons agreed.

"Like when he teaches her to spit," Elyse offered.

"What?" Sara asked.

"In *Titanic*."

"Charlotte needs to be more sympathetic," Marty added. "Why should we like her?"

"But she *is* sympathetic," Sara pressed. "She's still recovering from the loss of—"

"We'll fix it," Mr. Emmons interjected.

"I think the audience will understand if she's a little . . . ambivalent. She's still getting over the death of all her siblings," Sara resumed, trying not to look at Mr. Emmons's face or Marty's manicured nails. "What's more, it's important to establish the mores of the time—women simply didn't stay single in their thirties, and here she is turning down a man's proposal. She'd turned down two other men who were perfectly respectable matches because she wasn't in love. That just wasn't done at the time and it tells you a lot about who she was." She looked cautiously at Mr. Emmons. He wasn't happy.

"But she lets Nicholls twist in the wind for another year and half," countered Elyse. Elyse was in her thirties and not nearly as content with single life as Charlotte.

"The second time he proposed, yes, she was interested, but they had to wait for her father's approval—that's how it was done," Sara explained again.

"I mean, c'mon," Marty said, leaning back in his chair. "The guy proposes, she refuses, he leaves town, comes back, proposes again, and she says, 'Lemme go ask Dad'? No. This is a big romantic moment—this is a big *do me now* moment. Here, it's like he's just sloppy seconds after this professor. Nicholls has gotta be the big love," Marty declared emphatically before adding, "Just a thought," in a pretense of diplomacy.

"He was. Eventually," Sara explained. "It was a more sober, mature love—that's the point. She grew to love him. She had doubts about him and so did her father and her friends—she wasn't sure they were well matched. The point is in the last year of her life she discovers a quieter but equally intense love that grows out of mutual respect."

Marty joined his fingers thoughtfully. "Yeah, but

what's the fun of that? You know? At the end of the day that just makes him look *whipped*."

For years after her death, there was debate among Charlotte Brontë fans that portrayed Arthur Bell Nicholls in fairly unattractive terms. Some claimed that he was not sufficiently supportive of Charlotte's genius, that he attempted to censor her correspondence and was overly critical of her work, preferring a dutiful curate's wife to an accomplished author. There were ultimately pro and con Arthur camps. But in the end, Arthur Bell Nicholls prevailed. Not because right was on his side. Not that it wasn't. Charlotte Brontë was a lonely, depressive virgin when she married at thirty-seven—who could blame her if she decided to give herself over fully to the simple joys of matrimony during her brief life? Charlotte expressed unexpected happiness in her marriage. But that had nothing to do with it. One hundred and fifty years after Charlotte's death, Arthur Bell Nicholls won sympathy for all posterity because the actor playing him in the movie version had a very powerful manager who didn't like his client appearing weak.

Sara was beginning to realize that Mr. Nicholls's posthumous reputation would be preserved by the ambitions of an up-and-coming British actor who was looking to cross over into the mainstream Hollywood market. He had the pedigree: a couple seasons with the Royal Shakespeare, minor parts in TV, even a splashy bit as a psychopath in a British film that had become a sleeper hit. Now he would do the obligatory costume drama, receive respectful notices for his understated, dignified performance, and then meet his reward alternating roles as befuddled, romantic Englishmen and scary, brilliant psychopaths (versatile as well as deadly handsome, he had range!).

The British actor was in a good position to negotiate. The Actress was vacillating, wondering now if the project was as "interesting" as she'd originally supposed, wondering if she was being paid enough. It was all well and good to lower your quote for a prestige project, but it had to be real prestige. Charlotte didn't seem sufficiently complex. Mr. Emmons would sigh patiently. *Yes, of course. Whatever she wants, she does know we're in preproduction, doesn't she?*

The June start date had been pushed back to July, then August, and now, good God, September. Fear of losing the Actress amplified Mr. Emmons's fear of losing anyone else. Especially the up-and-coming British actor—he was getting a lot of buzz. By now, casting him had been a stroke of prophetic luck. As long as the Actress's delays didn't cause the British actor to move on to something else. *Make Mr. Nicholls more sympathetic? No problem.* Mr. Nicholls should be the lover standing at the gate all those years just waiting for Charlotte to pull her head out of the clouds and see him. Charlotte stops looking for the Byronic ideal of her fantasy world and finds paradise just sitting under her nose. All she had to do was look for it. . . .

"I don't know," Marty said, staring out the window pensively. On a clear day you could see Catalina from his office but, as he always joked, it was never a clear day. "I just think his proposing to her twice makes him look like a total whipped pussy." He shrugged as though maybe he was crazy, but that's what he thought. Mr. Emmons rushed to assure him of his sanity.

"Yeah, I tend to agree," Mr. Emmons confirmed.

"But it's so powerful when she's dying that she discovers this quieter love," Sara protested.

"Sara." Marty leaned forward. "I totally admire your knowledge here, but trust me—quiet love is for PBS. This is a movie. People don't want quiet love—they get enough of that in real life!" He laughed. "In fact, we were thinking of ending on the wedding. Cut all the death stuff. Dignified title card at the end. It's just so much death with the siblings already, y'know?"

Mr. Emmons nodded in agreement.

"I mean, Jesus, Emmons." Marty laughed. "I think you got a bigger body count here than in all your *Deadly Force* films put together!"

Mr. Emmons and Marty shared a good laugh. Sara's face felt flush.

"And Nicholls's profession?" Elyse asked.

"Maybe a blacksmith?" Marty suggested.

"Nicholls was a curate," Sara reminded everyone. She could hear Mr. Emmons sigh.

"We thought something more physical," Marty said, "active—"

"Manly. He is Charlotte's romantic interest after all," Elyse explained nonchalantly. "Nobody even knows what a curate does today."

"Who knows what a *blacksmith* does?"

"Everyone," Marty said.

"True," Mr. Emmons agreed.

"Are a blacksmith and a 'smithy' the same thing?" Elyse asked.

"A curate is like a reverend—" Sara started in. Hadn't she already explained this?

"Which is totally what her dad is—we don't need two," Elyse decided.

"Did their village have a sheriff? Or I guess the English equivalent?" Marty asked, brainstorming.

"Scotland Yard?" Elyse asked, excited now.

"Or a doctor? Simple, active, noble," Marty said. "But decent. Which reminds me, the scene where he asks her to burn her letters . . . ?"

Sara could feel her stomach churn. "Yes?"

"Maybe . . . instead . . . he could talk her into keeping them because he recognizes her genius? Just a thought," Marty suggested.

"Oh, that's good, that's great!" Elyse agreed.

"We'll look into that," Mr. Emmons assured him.

"And we're still on budget with actor salaries?" Marty asked, all innocence. He'd heard something. Mr. Emmons straightened his shoulders, a man ready for any challenge.

"Absolutely," he assured.

Marty smiled. Elyse smiled. Wicked carny barker smiles, Sara thought.

"Sara. Please. Let me do the talking," Mr. Emmons asked as they sat in traffic.

"Sorry. It's just not what we'd talked about. It's just so totally fabricated. What we had before played fast and loose, but at least it was consistent with the spirit, but—"

"Let me deal with Marty, Sara."

"If you don't want to tell Brontë's story, then make it about some anonymous—"

Mr. Emmons was already dialing his cell phone. "Nykki, hi, Emmons, listen, Marty had some terrific suggestions on the Brontë project. . . ."

Sara's current strategy was to encourage a more "inspired by the life of" rather than a "story of the life of" affair. This assuaged her guilt on two counts: She now felt personally responsible to Charlotte Brontë for the gross misrepresentation of her life, and yet she was also letting down Mr. Emmons. The sweeping, romantic epic he'd labored mightily to create simply vanished under the weight of one simple, inescapable fact: Charlotte Brontë's life was just not the story he wanted to tell—where he wanted grand opera, he got bleak, consumptive dirge.

Sara didn't feel guilty about abandoning academia. Hadn't it already abandoned her? But the Brontës were another story. She just wasn't a natural abandoner of things or people, and she had to stay with the project in spite of her growing despair of ever representing them properly. She felt a thick guilt building daily that she appeased by apologizing compulsively for everything: "I'm sorry they don't have soy milk," "I'm sorry there's traffic," "I'm sorry you're so angry."

It seemed to Sara that as Mr. Nicholls became nicer, Mr. Emmons became less so. She began to wonder if there was some sort of universal constant governing sympathetic traits. As sympathetic behavior was poured into Mr. Nicholls, it seemed to drain out of Mr. Emmons. Naturally he was irritated by the endless delays, the vain protests of his leading lady, the knowledge that the clock was ticking and he was taking on water.

Mr. Emmons had been collecting Eames furniture for his architecturally significant home. Sara had begun to feel like the natural addition to his lot. Her presence in his life said what his taste in furniture and cars communicated—a refined understanding of what mattered; uncluttered simplicity, clean lines, function.

Weekends spent "unwinding," tooling around in Mr. Emmons's Facel Vega, looking for more furniture to acquire, had become a chore. The midcentury modern jaunts into Palm Springs for the weekend seemed to inspire a phony enthusiasm in Mr. Emmons that extended to Sara herself. Sara could feel his gaze drifting from the clean lines of perfectly joined cabinets to the eccentric charm of a chrome-and-leather Deco couch or a garish, stuffed armchair. He'd stare accusingly at the simple, overpriced honesty of a dinner table, sliding his hand over its perfectly formed edges, and intone with melancholy reverence, "Now, *that's* craftsmanship."

Sara looked at the leather seats of the prized Facel Vega, all that tastefully rich vintage luxury. Six months Mr. Emmons had waited for it from France. She sighed and stared back up at the gridlock that ensnared her.

"I'm sorry Brontë doesn't have the life you thought she did."

"What?" Mr. Emmons asked, surprised by the apology.

"I feel sometimes you blame me that Charlotte's life wasn't more . . . cinematic."

Mr. Emmons looked at her, regretting all his previous churlishness. She was sweet, really, in ways you don't find in real live girls anymore. Simply sweet. Mr. Emmons smiled warmly.

"I'm sorry I'm such a bastard," he said. "I get into L.A. mode and it's like I'm not even human. I'm sorry."

Sara smiled uncertainly.

"We need to get out of here, Sara. I'm more relaxed elsewhere. Let's take a long break after—"

A battered Hyundai swerved in front of Mr. Emmons's Facel-Vega-six-months-from-France. He slammed on the brakes and paused only briefly before yelling out his open window, "Watch it!" His cell phone rang and he answered it in one fluid motion.

"That's ridiculous. We had a verbal agreement. I'm not paying ten million—that's outrageous. Uh-huh. No. Because it's just not going to happen is why. Uh-huh. I'm not going to sleep on it. You don't double a star's salary in preproduction is why. That's not— The delays aren't my fault. All right. Fuck you, too." Mr. Emmons violently pitched his cell phone out the window.

"Fuck!"

"What happened?" Sara asked tentatively.

"She still wants ten million. That was her agent."

"Can she do that?"

"Oh, fuck, Sara. She is doing it, that's the point. Fucking shit. She knows we're over a barrel without her. Fuck."

"I'm sorry."

Later that night, Sara covered Mr. Emmons with a blanket as he dozed on the bed. Wine was supposed to be the one substance he could handle in moderation, but in the last few months marijuana and the occasional snort had been sneaking onto the list. He'd have a hard day, then a hard week. Sara watched him and tried to console herself with the thought that in speedy, fated romances it can't be unusual to look at the beloved and wonder, Who the hell are you? It must have happened with Juliet, too. That's the problem with fate—it moves faster than the human heart.

Sara woke early the next morning to the sound of the phone. She turned to see if Mr. Emmons was getting it, but he was already up and gone.

"Hello?"

"Sara, it's Claire. Is it too early? Everyone here gets up *so* early. I'm sitting here in my room at the W and I'm staring out at this place and I thought of you. How are you?"

"I'm fine," Sara said, still waking up. She hadn't heard Claire's voice in months.

"Listen, I'm in town and thought we could have lunch. I know you're busy, but you can't say no. One o'clock. Is that all right? There's a photo shoot or something very boring my publicist tells me, then I have a lecture at five at UCLA. Is that a problem?"

"I think—" Sara began. She was seized by what the doctors would call a panic attack but what she recognized as simple homesickness. Claire's call had aroused some vague seizure of anxiety and now the morning would be lost to deep breathing. She would see Claire for lunch and Claire would be very impressed. Sara was buffed and shaped, polished to a neutral shade of near-perfection. She'd never been in better shape—in fact, had never been in shape.

Now she had biceps and triceps and her skin was exfoliated, her clothes pressed and stylish. Hearing Claire's voice reminded her that the year of separation with Paul was up. Today. What a day.

"Great!" Claire said. "I have a little confession."

"A what?"

Confession implied a sense of consequence, of culpability, qualities Claire carefully avoided.

"Well, not really a confession—I just can't wait to see you."

"Me, too," Sara said.

friends

I can be on guard against my enemies, but God deliver
me from my friends!

Charlotte Brontë, to G. H. Lewes, 1850

"D'you know what Kennedy used to call Sinatra?" Claire
practically glided onto the patio, settling effortlessly into
her seat. Busboys rushed to her aid, proffering water of
every variety.

"Chicky Boy! Isn't that perfect?!" Claire announced
loudly. Sara noticed a man turn around at a far table—a
Merv Griffin man. Sara had noticed early on that there
were entire armies of men in Los Angeles restaurants who
faintly resembled Merv Griffin but weren't Merv Griffin.
Usually they had been mildly successful agents or produc-
ers in the seventies and now they were plump, affluent,
and tan, sitting around restaurants discussing real estate

and the size of their prostate. Sara thought of them all as the Merv Griffin men.

"Sinatra wanted to be JFK and JFK wanted to be Sinatra. That just about sums up the twentieth century, doesn't it?" Claire asked, lighting a cigarette.

The Merv Griffin man walked over to Claire and reminded her that there was no smoking. Claire pouted as she stubbed out her cigarette on the Spanish brick tiles.

"It's like being in boarding school again," she whispered. Sara noticed she'd gained a little weight, noticed in the petty, prideful way that people observed these things.

"You look great!" Claire announced without a trace of envy. This annoyed Sara.

"You do, too," Sara replied.

"I forgot to kiss you!" Claire said, leaning in—kiss, kiss à la française. Sara always forgot whether it was two or three and secretly resented this convention of Continental sensuality enforced by smug Europeans on their uptight American counterparts. Was it two or three? Sara wondered when Claire kissed her again, dead center. Sara felt a confused rush of embarrassment. Claire sat provocatively back in her chair, lighting another cigarette, just waiting for Merv to stop her.

"I've put on weight," Claire said.

"It looks good on you," Sara said, realizing it did. It softened her hard edges. Claire wore a simple, shapely, and low-cut linen dress, a light copper-red with a skirt that flounced in a way that seemed disarmingly un-Claire. She looked happy and girlish, flushed and sensual—she looked like she was in love.

Claire leaned across the table, whispering confidentially, "I'm in a family way," and laughed her throaty laugh. "Isn't that the most curious expression?" she asked as she took another drag of her cigarette, sending Merv a seductive smile.

"Not so curious," Sara said, her stomach tightening, feeling strangely, suddenly jealous. Sara had wondered how long it would take for Claire to decide to have a child. It was exactly the right move to counter all the negative publicity in the wake of *the first coming* and magenta blue. She'd been forced to resign from the university, she'd settled out of court with magenta blue's family, she'd weathered the battering of her image, even worse, she'd lost control of it.

"It's like a brush with death, really," Claire explained. "Scandal is a death, a social death. But life seems fuller, more precious when you go through a social death. Luckily, I'd spent my whole life training for this—it's enjoyable in some aspects. A marathon runner enjoys the marathon even if it is grueling. It made me really appreciate what Diana had gone through—no training at all. She must've been at sea—it's a shame I couldn't have been there for her." Claire shook her head sadly.

"Who's the father?" Sara asked.

"I'm thinking of naming it Eve."

"It's a girl?"

"No, my magazine. *Labia* puts people off. It was good at first but it's not serving our needs now that we're trying to expand. Eve is good, but I have to confess, apart from historically and biblically, I just have never found her to be a very compelling persona. Have you?"

"What about magenta?"

"As a name?"

"No, the person. What's happened to her?"

"Well, vis-à-vis me, nothing. Of course you heard about all the suicide nonsense."

"Suicide?"

Claire rolled her eyes. "Frankly, I've always found female suicide to be a retrograde cliché both in literature and life. I mean from Cleopatra up to Sylvia Plath, I've always had a faint suspicion that suicide is merely an average woman's cheap way of ascending to greatness."

"She killed herself?" Sara asked, stunned.

"Tried, anyway. I can't take suicides seriously. They're so coercive. How's Brontë?" Claire asked pointedly. It was an old tactic of Claire's, confusing her listener. Sara shook her head, not sure how to respond.

"Still in preproduction. Pre-preproduction. But going great. We're in a really good place with—"

"Did you know Princess Grace investigated the supernatural?"

"No."

"Cults—you know the Swiss one? I think it was Swiss. Do you think it's possible to change another person's life?"

"I guess . . ."

"But without becoming directly involved. How can you effect change with the least effort, without actively manipulating?"

"I suppose if you were able to remove the obstacles from a person achieving what they want?"

"Exactly! After Diana I got to thinking, and part of my

project when I started teaching was to help other women, in the ways I'd failed, and I really felt I'd failed, to help Diana. I was so depressed. Whole days passed I couldn't account for. When I saw you at that party, that first night, I thought to myself, That's it! I'm going to save the silent Victorian— I'm going to save her from herself!" Claire nodded proudly. Sara was having difficulty breathing.

"It took so little, really. Just the slightest push. And look at you now." Claire shook her head in admiration of Sara.

"You see, my argument was that if your intention was to promote good, the result would be good. At base, life really is that simple. Goodness begets goodness—the Dalai Lama told me that. He's lovely, you know. I felt a purity in my heart, and that purity translated to the result."

"How can you presume to know what's good for me?" Sara asked, her breaths getting shorter, shallower.

"What's so amazing is how easy it was. I did so little. And look how much happened. I even changed my own life. Of course, I worried when Denis got involved—he has a tendency to screw things up. But you got out of that mistake quickly—I was proud of that, too."

"Is that why you talked Paul into going to France that night?"

"That's who!"

"Who?"

"The father."

"The what?"

Sara felt a sudden quickening inside her, and this is what she determined had happened: All the blood in her feet decided it wanted to be in her head, and all the blood in her head decided it wanted to be in her feet, and as the blood raced to opposite ends of Sara, it collided in the middle, forcing her to crumple in half like a snapped branch. Sara wasn't sure if she'd cried out, but she noticed the Merv Griffin man giving her a look of concern.

She took a sip of water and realized she hadn't moved, hadn't made a sound.

"Isn't that funny?" Claire asked. "I ran into him at a restaurant in Paris. We're in this really beautiful phase right now where we just ask each other a lot of questions. He says he's lost in the loops of my hair."

Sara recognized both parts of their conversation. "The beautiful phase just asking each other a lot of questions" was stolen from *Interview* editor Ingrid Sischy's comment about her collaboration with Elton John on his memoirs. Paul's appropriation was a little more subtle— an oblique rip-off of a line from Yeats. Sara felt a stab of rage, realizing they'd both misquoted Yeats.

"That's from Yeats, actually," Sara managed haltingly. Why the hell was she talking about *Yeats?* "What about Therese?"

"On the rocks, of course. You know Paul. Can't make up his mind. *Che sorpresa!*"

Sara had to suppress the mad notion of stomping across the globe and demanding that Paul tell her whether he knew he was sleeping with a woman who used the words *navy blue* as a verb.

"How can you be so . . . I don't understand . . ."

"Oh, I wanted to ask you before I forget, to participate in the Diana Symposium coming up in Paris. I know it's coming up soon, in fact I meant to ask you sooner, but . . . blame it on baby-brain, I guess," Claire said cheerfully. Sara felt queasy.

"This is going to be a very special one," Claire continued. "I thought we could do that Brontë/Diana thing. Being pregnant, I feel so connected to this event in a way I never thought I could. You know, Diana was pregnant when she died."

"Claire. You're insane."

"I should think you'd want to thank me! You're making a lot of money, you look great, you have a wonderful home, you're with a fabulous, powerful man, you're living a dream!"

"Mr. Emmons is a selfish child and so are you. What about magenta? Do you have any sense of moral culpability, any sense of consequence? Does it all just slide off of you? You're ridiculous and sad. You and Paul deserve each other!" Sara looked around her. She was making a scene, acting out of character, being a nuisance. The waiters were scared. The Merv Griffin man looked intrigued. But not Claire. She looked proud.

"My silent Victorian speaks!"

the full weakness

Man is indeed an amazing piece of mechanism when you see—so to speak—the full weakness—of what he calls—his strength.

Charlotte Brontë, to Ellen Nussey, 1854

Sara didn't remember leaving the restaurant. She didn't remember coming home or sitting down to a dinner of overcooked trout. She did recall taking the long way home, jumping off the 101 at Las Virgines and driving west through Malibu Canyon—she loved the immensity of nature in Los Angeles, the way it interrupted the landscape with its monumental presence and reminded the tiny captains of industry of the brevity of their reign. The road cut through the tall peaks that, with the sun setting, could feel like they were swallowing you whole—you and all the SUVs riding your tail and speeding ahead of you. *Paul and Claire, Paul and Claire* was all she could think as she passed through the ancient hills.

She remembered thinking that for all her revolutionary talk of pan-erotics and ambisexuality, Claire was nothing more than a good old-fashioned jezebel. She was a cliché, and a tired one at that. And it was a cliché, she observed with grim pride, that was deeply, conventionally, gendered.

Still here she was, sitting across from Mr. Emmons having dinner.

"The trout's dry," he remarked unemotionally.

"It is, a little," Sara replied, relieved that she could manage this simple call-and-response conversation.

"Where were you this afternoon?" Mr. Emmons asked, a slight edge to his voice.

"Where?"

"Yes."

"I had lunch with Claire."

"Yes, I know, after that. Where did you go?"

"When?"

"After that." Mr. Emmons was clearly irritated. "The answer's not written on your plate, Sara."

Sara looked up at him. "I don't—"

"Sara, d'you mind telling me what's going on? Like I need this now of all times. . . ." Sara tried to straighten, pressing her back flush against the chair.

"What?"

"Sara, where's your necklace?"

Sara felt her neck. The Brontë pendant was gone, replaced by a silver-beaded choker.

"I don't know. I had it—"

"They phoned me this afternoon."

221

"Who?"

"The boutique. They said you took off your necklace and tried that one on and then ran out of the store. What the hell were you thinking?"

"I did?"

"My God, if you're going to pull shit like that, at least go to a store where they don't know me!"

"I really don't remember." Sara felt a panic attack coming on.

"What is your problem, Sara?" He looked at Sara with an unflinching stare, turning his gaze from the necklace back to her furrowed little face. He took an angry bite of the dry trout.

"It's been a strange day," she explained.

"You're not the only one. I got our star down to seven and a half, and it sure as shit wasn't pretty," he said as he poured himself more wine.

"Don't you think maybe you've had enough?"

"What?" He glowered, glassy-eyed.

"Are you *high*?"

"I've had a fucking hard day."

"Seems every day is a hard day lately," she said.

"That's beautiful, that's just great. You sure don't seem to mind the lifestyle my hard days buy," he said, pushing the dry trout aside.

"It's not my lifestyle, it's yours. I never asked to live like this. I mean, why am I even here?"

"What?" Mr. Emmons asked, rubbing his temples.

"What do you keep me around for? Why do I always

feel you're just putting up with me? Do I match the furniture or something?"

"I don't even know how to begin to answer such a ridiculous question."

"I don't find it ridiculous."

"I do. And I'm insulted."

"I'm the one who should feel insulted. I'm just an accessory to you."

"That's ridiculous."

"No, actually it's the first true thing I've said to you. What are we playing here? I don't want this life. This isn't . . ."

"What?"

"This isn't a real life," Sara said, realizing. "I've just been pretending that I have this great life to impress someone who doesn't even care."

"I do care," Mr. Emmons said defensively.

"I didn't mean you," Sara said as she folded her linen napkin, noting how beautifully the pale marine blue of the napkins played against the blond bamboo place mats. She should be flattered. Mr. Emmons had excellent taste in all things. Sara smiled faintly at him, which only added to his confusion. Asking him to explain her presence in his life, his town, his bed, and his business was like asking a dog to do long division. She pressed the napkin with the palm of her hand, rose from the table, and walked away.

"*Sara,* we have meetings all week!" Mr. Emmons reminded her as she stuffed clothing into her bag. Even as she slammed the door behind her, he couldn't believe it. He didn't think she was capable of such a gesture. But he wasn't about to go after her. He wasn't the type of man to go running after a woman. It wasn't *his* type of gesture.

Sara stood staring at the other side of the door, equally amazed. Dramatic gestures were never her forte. She remembered all the times she'd seen *A Doll's House*, imagining what comic revelation must have taken place offstage, on the other side of the clapboard set where Nora stood alert and perplexed, looking up and down the road ready to meet her great future and thinking to herself, Fuck. *Now* where?

dread to feel

... the craving for companionship—the hopelessness
of relief—were what I should dread to feel again.

Charlotte Brontë, to Ellen Nussey, 1850

Mr. Ives's handwriting was impeccable and his directions
precise. Twenty miles out of Florence, Sara got off the bus.
There was the café on the corner he'd described in exact-
ing detail, almost down to the patrons she would find inside. And sure enough, she found someone who would
drive her the four miles to the convent.

"*Va'al letto dei sogni?*" her driver asked.

"*Sì,*" she answered, she was going to the bed of
dreams. Sara was embarrassed by the revelation, but her
driver, Scarpa, seemed unmoved. Lots of people came for
the bed, he explained, shrugging his shoulders. Young, old,
single, married, all with the same shy, shell-shocked look

on their faces, Sara imagined, trying to conjure the image of her predecessors.

"Creda?" Do you believe? Sara asked him. The man smiled; he was in his late forties, she guessed.

"I think business is good for Signora," he said simply. Sara asked if that meant the woman who ran the hotel had made up the story. The man shrugged again, suggesting he was willing to believe people were, perhaps, cynically motivated. Sara didn't care to hear the rest. Misery had made her superstitious, and mercenary motives only clouded the issue. She stared out the window, where murky green Tuscan hills rose up to meet more murky green Tuscan hills.

She remembered Claire talking about Princess Grace and Princess Diana. They had both become involved with psychics and the paranormal, both apparently familiar with the corrosive discord of life inside a fairy tale. Their presumed happiness must have weighed them down—so much better to be an unhappy commoner like herself, Sara decided. If she were famous, she'd have to shield her face from the cameras as she emerged from Scarpa's car, fending back tears, trying hard to pretend she wasn't having a breakdown. A breakdown? Is that what she was having? How did one tell exactly?

Sara had always thought there was something romantic about nervous breakdowns, that they were only for Fitzgerald heroines and alcoholic starlets. Somehow it seemed less exotic now; she was just a scared, dumb girl who'd foolishly put a very expensive flight to Italy on her credit card for reasons having vaguely to do with dry trout and a purloined necklace. This was not what she'd imagined at all.

She remembered the photos of Marilyn Monroe checking into a psychiatric hospital. It was in one of her parents' it's-okay-to-be-crazy books. Marilyn was on the verge of tears; in one picture her head tilted down, then in another, up, as if she'd actually absorbed a blow from the camera's flash. Her hair looped in loose curls on top—she must have set it the night before. Sara thought Marilyn never looked better. Marilyn made mental disintegration unbeatably sexy. She wore a white oxford cloth shirt, Sara remembered, and her hair fell casually over the creases of distress lining her face. People always looked better in black and white and, from a purely aesthetic standpoint, Sara was grateful Marilyn's downfall was timed to the use of black-and-white newsprint.

"Ecco!" Scarpa announced as they rounded a curve up one of the murky green hills. They pulled up in front of the convent. Sara paid the man and got out.

"Buona fortuna." He winked as he took her money.

"Grazie."

The woman Claire described as possessing "crone energy" appeared at the front door. It was late afternoon and she was tending to dinner. She was stooped and small yet strangely sturdy, as though she'd been made of the same stones as the medieval building. She led Sara down a long, dark corridor, unlocking the door with an old skeleton key dangling from a large steel loop. The woman spoke in broken English. When Sara remarked how lucky she was to get the room on such short notice, the woman shook her head mysteriously.

"If you are called, the room is available," she said,

lifting her arm in a flourish. That was a bit much, Sara thought, already doubting the authenticity of the room's powers.

"Your passport?"

Sara handed the woman her passport. She gave a dark, ominous nod to the bed before informing her that the price of breakfast, but not dinner, was included in the price of the room. Checkout was at eleven. Payment in cash, *per favore*.

Sara didn't want to talk to anyone. She was grateful to be in a land where she barely knew the language. She felt herself inside and outside every conversation, watchful and observant, and was happy now to be burdened with only the simplest of conversation. She sat alone at dinner. Mark and Mary from Maryland sat at the table next to her, trying to guess her nationality, assuming from her silence that she didn't speak English.

"American," Sara finally volunteered when it became too awkward to continue to ignore them.

"I never would've guessed!" Mary said, as though this were a compliment. "I would've said French, maybe Romanian." That seemed like an odd combination. Sara just smiled. Mark and Mary were in their late fifties, and having finally settled into a period of affluence and reduced ambition, they'd entered the portion of coupledom in which they bought matching hunter green and purple windbreakers and planned foreign walking tours.

"Loved Rome, I don't care what they say. It's Rome!" Mary announced.

"Did you try the squid?" Mark asked. Sara shook her head. "It's great," Mary informed her. Mark nodded cheerfully.

Mark and Mary seemed remarkably in sync, almost interchangeable in their windbreakers and determined optimism. In another time, Sara would have regarded them with condescension, snidely wondering what seven habits of highly effective people had allowed these two wholly unremarkable specimen the luxuries of travel to spectacular sights as well as complacent residence in the richest country in the world while other hardworking, noble, brave individuals went to bed hungry and stared at the same damned four walls all their lives. What annuity-selling quota did they reach to get this lucky? Sara would wonder in mute disregard. But now she didn't wonder. Instead she observed how closely their movements matched and complemented each other's, she watched with envy the seemingly effortless simpatico of their matching windbreaker union.

"What other countries are you going to?" Mary asked. "Are you traveling alone? How is that, female and all?"

"None. Yes. Fine," Sara answered. "I'm very tired, if you'll excuse me?"

"Are you staying in the bed of dreams?" Mary asked in a furtive whisper.

"Yes, I am. It's research," Sara heard herself say. "I'm a scholar."

"A dream researcher?" Mark asked authoritatively, as though he had a ream of charts and graphs hidden inside his windbreaker.

"No," Sara answered, and without explanation left for bed.

"The bed not always work first night," the old woman told Sara the next morning. Sara had stared at the ceiling the entire night, wondering what the hell she was doing there. She shouldn't have slept on the plane, that's what screwed things up. She paid the old woman for her first night and reserved the room for two more nights. After breakfast, she started walking toward the café, looking for something to give her day structure.

She had brought no books, no magazines, nothing that could confuse or alter her thinking, and this, she realized, was a huge mistake. She would go to the café, buy an Italian newspaper, and teach herself enough Italian to read it.

"Sogni?" Scarpa asked as she entered the café. Sara shook her head and ordered a cappuccino at the bar. She was determined to stay awake all day. She ordered another and started reading an Italian newspaper that was sitting on the counter. A Greek ferry had sunk, killing dozens of people, while Sara had been trying to sleep. A lucky man in Rome had won a small fortune on a reality TV show and had promised to buy his mother the house she'd always dreamed of and start his own recording career.

Sara looked around. The café was filled with the usual late-morning café dwellers: the retired and the unemployed. Sara noticed for the first time how much attention she was drawing from them; tables of twos and threes, pensioners and young men still living at home, looked back at her. She was the only woman in the room and she worried now that she'd made a horrible cultural gaffe, that she'd wandered into an all-male café (was there such a thing?). Many of the men studied her with unabashed directness; there was no doubting their interest in the lonely American girl. She probably wasn't the first of her type to visit the bed of dreams, and she supposed she belonged now to a familiar sorority of special interest to these men.

In spite of her discomfort, she still felt quietly pleased with the attention. Look at all the men who want me, Paul, she thought to herself, realizing it was Paul, not Mr. Emmons, she fantasized about making jealous. Maybe I'll go with one of them because that's how over you I am. Maybe I'll have to sneak past the living room because that's where his mother sits and watches soap operas and drifts into sleep and I'll lie on the twin bed he's had since he was five and I'll stare at the water stain on the ceiling shaped like a dinosaur and I'll see the Britney Spears poster and worry that he's a teenager as he makes efficient, indifferent love to me and I notice he makes different noises and has different moves and his neck smells strange and sweet like hotel soap and when it's over he's suddenly nice and hopes I was pleasured, too, because that's how modern men are even in Italy and I won't care that I didn't much enjoy it, in fact scarcely sensed its beginning, middle, and end—all because That's How Over You I Am.

Look at how much I do for you, Sara thought, imagining him across from her at the table. Look at how much I do all in return for the enormous favor of not loving me enough. Sara looked around the café again—maybe every relation was just an answer to a previous one. She looked her potential lovers over, tenderly, worried about who they, too, were trying to impress. How many of these little internal dialogues with absent lovers were going on all over? Look at how peaceful and content I am in my solitude, in my life, without you. The sipping and the reading and convivial male conversation—it was all just part of an enormous ruse that Sara could now see clearly. She met eyes with a young man in a Che Guevara T-shirt. A young Communist, she thought; he'll do. He smiled. She smiled. And then she shook her head because she knew already what it would be like.

Walking back to the hotel, she had a dizzy spell and decided to sit down under a tree about thirty yards from the road. She lay down for a moment against the thick roots, and the next thing she knew, several hours had passed and it was dark, very dark. Following the road back, Sara looked up and realized it had been a long time since she'd seen so many stars. Usually she would be afraid walking alone at night. Nobody knew where she was or what she was doing, and for perhaps the first time in her life she realized she was totally unaccounted for. If she suddenly vanished, it would be days before anyone she knew would even think to miss her. This should have been an ominous thought and yet she found it strangely liberating.

It took forty minutes to reach the hotel. Signora was annoyed to be wakened so late. Sara tried to explain but was too tired to bother. She fell into bed and had a ten-hour dreamless stretch of sleep. When she awoke, she realized she'd missed breakfast and simply went back to sleep. She had an insatiable hunger for sleep and thought that maybe her exhaustion stemmed from her inability to dream. But what did she hope she'd dream, anyway? What could the deathbed of a medieval novitiate tell her that she didn't already know?

As she drifted off Sara remembered reading that the boxer Floyd Patterson slept constantly while he trained. She'd always found this strange, but now it made perfect sense. Sleep—the perfect antidote to anything. So much better to sleep through anxiety than to actually experience it.

Then finally, a dream. In the dream she was trying to get a loan from a bank, but instead of going to a bank, she went to the beach and one of the Merv Griffin men refused to grant her the loan because Paul wasn't there to cosign it. When Sara tried to explain that she and Paul weren't together, Paul showed up and said they didn't need the loan because he had the money. Then Ethel Merman showed up and started to sing.

When she woke, Sara remembered another reason why she'd make a crappy therapist: She didn't believe in dreams. She sort of believed in them, but mostly she thought they were brain-slop, the detritus of thoughts that didn't make the cut to the big leagues of consciousness. Subpar thoughts. She realized she'd slept through the day. It was night again and so she fell back asleep.

Claire stood on a stage. It was Claire but not Claire, Sara realized in the dream—and she was still pregnant. Sara sat next to her on a dais and in the audience she saw everyone from her year of separation: Paul, Mr. Emmons, Denis, Nykki, Mr. Ives and Mr. Burke. They all stared at Sara. Didn't she have something to say to them? Sara tried to speak, tried to warn them of something, but nothing came out of her mouth. Finally, when words did come, they were nonsense. Everyone could see what an idiot she really was. Then Paul was lying on top of her, slowly pressing the life out, suffocating her.

Sara looked around for help, but all she could see was Claire laughing, amused by her struggle. But Sara could sense that Claire was in terrible danger, too. Sara wanted to warn her, or at least tell her not to look so damned smug. Then a three-legged dog walked up to Sara, amused by everyone. The dog was laughing. He licked her face. *Nothing very bad can ever happen to you*, he seemed to say. *No, everything is very bad*, Sara wanted to tell the dog, *just look!*

Sara realized this was a dream and that it was very important for her to wake up. She heard the door rattle, as though someone was forcing the lock. Sara thrashed in her bed, her arms immobilized at her side. Her mouth stretched into a scream, the sound seemingly frozen in her throat. Hands grasped her by the shoulders, shaking her forcefully. She opened her eyes. The old woman towered above her.

"No screaming, okay? No scream?" the woman asked, as though it were a polite request. Sara sat up in bed, the dream still playing vividly in her memory.

"Okay, now?" the woman asked, offering her a glass of water. Sara nodded, yes, she was fine.

"What time is it?" Sara asked. She had to get to Paris and warn Claire—of what? Something, she felt certain of at least that much.

"Almost eleven. I have people in room one hour. You pay now, okay?"

"Yes," Sara assured her weakly, she would pay.

calmness

. . . the remembrance of a person whom one believes one will never see again but whom, nevertheless, one esteems highly, harasses the spirit too much and when one has suffered this kind of anxiety for one or two years, one is ready to do anything to recover calmness.

Charlotte Brontë, to Professor Heger, 1845

"Oh, honey, you'll have to ask your father about dreams. I just do closets," her mother said, sighing with concern.

"Why were you in Italy?" her father asked.

"Why are you going to Paris?" her mother asked.

"I had this dream," Sara began.

"Of Paris?"

"They're boarding my flight."

"You all right?"

"Yeah, I'll be fine, thanks. Bye."

Sara had realized the date, August 31, the anniversary of Diana's death, and remembered it marked the beginning of Claire's symposium in Paris. The train from the

airport was easy enough. Sara had enough French to manage that much. What complicated matters was transferring
trains at the Gare du Nord. Sara searched for the train that
traveled to the hall that was hosting the Diana Symposium. It was near the Ritz. She remembered this much, as
Claire had gone to great lengths to secure the site of
Diana's last supper for a cocktail reception in what seemed
to Sara a needlessly morbid gesture.

Announcements blared in French, between the sing-
song chiming announcements of trains departing and arriving. Sara felt a panic rising. She couldn't find her train.
It seemed simple, but each time she stopped to examine
the Metro maps on the walls of the station, an oily gentleman would ask, in heavily accented English, "*Bonjour,
cherie,* may I help you?" Sara remembered the armies of
creepily helpful Frenchmen from her college year abroad.
And here they were again ten years later, seemingly unaged
and still unaffected by her obvious repulsion.

"*Allez!*" she would mutter, then guiltily tack on a
"S'il vous plaît." Sara skittered away from gentleman
number three and stood with defiant American independence, her map spread in front of her.

Another man tapped her on the shoulder. Sara
wheeled around. "*Allez!*"

It took a few seconds for her eyes to adjust their focus
on a young man seemingly lit from within. He looked
amused by her irritation—not in a patronizing way, but
in the way saints are amused that humans take *anything*
seriously.

"Can I help you?" he asked gently.

Sara searched her memory for her destination. He was in uniform, he worked for the Metro. At long last she'd found the man who possessed what she needed most in the world: a benevolent spirit and accurate train information. Sara blinked; was there light behind him as well? Had she just wandered into the Annunciation and here was her St. Gabriel lovingly bathed in chiaroscuro offering her a lily? In one fluid motion, St. Gabriel seemed to lift and float above her, suspended, hovering.

"You okay?" he asked.

Sara nodded weakly. A crowd gathered around her and they seemed suspended as well. Sara stared up at them; they all looked well read and knew how to wear scarves. She felt foolish and groggy and deeply un-French as she looked down and saw she was sprawled out on the ground; she must have fainted. Now she was blocking a main artery of rush-hour foot traffic, and while she lay buffeted by an inner circle of compassion, she felt the hostile bustle that whirled just outside.

"I'm fine. Yes. I'm— Yes, I forgot to eat."

St. Gabriel just smiled placidly. A fellow traveler produced a bottle of water from her leather tote bag. Why are people always putting down the French? Sara wondered. They're just lovely. She nodded that she was fine and everyone could go back to the hustle of a busy train station. In twos and threes, they agreed and left her. St. Gabriel remained, helping her to her feet.

"You are okay?"

"Yes. Thank you. I need to go . . ." Where? Sara

struggled to remember. "North," she managed, "I'm trying to—"

The man smiled kindly and nodded. He waved to a
passageway beyond the ticket kiosks.

"You promise to eat soon? So no more fainting?" he
asked with grave concern.

Sara nodded and mindlessly moved to where he had
pointed, already missing her saint of the Gare du Nord. She
turned back around and he was still watching her. He gave a
reassuring nod, as if to tell her, *Yes, that's the right way.*

something other

The whole thing is something other than imagination paints it beforehand: cares—fears—come inextricably mixed with hopes.

Charlotte Brontë, to Ellen Nussey, 1854

Claire sat erect in her chair, her best navy blue suit of the season catching the light in a way that made her especially pleased; everything was coming off even better than she had expected. She spoke from the dais with a lilting French accent—the French part of her always became more pronounced in France.

"There's a notion in *The Tibetan Book of Dead* of the 'between traveler,' someone hovering between the two worlds of life and death who is compelled to navigate new territory, mapping a way into the next life. We're all able, after a death or ending of some sort, to seize great opportunities. We are suddenly able to respond to the smallest signs, our mental powers are heightened, we can become whatever can be imagined, we can remake the future entirely. The 'between traveler' has the openness and the ability to be powerfully transformed by thoughts and visions.

"I feel this concept exemplifies the place," Claire continued, "the spiritual place, Diana occupied during the last years of her life. What death did she experience? The death of an illusion, a romantic dream of sorts, a fairy tale. As she said herself, 'Being a princess isn't all it's cracked up to be.'"

Claire's audience at the Diana Symposium nodded approvingly, knowingly. Sara slipped in a door at the back of the hall, narrowly evading the prim registrars at the desk outside. She looked around, taking in the audience, which consisted primarily of academics in nerdy-hip eyeglasses and doughy middle-aged English Dianaphiles whom Sara imagined with vast collections of commemorative plates.

The lecture hall had to be hundreds of years old. Sara had noticed a plaque outside commemorating its history as a host to meetings of both the French Revolution and the Resistance. Banks of low-hanging lights, which once burned for the Enlightenment, Fraternity, and Liberty, cast their now-electric brightness on the Age of Claire.

"Once she had discarded the illusions that come with a fairy-tale life," Claire continued, "she was finally free to live."

Sara noticed something strange about the dais. It featured Claire, but as the lights grew brighter onstage, Sara could make herself out there as well. She blinked. Was she still dreaming? The sign onstage announced MYSTICISM AND SPIRITUALITY: DIANA AND BRONTË.

"There's a theory that the ultimate obstacle to a religious experience is religion—the fetishized outer trappings. What Diana discovered was that romance was the final obstacle to human love. Once she'd discarded that, there was nothing she couldn't do. She was an avatar of modern spiritual evolution—she represented the Buddha going outside the palace walls to find suffering and true compassion. She wasn't merely 'between,' she was 'beyond.' Beyond illusion, beyond striving, beyond desiring. Which is why when people ask me, 'What is the significance of Diana, Princess of Wales?' I just have to laugh. . . ."

"The same thing happened with Charlotte Brontë," Sara heard her onstage self say. "Brontë reached that point after losing—"

"Pardonnez-moi, mademoiselle?" Sara turned to see a tall, lanky man with a kind, businesslike expression grasp her arm.

"Non!" Sara protested, exhausting her current command of French. The man, who was stronger than he looked, pulled her out the door and into the outer lobby, where they were greeted by two burly security guards.

"Parlez-vous anglais?"

The tall man nodded as one of the burly men frisked her.

"This isn't necessary. I'm not—"

"I'm afraid it is. There have been some threats against Mademoiselle Vigee. We cannot be too careful," he said darkly. The burly man shook his head to indicate Sara was unarmed.

"That's just it. I think Claire's in danger. I know it."

This information, intended to make Sara seem more innocent, only aroused the tall man's suspicion.

"And you know this is true how?"

"Sara?"

Sara turned to see Burke sitting next to Ives on a leather couch in the foyer. They rushed to her.

"What are you doing here?" Burke asked.

"I went! I went to the bed of the dreams!"

This piqued Ives's interest. "You really went?" he asked.

"Yes."

"Sara, I wouldn't invest too much in that bed. To be honest, Nykki and I aren't doing very . . ." Burke offered tentatively. Sara saw a flicker of contentment spread across Ives's features.

"Nykki—that's who's inside?" Sara asked, realizing Claire could easily enlist her as an eleventh-hour replacement for Sara.

"Yes," Burke answered glumly.

"Tell them I can go in."

Burke sighed and gestured to the tall man, who allowed them all inside.

Claire was still talking. Nykki watched her with a glazed look. Sara wandered down the side aisle, scanning for something.

"Camus said you live your way into your death," Claire was saying. "Your life contains the seeds of your demise. Now, look at Diana. All that work with land mines? She sensed a violent, explosive demise. She must have. Camus, by the way, also died in a car crash. He was afraid of cars and had a train ticket for his voyage in his pocket. And Brontë was obsessed with illness, wasn't she?"

"Um . . ." Nykki searched. "All her siblings died of illness, so yeah, you'd think—"

"I think it was Yeats who said that Charlotte Brontë was the flame that longed for the fire."

"No, he didn't!" Sara blurted from the audience. All heads turned back to look at her.

"Well, I know he said something to that effect," Claire assured her, not missing a beat.

"Yeats never said any such thing. What's more—"

The security guards were already striding down the aisles as everyone rustled in their seats, excited.

"What's more, I find it interesting that you espouse a philosophy of sisterly support while in private you embrace every negative stereotype of female sexuality from the black widow to jezebel."

By now a guard had a grip on each of Sara's arms and prepared to goose-step her into a long academic exile.

"I think," Claire began, signaling to the guards that she could handle this little squabble, "Virginia Woolf said it best: 'Women are hard on other women.' When I find a woman I admire, I demand a lot of her. If I see her not achieving the excellence she's capable of, I feel no remorse in giving her the slightest push toward her real destiny."

"Was it this 'slight push' that encouraged magenta blue to attempt suicide?"

This one hit Claire between the eyes; her audience perched on its seats for the return volley.

"Claire," Sara continued, "you have no insight, no real feelings—how dare you assume you know what's best for us?"

"Ugh. The Wounded Woman. Stale, stale, stale clichés . . . ," Claire sighed feebly, trotting out the old warhorse.

"You should talk about stale clichés, jezebel," Sara said.

"Excuse me?" Claire protested.

"You're *carrying* Paul's child."

"What?" Sara heard a faint male voice unmistakably— "Paul?" Sara called out. Of course he'd be here.

"That's not true," the muffled voice managed, coming closer.

"What?" Sara asked.

"Well," Claire explained, "he's like the spiritual father—"

"Come with me," Paul whispered, now at Sara's side as he tugged on her elbow. Sara followed him up the aisle. She could hear Claire regain her composure. Heckling was a fact of life for her. She took it as a compliment.

"Are you all right?" Paul asked as they hit the busy sidewalk outside. The sun was just lowering on the horizon and the streets were filled with the late-summer, after-work foot traffic, people making their way to the bars and cafés. Sara joined them, walking briskly as Paul followed her.

"Really? I mean—really? You and *Claire*?"

"Sara, Claire and I aren't together."

"She said it was yours, the baby."

"She calls me the spiritual father because I brought her together with the father—Dell? The Tupac Shakur/ Beckett guy? He was crashing at my place when I met her here. I guess he insulted her at some panel and she found that really sexy. I don't know. She won't admit it—she's got some weird thing about biological paternity being a bour- geois cliché. She's always misusing words. . . ."

Sara stopped. "So you're not together?"

"No."

The relief made her want to cry. Seeing him standing in front of her, so familiar, made her body ache. The anger she felt just a few minutes before was gone.

"You know, I always meant to call you," he said ten- tatively. This wasn't how he'd envisioned seeing her again. Her gaze wandered; she didn't want to look him in the eye. She stared off at the funky bookstores and secondhand music shops that were slowly being edged out of the neigh- borhood by airy boutiques selling overpriced sheets and candles.

"When my fellowship ended," Paul continued, eager to explain without quite knowing why, "I came to Paris and washed dishes and got depressed and was ready to come home. But then I ran into Claire at the restaurant—"

"You washed dishes?"

"Yes." He nodded sheepishly. "I did the whole Orwell down-and-out thing. Dreams do come true."

"And?"

"The only thing worse than washing dishes is wash- ing dishes for the French."

Sara laughed involuntarily, the overeager laugh of someone desperate for release.

"It's not that funny."

"Yes, it is."

Paul looked at Sara, noticing her new gym-toned body, new smartly mussed hair, new fitted leather jacket; all that unfamiliarity made him feel weak. She looked great. How exhausting it all is, the attractiveness of exes.

"You look good," he said without emotion, just a fact, just the sweet lull of small talk.

Sara had once started one of many versions of her thesis on the Brontës by observing that all great stories are about a return: Jane Eyre returns to Rochester, M. Paul returns to Lucy in *Villette*, Heathcliff returns to Cathy and Wuthering Heights. She remembered this as she noticed they were standing in front of a music store that blared ironically kitschy American pop tunes: *I just wanna keep on lovin' you*.

Of course! Like the philosopher said, "Every pain and every joy and every thought and sigh and everything immeasurably small or great in your life must return to you." All stories are about a return. Sara's head was swimming now. Maybe this long, circuitous path was heading right back to Paul, just as she'd always secretly longed to believe. Believed without even acknowledging to herself that she believed. Here it was like an unexpected inheritance.

"Go for a drive?" Paul asked.

"Okay."

They walked the short distance to a green Peugeot, which Paul unlocked.

"You have a car?" Sara asked as she got in, noting a stack of Colette books in the backseat. Paul couldn't stand Colette.

"A friend's," Paul said as he started up the engine.

He was trying to spare her feelings with a white lie, and this fresh humiliation flushed her cheeks. This was his girlfriend's car. They were probably back together, had probably never split, given the general reliability of Claire's information. He had found passionate love and it wasn't with Sara. Deal with it, she told herself. Once and for all, just deal with it. How many more times would she set herself up like this—read too much into things and assume too much? How was it possible that she'd deceived herself yet again?

"Can I ask you something?" she said, her anger at herself naturally finding a target in Paul. "What were all those years together? Just pretending?" Her delivery was more vehement than she'd intended, her emotions rushing to the surface yet again.

Paul exhaled slowly. "This is exactly why I've avoided this conversation. You've always got this victim story going."

"I what?"

"That whole loss and disappointment thing you do— it's like you're in training for martyrdom—"

"Loss and disappointment thing? You think I like this? You think this fulfills me?" she asked.

"I don't think you like it, I think you love it. I think it gives you reason to live in ways you could never cop to. I mean, what was that scene in there? It's not Claire's fault if you're not happy. And it certainly isn't mine. I couldn't handle being the reason for all your unhappiness. I know I wasn't the biggest help sometimes, but—"

"Oh, my God, don't even try to play this off as some neurotic wish fulfillment that I created. You're here so you could screw around," Sara said. *Gallia est omnis divisa in partes tres:* blonde, brunette, and redhead, Sara thought.

"Sara—"

"You've just got this fantasy version of your life in your head, and anything that even slightly deviates gets cast out without a thought."

Sara stared out the window as the car whipped through traffic, moving at a powerful clip. They drove along the Seine, a spot she'd imagined strolling happily hand in hand with Paul on their honeymoon little more than a year ago. They were coming up on New York Avenue. Only minutes earlier she would have read this as yet another sign of happiness foretold instead of what it really was: the dry laugh of Satan.

"I didn't cast you off without a thought," Paul said finally. "You're being unfair."

"Well," Sara said, throwing her hands up, "then walk away. That's what you're good at."

Paul raced around a taxicab, pulling sharply alongside a divider. "Fuck. Slow down, Paul."

"That's not fair and you know it."

"You bailed. Things got tough and you walked."

"I didn't like who I was becoming—what we were both becoming."

"Which was what?"

"We weren't . . . I don't know . . . alive? We were turning into a Bergman film. Didn't you feel it?"

"And your answer was just to dump everything we ever had?"

"No. I don't know. I did it for both of us."

"Don't patronize me. You wanted to leave. You left. Fine. Things weren't perfect, I agree. But at least I was willing to try. You? You can't handle mess or imperfection or anything remotely human. But that's your decision and I accept it—just don't try to enlist me in helping you feel good about it."

Paul sighed loudly. He had hoped for a bittersweet evening sunset of rueful half smiles and shared jokes—in Paris, no less. What better place for a nostalgic interlude with an ex?

"I mean, why are we doing this? Why are we driving around Paris in your girlfriend's car pretending everything's okay? It's not okay. It's not even close to okay."

"There's this park I thought you'd like. It was a stupid idea. And this isn't my girlfriend's car, just a . . . someone. It's complicated. . . ."

"Thanks for the clarification. Maybe you could drive me back?"

Sara stared out the window as the small cars whipped past her. She saw a sign along the road, something apparently meant to calm the frazzled drivers: UN PEU DE ZEN, MOINS DE HAINE—a little Zen, less hatred. She spotted a dog with his head out the window, the wind flapping through his big ears. If I could have one moment like that,

I'd be happy, Sara thought. Just one unself-conscious moment of animal joy. *Un peu de Zen.* Paul was right. His sudden bolt for the door was indefensible, but his observation
was correct. She hadn't been happy and she still wasn't.
From the looks of it, neither was Paul.

Or maybe he was. If it was possible that his Colette-
loving "someone" with the green Peugeot gave him dog's-
head-out-the-window joy, she could let him go. She could
forgive him for not loving her enough. She could be happy
just like that dog. She could be magnanimous and spiritu-
ally generous. For once, she felt face-to-face with love, the
sweet animal thing itself. Perhaps she was capable of, at
long last, loving Paul by letting him go.

She felt suddenly able to love anyone and everyone
for no reason other than she was alive in this moment in
Paris admiring a dog's capacity for joy. It had to be a
miracle of sorts. There were no accidents, really, were
there? She could visualize the people who gave her the
most difficulty and send them love. Paul. Claire. Mr. Emmons. Everyone who'd turned down her grant proposals.
Her indifferent thesis adviser. She could thank them for the
lessons they gave her, just like her yoga instructor, Jasmyn,
had suggested. It all seemed within grasp. If she could only
have a brief taste of that dog's experience of happiness.

"Are you happy?" she asked.

Paul tensed his grip on the wheel and exhaled
sharply.

"What's happy?" he answered.

Sara watched the dog enviously. The wind picked up
and threw one ear up and over—this only made the dog

happier, and it seemed to Sara he was smiling at her. *Come play, come join me,* his smile said. Sara rolled down her window and edged her head delicately out the side. The sound of the cars was loud and the wind hit her ear like cold pleasure. She remembered her St. Gabriel at the train station and remembered she still hadn't eaten anything— in fact, she was feeling light-headed.

They were approaching a tunnel. Sara noticed a red heart, graffiti drawn on the approach to the tunnel—dry laugh of Satan. She saw two names scrawled next to the heart: *Dodi and Diana.* This was the tunnel, the Alma Tunnel, where, as Claire had informed her, pagan sacrifices to the goddess Diana were once performed, and centuries later the People's Princess met her own fate at the thirteenth pillar.

Sara looked around and was struck by how beautiful Paris was in contrast to the dumpy and industrial Alma Tunnel with its anonymous white pillars. It was possibly the least picturesque place to die in a city teeming with pretty sites far more fitting for one's last sigh. Claire had said the spot of Diana's accident was considered magical, a place where souls ascend directly to heaven, apparently avoiding the bureaucratic tangle involved with dying elsewhere. But the tunnel didn't speak to Sara of the transmigration of souls. It looked like what it was: a death trap for drunk drivers, nothing more. And this suddenly struck her as deeply, sadly funny. It summed up the whole rotten ride. She looked at the dog and smiled. He smiled back as they entered the tunnel. She could almost touch him if she just leaned out the window a little farther—

"Sara, Jesus!"

Sara turned to Paul as he cranked the steering wheel left, overcompensating for the dog's car, which had tried to change lanes in front of them while Paul had been distracted by Sara. The Peugeot's front smashed into the tunnel's center divider, sending it spinning. Sara's head fell from the window and slammed sharply onto the dash. That's not fair, Sara thought, just as I was beginning to feel happy, that's not fair. She felt a burning. She smelled smoke. But the smoke was a color, an object, a rose—a red rose that blossomed and melted and burned in her head. That was the last thing she remembered.

the event

Life is so constructed, that the event does not, cannot, will not, match the expectation.

Charlotte Brontë, Villette

All week, that week, everyone wanted to confess to Sara. She recalled having a fantasy somewhat like this as a child, in which she was hospitalized after doing something vaguely heroic, hovering between life and death, and everyone she knew would show up and apologize, weeping profusely for being so mean. As a child this manifested as her parents showing up at her bedside to beg forgiveness for not allowing her to watch *Charlie's Angels* because it presented a retrograde version of feminism.

But it lost something in translation, Sara noted briefly as she drifted in and out of consciousness—the real-life version of her fantasy wasn't nearly as fun as she'd imagined. Perhaps it was the tube shoved down her throat.

"Sara? Sara, can you hear me? She squeezed my hand—she can hear?"

"*Non, monsieur*, is just a reflex. Is typical."

"She can hear me. Sara? It's me—Byrne. Mr. Emmons. I came as soon as I heard. I'm so sorry, sweetheart. I've been terrible. I don't blame you for leaving. I wanted to follow you, but I don't know . . . I'm such a miserable fuck-up. . . ."

Sara heard tears, coughing. He blew his nose.

"Sorry. That's all I say, I know, I know. Anyway, I knew right after you left—knew I was the biggest jerk in the world. And then— It's karmic, I tell you. Well, you probably read in the trades. Maybe not. We lost our star. Now starring in Marty's pet project—some rancid crap about Amelia Earhart. Wonder how that happened, huh? Anyway, I'm total fucking dead in the water and I didn't even care. Didn't care. Just wanted to see you again. You've changed me, Sara. I know I can be such a bastard, but I've realized what matters. I'm renting out the house, sold the Vega even—it's all just *stuff*, I realized, I was putting all my energy into stuff. I'm out of L.A. mode—back at the meetings. Clean a whole week."

Sara drifted back out. His words became unintelligible, more like a quilt covering her ears. Words were something to lie in. But she liked the conventions his words invoked. The penitent cad was always one of her favorite stock types.

"Sara?" Paul. Two penitent cads, what fun. "Sara? Sara, can you hear me? I called your parents. I hope you can

hear me. I've been thinking and—I think you may be right about some of the things you said. I should have thought things through and not left so suddenly. . . . I don't know . . . I'm sorry. I do wish now I'd done things differently and not burned so many bridges. I think part of me just wondered what would happen if everything I knew was taken away, like if I just burned down the house what would happen? But now I guess I see that, well, life's short and being wasteful is just . . . I don't know what I'm trying to say. I wanted to call you. A million times. I thought I'd made a mistake leaving, but then I wasn't sure and I couldn't put you through that twice. Not if I wasn't sure. I wanted to call you. I guess I just didn't have the courage."

"My poem is all about you this week. *Cherie,* you are more beautiful on a ventilator. Do you know the asshole doctors don't let you smoke in these places?"

"I have to confess I've always envied you. Success has always come so easily to me that I never know what it's like—what you go through, I mean. Your passions are pure because they're so unsupported—year after year nobody gives a damn except you for your work, but you just keep at it. That's what I envy. You know what you truly love— it's pure. For me, it's always complicated by huge advances and media and public admiration. If I weren't getting all those rewards, would I still love my Diana Studies? I don't honestly know. I don't. I've never been challenged by the crush of indifference you've confronted. You don't know

what it's like, this doubt of your core beliefs. In a way my road is much tougher, when you think about it. You never have to wonder if you would look for Brontë letters without hope of material reward because you already have! I'm not sure if I could do it."

Sara's eyes fluttered open. Claire clapped her hands.

"You're awake. I feel so Prince Charming! It's so mythic—the one who awakens another. I feel—"

"Claire. Am I all right?"

"There was blood and I guess some fluid in your brain, which sounds pretty bad, but then it drained off or something—I kind of zone out when science is mentioned. I find its pretense of authority coercive and unreliable. Anyway, it seems you're better. They were just waiting to see if you'd wake up and be able to talk, which obviously you are. You should see the parade of men you've set off. And the papers—they're calling it the 'Curse of Diana.' Of course, they would try to vilify her as if they didn't get enough of that during her life. Why not call it the 'Blessing of Diana'? I mean, you *lived*. They've gone mad, the papers, since this did all happen in the Alma Tunnel, where she had her accident, and on the anniversary of her death— Oh! I sort of told them you were attending the conference as well. It works better PR-wise."

Sara could barely follow what she was saying.

"Is Paul all right?"

"Paul is adrift. I think he's depressed. You were right to cut him loose. And Therese—nice but what can I say? Can't finish a thesis on Colette? Frustrated and self-defeating?

Very you circa twelve months ago, only French. I think Paul is one of those men doomed to date the same woman all his life. He's been hanging around here like an old dog. I think you've become his reason not to commit to her. How do you like that? So predictable, that one. But you're beyond him now—the only women that suit him are frustrated and self-defeating. Anyone who evolves beyond that simply frightens him."

"I'm still frustrated and self-defeating," Sara said defensively.

"No, you're not. Flying off to some silly bed in Italy, yelling at me in public, twice? That's lunatic and impulsive. Sara, this is real progress. Paul tells me the whole accident happened because you were climbing out the window."

"I wasn't climbing out."

"Then what?"

Sara rubbed her head. What was she trying to do?

"I think I was trying to be a dog."

"Perfect!"

"Claire, is Paul all right? He wasn't hurt?"

"The only one who can hurt Paul is Paul. He's fine."

"And the other car?"

"Some dog lost its leg. But everyone else was fine."

"Oh."

Sara looked out the window and saw that it had been raining and worried about a three-legged dog. An oppressive gray sky threatened more rain.

"Do you think maybe you should tell someone I'm awake?" Sara asked finally. Claire nodded that she had a good point and started dialing her publicist on her cell phone.

"I mean like a doctor."

"She's awake! I'm so Prince Charming. It's so mythic. Be sure the release clearly states I was at the bed-side when she woke up."

courage to break it

At last sheer pain made me gather courage to break it—I told all.

Charlotte Brontë, to Ellen Nussey, 1854

Sara had heard that brushes with death had a clarifying effect on the mind. Values came into stark relief, decisions became simple and easy. She found the opposite to be true. Her recovery had been plagued with drowsiness and indecision. Nothing had come into focus except a vaguely generous fellow-feeling and relief to be alive. She felt cheerful enough, but it certainly didn't help her make any decisions. And everyone was offering her something, as though the accident had clarified and intensified the feelings of those around Sara but not Sara herself: Paul and Mr. Emmons and Denis had all expressed a now clear and intense desire to be with her, Claire had offered a no-strings-attached research fellowship. Everyone felt certainty, except Sara.

Her parents had flown to Paris on her release from the hospital and were staying in a hotel just blocks from Sara's new temporary home: Claire's Paris apartment. It was an arrangement Sara had initially resisted but now actually enjoyed. For starters, Claire's place was enormous, several floors in a beautifully restored old building. Claire had given her more freedom than she expected; some days she rarely saw Claire at all and could spend her time just reading and going for the occasional walk when she felt strong enough. Staying there also granted her some distance from her hovering, concerned parents.

"Here's the thing you have to remember," her mother cautioned her over lunch shortly after Sara's release. "Some people are just tremendous shits. I know you'd like to be romantic about it and think things can be put back together, but sometimes they just can't."

"But don't you think a person sometimes deserves a second chance?" Sara asked. She longed for her mother to just give her the answer, but the woman still possessed a therapist's irritating tendency toward the opaque.

"Absolutely!" her mother said, growing more animated on her second glass of wine. Sara soaked in the warm steak and coffee smells of the café. She ached to stay here forever, poised between choices, reassured by the clanking of glasses, the soupy egg whites on her plate. Toast. Mother. The pleasure of watching people rush through their lunches to get back to work while you yourself had nowhere to go.

"So you think I should give Paul another chance?"

Sara asked, baiting. Her mother raised her eyebrow inquisitively. Could be yes, could be no . . . damned therapists!

"I think some people should be given a second chance and some people should have the doors locked against them," her mother said unhelpfully.

"But how do you know?" Sara asked plaintively.

"Oh, honey," her mother said, sliding a bit of arugula out of her front teeth, "this is why I do closets. When it comes down to it, I have no idea. I really don't know who deserves what."

"Thanks," Sara said ruefully, staring out the window. Suddenly she wanted to be one of those women striding purposefully down the boulevard with an ironclad schedule to keep. Oh, clear purpose, Sara thought, how you evade my clutches at every turn.

"If you really want my advice," her mother began, tantalizingly. Sara's ears pricked up. "Pay attention to how you feel. In the moment. Get all these men together in one room. . . ?" Sara began laughing and so did her mother.

"What the hell?" she continued. "Pay attention to how each of them makes you feel—the way you paid attention when you were seven and deciding who to play with and who to avoid because they're mean. You have the freedom to choose your life right now. Choose what's right for you."

Sara looked at her reflection in a spoon and took a deep breath. She didn't ever want to leave her chair. Her mother paid the check and looked up expectantly.

"You have enough energy for a little shopping?" she asked. Sara smiled and nodded.

❖   ❖   ❖

"*Am I early?*" Paul asked.

"Just a little. Come in."

Sara escorted Paul back to the sitting room. She was hoping he'd show up last. She was still most vulnerable with him.

"Claire does know how to live in style," he said.

"She does."

"And I guess you, too, now."

"I'm just a guest."

"I know but . . ." Paul smiled anxiously, taking his seat on a stiff navy blue sofa. "You look good."

"I feel good. I've started going on walks." Sara smiled apprehensively. She'd rehearsed this moment but felt the novice actor's last-minute reluctance. She couldn't play this moment adequately; she lacked the sophistication, the grace to entertain ex-lovers and chat about walks and apartments.

Sara's polite smile faded. In the past, that look always aroused in Paul the deepest anxiety. Her joy was fading and he believed it was his fault. He always worried that Sara's perception of him was in part a lie, or at least a fabrication, that she conveniently amplified certain virtues and turned a blind eye toward the rest. Did he really want to spend his life with a woman who only saw him in half-measures? As a version of some long-awaited love she'd nourished since childhood? But watching her now, he realized she looked new yet strangely familiar. She listened with a directness he'd never experienced. She wasn't waiting for him to say something that would disillusion her. She just seemed quietly amused by him.

Paul smiled. "How do you like that?" he asked, trying to reduce things to a little cosmic joke. "I leave to see the world and you're the one who sees it."

"You saw the world," Sara reminded him.

"You saw more than I did."

Sara nodded; that was probably true. Outside she could hear the chaos of traffic, but Claire's vast apartment was always strangely quiet inside. The olive-colored walls lined with books felt studious, intimate, serious. Sara felt awkward, as though trying to force an old familiarity. She knew more was necessary. She stood and walked over to a stack of books on an ottoman. She pulled one off the top and handed it to Paul. He smiled in recognition.

"My *Down and Out*," Paul said.

"I asked my folks to bring it when they came. I shouldn't have kept it." Sara shrugged, indicating there was more to tell but why bother? Why bother now with old scores? "It's yours. You should have it," she said.

All morning, Paul had sensed a strange optimism growing inside. He'd found himself smiling for no reason. He'd examined his life, searching for reasons for this quiet sense of excitement, and found nothing; all the objective evidence—no job, no money, Therese had finally walked out (smashing up her car with his ex-girlfriend in the passenger seat hadn't helped matters)—everything pointed him logically toward despair. But he felt none of it. He felt something. Something he desperately wanted to name. Love? Too common.

Curiosity, then? *Curiosity,* from the Latin meaning "care," transformed in later Latin to convey the sense of spiritual charge, hence the word *curate*. Curate, curator. Curator, curator—what a beautiful, noble word: *curator*. What is a curator but the person uniquely charged in overseeing the proper appreciation of a work of art? Not the airless "appreciation" they teach in night classes, but the intense, scholarly devotion to the thing itself. What thing? Sara? Himself? Both? Maybe.

He was a curator, he decided, and the thought of the word sprang in his chest like a newfound optimism, the kind of optimism that descends on a man for no real reason at all. He should tell her his secret; he was a curator.

"How come he is here early?!"

"How'd you get in?" Sara asked.

Denis held up his keys. Paul realized he would have to tell her about being a curator later. Mr. Emmons followed close behind. Sara took a deep breath.

"Looks like we're all here." Sara found a place center stage in one of Claire's low leather chairs.

"I realize this is a little awkward, but . . ." she began, trailing off. Yes, it was awkward, more awkward than she'd expected. This was the last time she'd ever take her mother's advice. Denis and Mr. Emmons both lit cigarettes. Paul politely opened the window. The sound of traffic poured in.

"You've all, over the past few weeks of my recovery, made your feelings known to me. The thing of it is . . . is I have pretty good reasons for thinking it wouldn't be such a good idea with any of you."

"Reasons?!" Denis exploded. "What are reasons? The soul dies when it—"

"Denis—"

"I believe she's trying to—"

"Mr. Emmons?"

"You call him Mr. Emmons?"

"Paul. Please. What I'm asking for is a year," Sara managed finally.

"A year of what?"

"Separation." Paul nodded knowingly.

"I need a year to myself. Claire has offered, and I've decided to accept, the first Diana Fellowship, in which I will be allowed to pursue my studies, research, travel, and write—fully funded. What I need is time."

"Are we talking complete separation?" Mr. Emmons asked, already angling for a loophole.

"We can write, I suppose. I realize this is unorthodox, but . . ." Sara looked around the room for maximum effect. "I need to know for certain and right now I don't have that certainty and I think a year to see how I develop and you and the world . . . I think there are compelling reasons why it wouldn't work with each one of you and I know I have my share of blame here. I just don't want to make the same mistakes all over again. You," she said, turning to Paul, "need to grow up and decide what it is you really want." And then turning to Mr. Emmons: "And I know you want to be a good man, but you're not, and I'm not the one to get you there. And Denis, well, you're . . . a poem . . . if that makes any sense."

Denis shrugged, sort of. Her little rehearsed speech had the intended effect of throwing cold water on their hopes so that only the strongest spark could survive it.

The men sat in humbled silence until Mr. Emmons penetrated it.

"A year? That's a very long time, Sara."

Sara expected this response and had a ready answer, "If timing is all you care about, you should love trains instead of people." She had meant this to sound worldly and wise but saw it met with blank stares. She was waiting for her sign. For something, anything. The feeling within that her mother swore would be there. But instead she felt foggy, achy, tired. Her legs felt heavy. She wanted a nap.

"And that's only in some countries," Denis said. Everyone turned to look at him. "You could not love a Spanish train, not if you like things on time. You know, there is this belief in Judaism that God takes each person to a field before his or her life and has them choose a bundle of troubles they will suffer in their life. When that person returns to the field, he always chooses the same bundle."

"But how could they return to the field?" Mr. Emmons asked briskly. "I didn't think Jews believed in reincarnation."

"What are you, a lawyer?" Denis asked indignantly. "I'm only trying to help."

"How?" Paul asked.

"I'm saying it doesn't so much matter who she chooses, she'll always choose the same bundle of troubles." Denis shrugged. Here he was again, explaining things to an American—his bundle of troubles.

"That's so fatalistic," Mr. Emmons countered. "People change."

Denis shrugged again. "Yes. I am a *fataliste*. So what?"

"I think that's very sad for you," Mr. Emmons told him.

"What does it matter what I think?" Denis asked.

"I wrote a paper about fatalism. . . ." Paul offered.

Sara could see her plan was unraveling. Where were the passionate protests? The dawning clarity, the awakening calm? She had provided them all with a suitably dramatic stage from which to perform, and instead the conversation had broken down into philosophical debate. She needed an object to ground her reality again. She looked at a book of Brontë letters, resting innocently on the shelf like an unseen director discreetly guiding her insensible actors. She tried to remember her favorite letter and what she thought of it—this would certainly ground her.

Biographers are often aided by the embittered, by those who relentlessly hold on to evidence far beyond the statute of limitations. Sara knew that she owed a tremendous debt to Professor Heger's wife. Thanks to her, Charlotte Brontë's last letter to Professor Heger remains preserved, sewn together with thread, the address of a shoe repair on the back jotted down, presumably by the professor before he tore it up and threw it away.

Why cannot I have for you exactly as much friendship as you have for me—neither more nor less? Then I would be so tranquil, so free—I could keep silence for ten years without effort.

Mr. Nicholls would burn this, too, if he could. So many men trying to destroy this letter and here it was, preserved for anyone to see. The letter had everything, every eternal problem played out: the inequality of affection, love, loss, rejection, shoe repair.

But Sara had never been able to reconcile one odd detail: The professor's daughter also presented this letter to him later, after his wife had died. That was a strange act. Sara had always assumed the wife had kept it out of some sort of proprietary impulse, a warning of her powers of detection should he ever consider straying; she needed to keep him in line and the letter gave her ammunition. But the daughter seemed a strange player in this drama.

Maybe Madame Heger didn't like Charlotte, maybe she felt threatened, but perhaps the fact that the professor could so easily discard the feelings of another frightened her even more? Maybe all three women were bonded by a fellow feeling that the man they loved was compulsively lacking in the realm of tenderness. Maybe the repeated presentation of the letter was nothing more than a plea that Professor Heger show remorse or regret or love or just any damned emotion that bubbled to the surface of that exterior.

In the past, Sara had always pitied heartbroken, outcast Charlotte in this little domestic drama. But now she saw the wife and daughter as perhaps the more pitiable figures. Charlotte moved on, became a literary star and married someone else, someone who loved her. Charlotte was the lucky one. She moved on. Now Sara was casting her lot with the Hegers, begging for a response she'd never get.

"I can't do this," Sara said uncertainly. She longed to walk out the door with Paul by her side, sure of their future happiness, his devotion unwavering.

"So you've said, darling," Mr. Emmons replied, his edge returning.

"I think I am in love with one of you. And I think I've been allowing these flirtations with the rest of you because I know deep down it would never work out and so I'm still being loyal to man number one, who come to think of it hasn't been all that loyal to me. So I think—in order to save myself from one of you and be fair to the rest—I'll have to say no to all of you. I'm so sorry. . . ."

Sara watched the suitors regard one another with new appreciation—there would be no victor today. She watched Mr. Emmons slap his thighs with his palms—another rotten hand he'd been dealt. She watched Paul rub the back of his neck the way he always used to, as if he could massage the answer to a thorny problem up into his head. Denis defiantly lit up another cigarette, digging in for an all-nighter.

Sara's heart felt queasy and sick. She wanted to fill the air with inane reassurances about the resilience of the human spirit and the abundance of love, but her words were gone. It hurt to be left and it hurt to walk away from love even when it meant self-preservation. She searched for something wise, witty, off-the-cuff to say. Something bittersweet and Parisian. But all she could think as she finally managed to lift her eyes and meet Paul's gaze was what she supposed any lover must feel at the end: I will always miss who I thought you were.

"If you don't mind," Sara said, "I think I'd like to be alone."

"Well!" Denis said, stabbing the air with his cigarette. "I want to know who it is you love."

Sara shook her head, the effort it took not to cry. She had told herself she wouldn't.

"Let's just say it doesn't matter," she said softly. Denis nodded impatiently; even he could see it was no use.

"Sara!" Paul protested, wanting to tell her about being a curator. But her eyes said not to. Her eyes told him to leave. He picked up his first edition with a sad, resigned smile and filed outside with the rest of the suitors. Sara walked to the window and watched them each disperse on their individual trajectories, tiny vectors of fate now pitched decisively away from her, into the city, and finally let herself cry.

only by halves

Do not condemn yourself to live only by halves . . .

Charlotte Brontë, to Ellen Nussey, 1845

"Whom did you choose?" Claire asked as Sara joined her on the terrace.

"I don't think any one of them is right for me."

"I could have told you that a year ago."

Claire watched the sun fight its way out from behind a cloud. Rain seemed imminent but Claire would have none of it and seemed to will the sun back to the fore.

"Are you still angry with me?" Claire asked.

This was as much as Sara had ever seen Claire acknowledge another human's emotional life.

"I was."

"And now?"

Claire repositioned the sun a little more to her liking, willed it out of her eyes.

"While you're doing your Diana Fellowship this year—if you do it—I wonder if you'd like to stay on here. This town house is so huge—even when Denis is here. You'd have your own entrance. You can come and go as you like."

"What's the catch?"

"No catch."

"There's always—"

"Maybe every now and then have lunch with me. Or maybe you could come to one or two of my prenatal yoga classes. . . ."

It occurred to Sara for the first time that Claire might suffer from plain old loneliness.

"I mean, you don't have to. I just realized it would be nice to have someone around who's trustworthy and reliable and, well, not Denis."

"I see."

"But, of course, the fellowship's yours either way. If you want it."

Sara stared at Claire. She looked remarkably alone even as she commanded the sun.

"I realized after our lunch, that day in Los Angeles," Claire intoned somberly, "that my plan to fix your life— Maybe I could have done things differently. Denis and I always had this argument—he says you can't do anything to help someone, that they're set on their own course, it's all fate. I say moment by moment you choose your destiny. People change—in fact, they do nothing but. The possibilities of human transformation are endless—just look at Diana. Anyway. That's what I thought I was giving you. A way into the life you were meant for. You just needed a little . . . push. But maybe it wasn't the push you wanted after all. And magenta—well, I do feel bad about that. I've felt very bad. I called her. She didn't want to speak to me."

Claire traced the bottom of her glass with a fingernail, drawing a figure eight that seemed to soothe her. Sara let the silence hang in the air, unsure whether to comfort or challenge her. Were they friends now? Adversaries? Sara still felt guarded in her presence.

"Well," Claire said finally, "I hope you'll take the fellowship. It's offered in the spirit of helping you. That's all."

Sara nodded, noticing the shadows on the wall, the curlicues of iron filigree from the balcony railings.

"Do you find me difficult?" Claire asked, worried.

"Well . . ."

"I'm just joking. Of course you do! Passionate creators are difficult! Of course, you know that, too." Claire laughed, a deep, open laugh that took in the whole afternoon. "I'm seeing an analyst now. He floated the notion that I may have control issues."

"You don't say," Sara said, smiling.

"You probably hadn't noticed—I'm very private."

Sara laughed softly to herself, the autumn sun filling her with new energy.

"He told me to keep a journal. He's brilliant. He suggested that I not force a story like I used to—like I was trying to with you, trying to force your life into a happy ending—it's false. I'm just trying to *be* now. I'm reading a lot of Zen. The thing is, I was trying to make everything a story—my life, your life—and then I realized that there's no need for a story, a story is not compulsory, just a life—that's the mistake I made, one of the mistakes, to have wanted a story for myself, whereas life alone is enough."

Sara looked out across the city. Claire's words sifted through her mind, settling in. She looked at Claire and narrowed her eyes.

"Claire, didn't Samuel Beckett write that?"

"He might have. He was always writing something or other."

"You are with Dell?"

"People aren't with anyone—people don't belong to other people. It's horrific. All this . . . *ownership* makes me gag!"

"Sometimes belonging can be nice."

"I suppose," Claire agreed, reversing herself instantly. She traced her wineglass with her finger pensively, then gestured to the bottle. "Do you want some?" she asked.

"Should you be drinking?"

"Why? Because of the pregnancy? We're in France, it's okay. Anyway, I watered it down a little. Now it tastes like a California merlot."

Sara smiled and poured a small glass for herself. Claire nodded approvingly.

"Maybe you're right, Sara. I've started to think you belong to me. In a nice way. My silent Victorian. I like that. I'd like it if you stayed."

"I do have a lead in Ireland. This woman I met in

New York has relatives in Cork. I always wanted to follow up on it."

"Ireland is easy. A short train ride. Then a ferry. The best is to drive up to Le Havre, then get a sleeper cabin for overnight. Or fly."

"If I stayed with you, I'd have the right to solitude?"

"Of course," Claire assured her.

"I mean days, possibly weeks. And I'd be traveling."

"All right."

"And I wouldn't be dragged into midnight parties with brilliant transgender amputee porn scholars?"

"I'm over that. The baby has mellowed me."

"And if I leave for weeks at a time, no guilt trips?"

"Guilt trips are American. I've never trafficked in them."

"All right, then."

Claire smiled and gave a quick sigh. She looked relieved and Sara realized how much she had risked in being so vulnerable. She was touching sometimes, Sara thought tenderly, but mostly when she wasn't talking. And then she felt it. The opening, the calm, that crazy heart chakra bullshit Jasmyn, her yoga teacher, couldn't shut up about. It was the unspoiled, sweet concern for another without hope, need, or fear of result. She felt like her three-legged dog with his head out the window. She didn't care what came next—here was just fine for now.

Sara felt a bead of sweat drop from her forehead. But it wasn't sweat at all, she realized. The sky had opened up and poured down heavy rain. Sara looked up. The sky was a creamy peach sorbet, streaked and bright with lemony chiffon swirls—it looked like a sky that had nothing to do with rain but was instead its cheerful consolation.

Claire hurried inside, taking her wine with her. She motioned for Sara to come inside, too, but Sara smiled and shook her head, letting the rain trickle down from the balcony above and beat an irregular Morse code on her head and shoulders. She watched the pedestrians below, who had suddenly transformed newspapers and raincoats into angel wings, held high overhead, waiting to take flight. They rushed madly, ducking into cafés and deep recesses of apartment entryways. They smiled at one another in the acknowledgment of an unforeseen, undesirable but purely manageable little catastrophe: the unexpected deluge.

Below them a car rear-ended another. Two men flew out of the cars, gesticulating wildly, cursing in French. "Calm down!" one kept yelling. "You'll pay!" yelled the other. Sara watched them, intrigued by their intensity. How quickly it all turns, she thought. She looked over to Claire, who was doing yogic alternate nostril breathing.

"Balance," Claire said through the open balcony door.

"I could go to the Gare du Nord," Sara said, staring down at the accident.

"You're going to Ireland *today*?"

"No. Just a walk."

"But the rain," Claire warned.

"I don't mind," Sara said, standing and pulling her raincoat tightly around her, already prepared.

Claire shrugged one of her Gallic, superior shrugs. Sara just smiled. Maybe she'd explain later. Or perhaps she'd just let it remain a mystery.

Sara hurried down the spiral stairs. She could see people hovering in the doorway as she opened it. The rain still came down in sheets, and a group of five wayward pedestrians stood sheltered under the awning of a brasserie next to Claire's building. Sara stood with them. A middle-aged businessman, two teenage girls with spiky hair and too much makeup, a twentyish Turkish man carefully shaking the rain from his boots, and an elegant woman in her thirties, poised, pulled together, calm even in the face of great obstacles, namely, rain. She had grace, the kind Sara always envied. Sara stood next to her, deciding whether to venture out in the rain. The woman smiled at Sara, as if inviting her into the club. They all watched as a weary police officer attended to the two crashed drivers as they tried to claw each other's eyes, slipping comically in the rain.

The graceful woman rolled her eyes watching them. Sara nodded in wistful agreement: *People!* The rain subsided. The Turkish man ventured out first, then the teenagers. Then it was just Sara and her new friend. They shrugged, put up their umbrellas and parted, walking off into the city in separate directions. Sara picked up her pace, her body feeling reenergized, the achy twinge that had settled between her shoulder blades since the accident lifting as her shoes slapped loudly against the wet Parisian pavement.

A young man on a scooter slowed down and honked, offering a lift to a cute thing like her. Sara smiled and shook her head—she liked the rain just fine—and walked on.

author's note

For those inspired to read more of Charlotte Brontë's writing, including her correspondence as referenced in these pages, I can suggest the following.

Jane Eyre is, of course, the best known of Charlotte Brontë's novels, using many of her most familiar themes and elements: orphans, lovesick governesses and teachers, darkly inscrutable men, and sudden financial windfalls. Less well known (and read) are her first novel, *The Professor*, which was never published during her lifetime (in spite of persistent appeals to her publisher), and her last, *Villette*. Both novels follow the professional and personal travails of an orphaned English teacher (*The Professor* is Brontë's only novel told from the male point of view) working abroad in a girls' boarding school in Belgium. Both novels also clearly build on Brontë's experiences studying in Brussels at the Pensionnat Heger.

Villette was Brontë's last completed novel, and while reminiscent of *Jane Eyre* in some respects, it represents for many her freshest, most mysterious evocation of the human experience. Virginia Woolf believed it to be her "finest novel." George Eliot announced upon its publication, "*Villette! Villette!* Have you read it? It is a still more wonderful book than *Jane Eyre*. There is something almost preternatural in its power."

As for Brontë's letters, *The Brontës: A Life in Letters*, edited by Brontë biographer Juliet Barker, reads like a novel itself with her helpful annotations. Most of the letters have been newly transcribed by Barker to maintain faithful accuracy to the originals.

For the truly committed Brontëphile, *The Letters of Charlotte Brontë: With a Selection of Letters by Family and Friends*, edited by Margaret Smith, is the largest, most thorough and accurate collection of Charlotte Brontë's letters in three volumes spanning the years 1829–47, 1848–51, and 1848–55.